"You will be the only occup... ...part," Philippe said.

Her body tingled. "Pretending to be your lover," Gretchen said breathlessly.

"Yes."

She felt deliciously hot all over. The thought of his mouth on hers made her knees weak. He wanted pretense. She wanted him, and was only just realizing it. All sorts of shocking, exciting images formed in her mind. "I have no idea how someone in a harem behaves," she said.

"Nor have I," he said with a touch of amusement. "We will have to learn together."

Some of the uncertainty left her expression.

"At least your virtue would be completely safe with me." He hoped. He didn't dare tell her what her touch did to him.

"How far would this pretense have to go, exactly?" she wondered aloud.

"It would have to be convincing," he said.

She lowered her eyes demurely. "You'd kiss me and...so forth?"

He lifted an eyebrow. "Yes. Especially and...so forth."

"Nobody tops Diana Palmer... I love her stories."
                                        —Jayne Ann Krentz

DIANA PALMER

LORD OF THE DESERT

MIRA

MIRA

ISBN 1-55166-617-0

LORD OF THE DESERT

Copyright © 2000 by Diana Palmer.

All rights reserved. Except for use in any review, the reproduction or
utilization of this work in whole or in part in any form by any electronic,
mechanical or other means, now known or hereafter invented, including
xerography, photocopying and recording, or in any information storage or
retrieval system, is forbidden without the written permission of the publisher,
MIRA Books, 225 Duncan Mill Road, Don Mills, Ontario, Canada M3B 3K9.

All characters in this book have no existence outside the imagination of the
author and have no relation whatsoever to anyone bearing the same name
or names. They are not even distantly inspired by any individual known or
unknown to the author, and all incidents are pure invention.

MIRA and the Star Colophon are trademarks used under license and registered
in Australia, New Zealand, Philippines, United States Patent and Trademark
Office and in other countries.

Visit us at www.mirabooks.com

Printed in U.S.A.

To Jim, Rhonda, Nancy, Amanda and Christian
(and Hugo)
with eternal thanks!

Chapter One

Tourists milled around the food court in the busy Brussels airport where the two American women were trying to decide what to do next.

The slender blond woman in the tan pantsuit was almost choked with mirth as she gazed mischievously up at her dark-haired, pacing companion in a green silk jacket and slacks. "Isn't it ironic that we could starve to death surrounded by food?" Gretchen Brannon asked gleefully.

"Oh, do stop," Maggie Barton groaned, looming over her laughing, near-hysterical companion. "We won't starve, Gretchen. We can get Belgian francs. There are money-changing booths everywhere!" She waved her arms around expressively at the nearby shops, almost colliding with a passing couple in the crowded food court.

Gretchen's green eyes twinkled. "Really? Where, exactly?"

Maggie let out a sigh as she tried unsuccessfully to remember enough French to read a sign.

Gretchen watched her through swollen eyelids. Unlike efficient Maggie, who could sleep on the plane, she'd been awake for almost thirty-six straight hours. "Can't you just see the headlines?" Gretchen persisted. "'Naïve Texas tourists found dead beside five-star restaurant...'!" She started laughing again.

Maggie was not amused. "Just sit right there. Don't move."

Gretchen submerged a mad impulse to salute. Maggie, twenty-six and three years older than Gretchen, worked for an investment firm in Houston where she was a junior partner. She had a take-charge manner that was occasionally a blessing. No doubt she'd find a way to get native currency and return loaded with food and drink.

Maggie came back with the money and sorted through it, frowning as she tried to remember how the currency changer had explained the coins. "We still have plenty of time to get something to eat and then take a tour of the city before our flight leaves for Casablanca this afternoon."

Gretchen blinked sleepily. "Great idea, about

the tour. Can you get a strong tour guide? I think I'll need to be carried..."

"Food. Coffee. Right now. Come on."

Gretchen obligingly let her friend tug her to her feet. They were an odd couple, with Maggie so tall and brunette and voluptuous, and Gretchen slender, medium height, fair and with long platinum-blond hair. They pulled the carry-on bags with them, having had the good sense not to bring more than that, thereby escaping the eternal wait at baggage claim for bags that often didn't even arrive with the passengers.

Maggie coughed helplessly. "Everybody smokes everywhere over here," she muttered. "I don't suppose there's a no-smoking section?"

Gretchen grinned. "Sure there is. It's where the smoke is being blown to."

Maggie made a face. "How about the food bar over there?" she asked, indicating a structure near the window. "It's almost deserted and nobody's smoking."

"I could eat dry bread crusts, myself," Gretchen agreed. "And if we don't have enough money, I'll even volunteer to wash the dishes!"

They had a nice order of pasta with tomatoes and mushrooms and homemade bread, on real china, with real silverware, at a counter. By the time they finished their second cups of coffee, Gretchen felt renewed.

"Now all we have to do is find a tour going our way," Maggie said brightly. "I'll call a tour agency and see if we can get somebody to come and pick us up."

Gretchen only sighed. She sat down and closed her eyes. It would be so lovely to have a bed and ten hours uninterrupted sleep. But they were still hours from their hotel in Tangiers, Morocco.

Fifteen frustrating minutes later, Maggie hung up the phone and mumbled some harsh words toward it as she nudged Gretchen, who was dozing.

"I can't read the telephone directory, it's all in French, I can't figure out which coins to use because I don't speak French, and I can't get anybody who answers the phone to understand me because *I don't speak French!*"

"Don't look at me," Gretchen said pleasantly. "I don't speak any French, even menu-French. I have to get by on Spanish, and nobody here seems to understand it."

"I speak Spanish, too, but we're in the wrong country to use it. Well," Maggie said irritably, "we'll just go outside and hail a cab. That should be simple enough. Right?"

Gretchen didn't say a word. She sighed and got

to her feet, dragging her carry-on bag behind her like a reluctant puppy.

The Brussels airport was large and modern and friendly. After a nightmare of dead ends they found a nice cab, with a pleasant, friendly driver whose English was every bit as bad as Maggie's French. Nevertheless, she and Gretchen managed to convey what they wanted to do and they saw some amazing sights. The tour was long and pleasant and educational. But eventually they had to go back to the airport or risk missing their connecting flight.

Buoyed up by coffee, food, and the sight-seeing tour, Gretchen was now wide-awake and eager for Morocco, land of camels and the Sahara desert, and the famous Berbers of the Rif mountains. She could hardly wait to see the ancient land in its desert setting.

Several hours and a fascinating snack meal of Middle-Eastern delicacies later, their plane set down in Casablanca, Morocco, where they had to find the concourse for their connecting flight up to Tangier. Among the interesting customs of the flight were the distribution of traditional Moroccan foods and free newspapers in an assortment of foreign languages to travelers, and the apparently routine custom of applauding the pilot when the plane had landed safely. Maggie and Gretchen joined in the general merriment and stepped out into another world, where men and women wore long, graceful robes, and women either wore head covers with veils or scarves tied tight around their heads. There were many children traveling with their parents.

Inside the Casablanca terminal, much smaller than they expected it to be, armed guards in camouflage gear shepherded passengers to the customs desk and from there into the various concourse rooms to await their flights. The washroom, though small and rustic, had an attendant who was an English-speaking treasure of information about the city and its people. They changed American currency for dirhams at the airport after they cleared customs and before they went through baggage control and the metal detector again before boarding their connecting flight.

Casablanca was huge, a mecca of whitewashed buildings and modern skyscrapers with the same maddening traffic congestion to be found elsewhere in cities. When the plane, a double-decker, lifted off, they had another beautiful glimpse of the sprawling exotic city on the Atlantic.

Only three and a half hours later, choking on unfamiliar smoke because the passengers on this particular flight were allowed to smoke, the graceful airliner drifted down onto the tarmac at the small Tangier airport.

Finally, their passports were stamped, their lug-

gage was checked, and they walked out of the terminal into the humid, almost tropical night air of
Tangier on the Mediterranean Sea. Many cabs
were parked along the road in front of the terminal,
their drivers with uncanny patience awaiting the
weary visitors.

The driver smiled, nodded courteously, packed
their luggage in the trunk of his Mercedes, and
they were, at last, on the way to the five-star Hotel
Minzah, on a hill overlooking the port.

The streets were well-lighted, and almost everyone wore robes. The city had a curious face, of
ancient things and venerable customs, of cosmopolitan travelers and mystery and intrigue. There
were palm trees everywhere. The streets, even at
night, were full of people, a few in European dress.
Cars darted from side streets, horns blew. Heads
poked out of perpetually open car windows and,
accompanied by strange hand waving, guttural
Berber spouted in friendly arguing as drivers vied
for entrance into the steady stream of traffic. The
faint smell of musk was everywhere, sweet and
foreign and delightfully Moroccan.

It was a leap of faith into the unknown for
Gretchen and Maggie, since they hadn't been able
to find a tour that featured only Tangier. They
booked through a travel agency and made up their
itinerary as they went. Stops in Brussels on the

way to Africa and Amsterdam on the way back from Africa had been deliberate, to give them a taste of Europe. It was turning out to be a grand trip, especially since they were now in Morocco, and everywhere there were glimpses into the ancient past when Berbers mounted on fine Arabian stallions fought the Europeans for ownership of their ancient, sacred homeland.

"This," Gretchen said, shell-shocked from long hours without more than catnaps, "is the most wonderful adventure."

"I told you it would be," Maggie agreed with a smile. "Poor thing, you're dead on your feet, aren't you?"

Gretchen nodded. "But it was worth every lost hour of sleep." She frowned as she looked out the window. "I don't see the Sahara."

"The Sahara Desert is six hundred miles from here," their driver said, glancing in the rearview mirror at them. "Tangier is a seaport on the Mediterranean, *mademoiselle*."

"There goes our desert trek," Gretchen chuckled.

"Oh, but there is much to see here," the cabdriver said helpfully. "The Forbes museum, the Grotto of Hercules, the Grand Socco…"

"The marketplace," Maggie said, remembering. "Yes, the travel brochures say it's enormous!"

"That is so," the driver agreed. "And perhaps you can hire a car and drive to Asilah, down the Atlantic coast, for market day," he added. "It is a sight worth seeing, where all the country people bring their produce and goods for sale."

"And maybe we can see the kasbah," Gretchen added dreamily.

"A kasbah," the driver corrected.

"There's more than one?" Gretchen asked, surprised.

"Ah, yes, the American cinema. Humphrey Bogart." He chuckled. "A kasbah is simply a walled city, *mademoiselle*. The shops are inside ours, here in Tangier. You will see it. Very old. Tangier has been inhabited since 4000 B.C., and the first here were Berbers."

He mentioned other points of history all the way through the city and up a small hill to a flat-faced building that blended in with small shops. Here he stopped by the curb and cut off the engine.

"Your hotel, *mademoiselles*."

The driver opened the door for them and gave their suitcases to the young man who came out of the hotel, smiling a welcome.

It wasn't what the women had expected a five-star hotel to look like, from the outside. But then they entered the building and walked into opulent luxury. The concierge at the desk wore a red fez and a white jacket. He was busy with another guest, so the women waited with their luggage, glancing around at the elegant carpet and dark, carved wood of the sofas and chairs under a framed mosaic in an open room adjacent to the lobby. The elevator was getting a workout nearby.

The concierge finished with his other guest and smiled at the two women. Maggie stepped forward to give her name, in which the reservation was booked. In no time at all, they were on their way upstairs with the young man escorting their luggage.

The room overlooked the Mediterranean. But closer, downstairs, were the beautiful flowered grounds of the hotel with a swimming pool and many places to sit and enjoy the view toward the Mediterranean under towering palm trees, unseen from the street outside. It looked like photographs Gretchen had seen of lovely islands in the Caribbean. The sea air was delicious to smell, and the room was exotic, enormous, with separate rooms for the bathtub and toilet. There was a telephone and a small bar, containing soft drinks, bottled water, beer, and snacks.

"We certainly won't starve," Maggie murmured as she explored the room.

Gretchen pulled a gown from her suitcase, changed out of her traveling clothes, climbed under

the sheets and went to sleep while Maggie was
wondering aloud about room service...

Despite the jet lag so often talked about, they
woke rested and hungry at eight o'clock the next
morning and dressed in slacks and shirts, anxious
to find breakfast and start looking around the ancient city that had once been part of the Roman
empire.

The concierge pointed them toward the elaborate
breakfast buffet and introduced them to a licensed
city guide who would pick them up two hours later
for a look at the city. They were cautioned by him
never, never, to go onto the streets alone, without
a guide. It seemed sensible to follow that rule, and
they agreed to wait for the guide inside the hotel.

"Did you notice the price of the buffet?" Maggie asked when they were seated for breakfast.
"Barely one dollar American, for all this." She
frowned. "Gretchen, how would you like to live
in Tangier?"

Gretchen laughed. "I like it here very much, but
how would Callie Kirby do without me in the law
office?"

Maggie gave her a long, silent stare. "You're
going to grow old and die in that law office, alone
and in a shell," she said gently. "Daryl's defection

was the worst thing that ever happened to you, coming right on the heels of your mother's death.''

Gretchen's green eyes were sad. ''I was a fool. Everybody saw through him except me.''

''You'd never really had any attention from a man,'' Maggie pointed out. ''It was inevitable that you'd go mad over the first man who treated you like a woman.''

Gretchen grimaced. ''And all he wanted was the insurance money. He didn't have any idea that the ranch was mortgaged to the hilt, and that there wasn't going to be any money. We'd have lost the ranch if my big brother Marc hadn't had a savings account big enough to pay off the part in arrears.''

''How sad that Daryl got out of town before your brother got to him,'' Maggie said coldly.

''Marc scares most people when he's in a temper,'' Gretchen reminisced with a smile. ''He was something of a local legend even before he left the Texas Rangers to join the FBI.''

''Marc loves you. So do I.'' Maggie patted her hand and smiled. ''I was like you, in a rut. I decided that I needed a leap of faith, a great adventure to pull me out of my complacency. So I'm going to Qawi to be personal assistant to the ruling sheikh of the whole country,'' she added. ''How's that for a leap of faith?''

Gretchen chuckled. ''About as big a one as

you'll ever make, probably. I hope you know what you're doing," she added. "I've heard some scary things about Middle-Eastern countries and beheadings."

"Not in Qawi," Maggie said easily. "It's very progressive in culture, with an equal mixture of religions which makes it unique in the Persian Gulf. And all that oil money is going to make it cosmopolitan very quickly. The sheikh is very forward-thinking."

"And single, you said?" she teased.

Maggie frowned. "Yes. You remember his country was invaded about two years ago, and there was a big scandal about it. I watched several news broadcasts that told about it. There were some rumors about him, too, of an unsavory nature, but his government explained them."

Gretchen sipped coffee. "Maybe he'll be gorgeous and sexy and look like Rudolph Valentino. Did you ever see that silent movie, 'The Sheikh'?" she continued dreamily. "Just imagine having a fantasy like that actually come to life, Maggie. Being abducted by a handsome sheikh on a white stallion and having him fall madly in love with you! I get goose bumps just thinking about it." She frowned. "Maybe I'm not cut out to be a modern woman. Probably I should be dreaming about throwing a handsome sheikh onto *my* horse and riding away with him as my captive." A long sigh left her lips. "Oh, well, it's only a daydream after all. Reality is never that adventurous, not for me. You're more the type for gorgeous, sexy men."

Maggie laughed hollowly. "I don't have much luck with gorgeous, sexy men," she said.

Gretchen knew she was thinking about her foster brother, Cord Romero. "Well, don't look at me," she mused, trying to lighten the atmosphere. "I only attract gigolos."

"Daryl wasn't a gigolo, he was a garden slug. You should only date men who belong to your own species," she said haughtily.

Gretchen burst out laughing. "Oh, you make me feel so independent and brave," she said, and meant it. "I'm really glad you asked me to come with you on this vacation and paid more than your part so I could afford it," she added gratefully. "Even if I do have to fly back alone. I'm going to miss you," she said quietly. "We won't get to go shopping together or even talk on the phone at holidays."

Maggie nodded solemnly. She was flying from here to Qawi. Her role as personal assistant to the ruling sheikh would be to assume responsibility for public relations, court functions, and organization of the household duties. It would be a challenge, and she might be homesick for Texas. But she'd told Gretchen once that anything was better than the hell of being around Cord Romero, who had made it obvious that she was never going to be part of his life.

Both had been orphans, adopted by a Houston society matron. They weren't related, but Cord treated Maggie like a relative. He'd married a few years back and his wife, Patricia, had committed suicide after he was almost fatally wounded and he couldn't, or wouldn't, give up his career as a government agent. Soon after her death, he left the field of law enforcement and went to work as a professional mercenary soldier, specializing in bomb disposal.

It was what he did now, and Maggie had managed to keep her distance from him quite comfortably until the sudden death of their adoptive mother. Maggie had married a few weeks later, but her elderly husband had been an invalid and died only six months after their marriage. She and Cord had avoided each other ever since. Gretchen wondered what had happened, but Maggie never spoke of it.

When Cord unexpectedly returned to Houston and moved in the same circles Maggie did, in between foreign assignments, she applied and got a job in another country. One which, ironically, Cord had casually told her about. He'd come back from a job in Qawi just recently, helping disarm old land mines from a guerilla invasion. When Maggie had looked into the job, she'd found that it paid handsomely—much more handsomely than her own position as a financial advisor. She was determined to make a clean break from Cord this time.

On the way, she decided to have a vacation. She'd invited her friend Gretchen along, mainly because Gretchen had been so very despondent after the death of her mother and the tragic betrayal of her one serious boyfriend. So far the trip had been wonderful. But soon, Maggie would fly on to Qawi and Gretchen would have to board a plane alone for Amsterdam, from which she'd fly back to Texas.

It would be lonely for Gretchen, but she'd get a glimpse of the world. She needed that. She'd nursed her mother through cancer twice in the past six years. Gretchen was twenty-three and she was as naïve as a teenager in a convent school. She hadn't had the opportunity to date much, with her mother so ill—and so possessive of her only child. Gretchen's father had died when she was ten and her brother Marc was eighteen, and that had made their lives much harder. Marc lived with Gretchen and the foreman and his family on their ranch in Jacobsville, Texas, when he could get home. Marc worked for the FBI, and spent much of his life out of town on job assignments. His job hadn't allowed him to help Gretchen with nursing their mother, although he certainly helped support them.

"Morocco," Gretchen said aloud and smiled at Maggie. "I never dreamed I'd ever get to go someplace so exotic."

Maggie only smiled.

"You're very quiet," Gretchen said suddenly, curious about her friend's unfamiliar silences. Maggie was usually the talkative one of the two.

Maggie shrugged, cupping her coffee cup in both hands. "I was thinking about...home."

"Shame on you. This is a vacation and we've just got here. You can't possibly be homesick yet."

Maggie smiled wanly. "I'm not homesick. Not really. I just wish things had worked out a little better."

"With Cord," Gretchen said knowingly.

Maggie shrugged. "It wouldn't have worked out. He'll never get over Pat's death and he won't give up his freelance demolitions work. He likes it too much."

"People do change as they get older," Gretchen said.

"He won't." There was finality and misery in the statement. "I've spent enough of my life hoping he'd wake up and love me. He isn't going to. I have to learn to live without him now.''

''He might miss you and rush over on the first jet to bring you back home.''

''That isn't likely.''

''Neither was my getting to go to Morocco,'' Gretchen replied mischievously. She finished her beautifully cooked scrambled eggs.

Maggie forced a smile. ''Oh well. The sheikh is relatively young and charming and a bachelor. Who knows what might happen?''

''Who knows.'' Gretchen was sorry that Maggie had decided on such a drastic action. She was going to miss her terribly. Callie Kirby, her co-worker at the law office in Jacobsville, was wonderful company, but Maggie had been her best friend since childhood. It had been bad enough when Maggie moved to Houston. It was a worse wrench to have her move out of the country.

''You can come and visit me,'' Maggie said. ''I'll be allowed to have company. We might catch you a prince yet.''

''I don't want a prince,'' Gretchen said with a chuckle. ''I'd settle for a nice cowboy with his own horse, and a kind heart.''

''Kind hearts are pretty rare,'' Maggie pointed out. ''But maybe you'll find him one day. I hope so.''

"You could come back with me," Gretchen said somberly. "It isn't too late to change your mind. What if Cord suddenly wakes up and realizes he's crazy about you, and you're two thousand miles away?"

"As you said, he knows how to get on an airplane," Maggie replied firmly. "Now let's talk about something *cheerful.*"

Gretchen didn't say another word. But she hoped most sincerely that Maggie knew what she was doing. It was one thing to be a tourist, quite another to be dependent in a foreign country. The job sounded almost too good to be true. And wasn't Qawi a very male-dominated society where women had separate quarters and separate lives from men? It did seem odd that the sheikh would want not only a female public relations officer, but one from a foreign country known for liberated women. Perhaps there was a subtle revolution in progress in Qawi. Gretchen hoped so. She didn't want her best friend in danger. But, she cheered herself, they still had a week in Tangier to enjoy. It was going to be a perfect trip. She just knew it.

Chapter Two

But all Maggie's plans for her vacation and her new job went up in smoke the next morning as she accepted an unexpected long-distance call from Jacobsville, Texas. "I hate to have to tell you this," Eb Scott, a friend of hers told her quietly. "Cord's been hurt. He was doing a job in Florida a week ago, putting a small explosive device in a barrel for remote detonation and it went off in his face."

Every drop of blood drained out of Maggie's face. She gripped the telephone receiver like a lifeline. "Is he…dead?" she asked in a hoarse whisper.

An eternity of seconds later he said, "No. But he wishes he was. He's blind, Maggie."

She closed her eyes, trying to see that proud,

independent man walking with a cane or a guide dog, trying to pick up the pieces of his life alone. "Where is he?" she asked.

"Gretchen's brother, Marc, was in Miami when it happened. He picked up Cord and brought him home when he was released from the hospital. Cord's at his ranch outside Houston." There was another hesitation. "I didn't know until Marc phoned me on his way back to Miami."

"Is Cord alone?"

"All alone," Eb said irritably. "He wouldn't come down here and stay with Sally and me in Jacobsville, or even with Cy Parks. He doesn't have any family of his own, does he?"

"Only me," Maggie said with a hollow laugh, "if I qualify as family." She hesitated, thinking fast. "I suppose he'd kick me out if I came home to stay with him."

"Actually," Eb said slowly, choosing his words, "Marc said he was calling for you when they took him to the hospital."

Her heart jumped. That was a first. She couldn't remember a time in their lives when Cord had needed her. He had wanted her, but only once, and he hadn't even been sober...

"I phoned Cord as soon as Marc said he'd taken him home. Cord told me he didn't think you'd want to look after him, but that I could call you if

I wanted to,'' Eb added dryly. "So I'm calling you.''

"What incredible timing,'' Maggie said, her nerves raw. "I'm on my way to a new job and I have a week's vacation left...'' She glanced at Gretchen, who was eavesdropping unashamedly, and grimaced. "I don't know how I'll do it, but I'll fly out this afternoon if I can get a flight to Brussels and then a nonstop flight home.''

"I knew you would,'' Eb said gently. "I'll let Cord know.''

"Thanks, Eb,'' she said sincerely.

"My pleasure. Have a safe trip. And Marc said to tell Gretchen to be careful about going anywhere alone while she's over there.''

"I'll tell her. Cord...the blindness...is it going to be permanent?'' she asked.

"They aren't sure yet.''

She thanked him and hung up. "Cord's been hurt,'' she said without preamble, "and I have to go home, today. I'm sorry to leave you in the lurch...''

Knowing how Maggie felt about Cord, Gretchen would have allowed herself to be carried off by bandits rather than express any fear at being alone in a foreign country. "Don't you worry about me. I can take care of myself,'' Gretchen said with more confidence than she felt after Maggie explained what was going on. "But what about your job, Maggie?"

Maggie stared at her friend and her mind went into overdrive. A plan was forming...

"You can do it."

Gretchen gaped at her. "What?"

"You can go to Qawi and take the job. Just listen," she said when Gretchen started to protest. "It's exactly what you need. You'll vegetate in that little law office in Jacobsville. You've already given up most of your life to nurse your mother. It's time you got a look at the real world. It's the chance of a lifetime!"

"But I'm a paralegal," Gretchen groaned. "I don't know how to organize parties and write press releases. And the sheikh is expecting a widow with dark hair...!"

"Tell him you've dyed it, and don't mention that you're a widow," Maggie said, dragging out her suitcase and heading for the closet where her clothes were hung. "You can use my ticket and I'll give you all my spare cash."

"This is a very bad idea..."

"It's a wonderful idea," Maggie countered. "You'll have the time of your life. You may even find an eligible bachelor."

"Oh, that's a great idea," Gretchen mused

whimsically. "I can be wife number four wrapped up from head to toe in somebody's harem!"

Maggie shot her a dry look. "You've got a lot to learn about Muslim women. They live by values we used to, and they have their own power. They have the vote in Qawi and several other countries, and their own independent finances. But there are plenty of Christian women and men in Qawi. Rumor has it that not only are the majority of the people Christian, but that the sheikh himself is one. His parentage is mixed."

"As I recall, there was a rumor about the sheikh's perverse sexual appetite," Gretchen reminded her friend. "You told me yourself."

"That was cleared up on the INN interview," her friend said absently. "Senator Holden said that the sheikh himself had started those rumors to get Pierce Hutton's wife to safety before her stepfather could harm her. They say he never got over Brianne Hutton." She started pulling clothes off hangers. "Mrs. Hutton isn't really pretty at all, but she has a beautiful smile and she wears clothes with a real flair. Maybe the sheikh was attracted because she's so blond."

"I suppose he's very dark, isn't he?" Gretchen asked.

"I don't know. I've never seen him, and there aren't many photos of him floating about. Even at his investiture, he was wearing a ceremonial *bisht* over his robes, along with a headcloth and an *igal*, and he managed to keep his face partially hidden from the international press." Maggie finished packing, her mind still on Cord even as she organized her papers and her purse.

"Maybe he's got warts," Gretchen said wickedly.

Maggie wasn't paying attention. She looked around the room. "If I've forgotten anything, send it back to me, will you? Here." She handed Gretchen a handful of Moroccan paper money and some coins. "I can't take this out of the country, anyway, and I won't have time to change it. You spend the next week here and then fly on to Qawi. By the time the sheikh finds out you aren't me— if he ever does—you'll be so comfortably situated that he'll probably keep you on anyway."

"Optimist." Gretchen hugged her friend.

Smiling, Maggie picked up the phone and spoke briefly and urgently to the kind man at the desk. "Thanks," she said after a minute. "I'll be right down." She went to get her things together, and spoke to Gretchen over her shoulder. "He's getting me a ticket. The car will be waiting downstairs. Mustapha's taking me to the airport. Remember, don't go out of the hotel grounds alone. Promise me."

"I promise. Maggie, you be careful, too. I hope Cord's okay."

"Without his sight?" Maggie asked sadly. "All I can do is what he'll let me do, and it won't be easy. But maybe I can help him adjust. At least he needs me. That's never really happened before."

"Miracles happen when you least expect them," Gretchen said comfortingly.

"I hope so. Cord could use one. Write to me!" she called as she grabbed up her hastily packed bag and went out the door.

"Of course."

There was such a hollow silence in the room after Maggie's departure that Gretchen could hardly bear it. There were television programs, but only on a handful of channels, and most of them were in Arabic or French. Only the news channel was in English. The room was a good size, but it was claustrophobic under the circumstances. Gretchen had to stretch her legs. She decided to go and play in the swimming pool. She might as well get a little sun while she could.

The afternoon was lonely, although she met other tourists and began to recognize them on sight. But she sat at a table by herself during the afternoon and evening meals and went up to her room early. She imagined that Maggie would be on her way back to Brussels by now to catch her flight home. She'd be alone, too.

She thought about their missed day trip and thought that perhaps the next morning she could get Mustapha to take her on the tour of the Grotto of Hercules that she and Maggie had planned for today. Then, she could go to the coastal city of Asilah the following day. It would be something to look forward to.

She slept restlessly, but felt oddly refreshed when she awoke the following morning. She put on a sleeveless yellow-and-white patterned long dress with a white knit jacket over it and left her hair long around her shoulders as she went to the concierge to see if he could help her find Mustapha.

In her haste, she ran almost headlong into a very distinguished-looking man in a gray designer silk suit. He caught her shoulders to steady her when she lost her footing and his twinkling black eyes searched her face amusedly.

"Oh, I'm so sorry," she gasped. "I mean, *excusez-moi, monsieur,*" she corrected, because he looked French. Sort of. He was elegant and he might have been handsome, except for the deep scars down one lean, clean-shaven cheek. His straight hair was as black as his eyes, and he had a grace of carriage that was rare in a man so tall.

He was darker than most American men, but not radically so, and lighter than some of the Arabs and Berbers she'd seen here. He was very tall. Gretchen only came up to his chin.

"*Il n'ya pas de quois, mademoiselle,*" he replied suavely, in a deep voice, as soft as velvet. "I am undamaged."

She grinned at him, liking the way his eyes sparked. "I'll watch where I'm going next time."

"You are staying here?" he asked with a polite smile.

She nodded. "For a few days. I'm on my way to a new job in Qawi, but I wanted a vacation first. It's beautiful here."

"A new job in Qawi?" he prompted with unusual interest.

"Yes. I'm going to work for the sheikh," she said confidingly. "Public relations," she added. "I'm really looking forward to it."

He was quiet for a space of seconds and his quick, intelligent eyes narrowed. "Do you know this part of the world well?"

"It's my first time out of the United States, I'm afraid," she said. She smiled again. "I feel so stupid. Everybody around here speaks at least four languages. I only speak my own and a little Spanish."

His eyebrows shot up. "Amazing," he murmured.

"What is?"

"A modest American."

"Most of us are modest," she told him, grinning. "Well, a few of us are rude and conceited, but you mustn't judge a whole country by a handful of people. And Texans are usually very modest, considering that our state is better than all the others!"

He chuckled. "You are from Texas?"

"Oh, yes," she told him. "I'm a certified cowgirl," she added dryly. "If you don't believe it, I'll rope a cow for you anytime you like."

He chuckled again at her enthusiasm. He couldn't remember ever meeting anyone like her except for once, a few years ago. He pursed his chiseled lips and studied her again, closely. "I understand that Qawi is smaller than even one of your states."

She looked around her with eyes that seemed to find everything interesting. "Yes, but America is pretty much the same wherever you go," she pointed out. "Here, the music is different, the food is different, the clothes are different, and there's so much history that I could spend the rest of my life learning it."

"You like history?"

"I love it," she said. "I wish I could have gone to college and studied it, but my mother had cancer and I couldn't leave her alone very much. I had to while I worked, of course, but I couldn't take classes, too. There was no time. And no money. She died four months ago and I still miss her." She smiled apologetically. "I'm sorry. I didn't mean to ramble on like that."

"I enjoyed it," he replied, and seemed to mean it.

"Mademoiselle Barton!" the concierge called to her.

It took several seconds for her to realize that the concierge had mistaken her for Maggie. Which was just as well, she supposed. She excused herself, went around the tall man with the briefcase in one hand, and went to the desk.

"Mustapha has already left to take a party of our guests to the Grotto of Hercules," he said apologetically. "But if you still wish to go, our car is at your disposal, and we can ask one of the other guides to accompany you."

"I don't know…" Gretchen said hesitantly. She didn't think she was going to enjoy the trip all alone.

"Excuse me," the tall man interjected, joining her at the counter. "I had planned to go see the

Grotto myself. Perhaps I could intrude on the young lady's company…?''

She looked up at him with pure relief. "Oh, that would be lovely…I mean, if you'd like to go?"

"I would." He glanced at the concierge and spoke rapidly and in a language Gretchen couldn't begin to understand. Comments passed back and forth and the concierge chuckled to himself. Gretchen was wondering if her impulsive acceptance was going to get her into trouble. She knew nothing whatsoever about the stranger…

"The gentleman is quite trustworthy, *mademoiselle*," the concierge said to her when he noticed her worried look. "I can assure you that you will come to no harm in his company. Shall I ask, uh, Bojo—another guide—to bring the car to the front door now?"

Gretchen glanced at her companion, who nodded.

"Yes, then." She hesitated. "But your briefcase…''

He handed it to the concierge with another brief spate of comment in that same musical but puzzling language and turned to Gretchen with a smile. "Shall we go?"

The hotel's stately Mercedes, with a tall, intelligent Berber at the wheel, easily identified by the way he wore his mustache and beard, slid easily into the flow of traffic. Their guide, like the taxi driver at their arrival in Tangier, had the window down and spoke volubly to other drivers and pedestrians with long, sweeping waves of his arm as he passed them. The stranger told her that he'd instructed Bojo to take them first to the Caves of Hercules, which she'd wanted to see earlier, and then on to Asilah.

"Bojo was born in Tangier. He knows half the population and is related to the other half," the tall man said, lazing back against his seat with crossed arms to observe her.

"Like back home in Jacobsville," she said, understanding. "Small towns are nice. Everybody knows everyone else. I don't think I'd be happy in a big city, where I wouldn't know anybody at all."

"Yet you left your small town to take a position in a foreign—very foreign—country," he said, and it was a question as much as a statement of fact.

She smiled absently as she looked past the driver's head to the narrow city streets ahead, lined with palm trees and pedestrians in brightly colored clothing. "With my mother dead, and no close relatives, I seemed to be looking at a dead end of a future back home."

"You are not married, then?"

"Me? Oh, no, I've never been married," she

said absently. "I had a boyfriend." She grimaced. "He thought I'd inherit a lot of property and money when my mother died, but the property was mortgaged to the hilt and there was only enough insurance for a simple funeral. He just vanished after the funeral. He's dating a banker's daughter now."

Her companion's face hardened visibly. He was studying her intently, but she didn't notice. "I see."

She shrugged. "He was nice to me, and at least I had someone for a little while, when Mama was the worst." She sighed as her eyes followed the coastline. "Before, I never got to date much. She'd been sick for a long time, you see, and there was only me to take care of her. My brother helped as much as he could, of course, but he works for the government and he travels most of the time."

"And there was no one else who could have helped you? A close friend, perhaps?"

She shook her head. "Just my friend Maggie, but she lived in Houston. Lives in Houston," she faltered. "I lived on our little family ranch with Mama that my brother managed to save. We have a foreman who lives there now and works for shares."

"This friend," he persisted in a deceptively lazy tone. "Did she come abroad with you?"

"Yes, but she had to go home unexpectedly." She frowned, wondering if she should be so forthcoming with a total stranger.

"And left you all alone and at the mercy of strangers?" he taunted in a soft, teasing tone.

She glanced at him with a suddenly impish smile. "Are you going to offer me candy and ask me to go home with you?" she asked.

He chuckled softly. "I abhor sweets, as it happens," he said, crossing his long legs in their elegant slacks. "And you seem a bit too astute to be picked up in such a manner."

"Oh, I don't know about that," she murmured. "I'm partial to chocolates. I could be a real pushover to anybody with a pocketful of Godiva soft centers."

"A fact I shall have to have to keep in mind, *mademoiselle...Barton,*" he said, so suavely that she missed the faint hesitation in his voice.

She searched his dark eyes, not liking to start off their friendship with a lie. "Mademoiselle Brannon," she corrected. "Gretchen Brannon."

He took the hand she offered and lifted it to his mouth. She grinned. "Mademoiselle Brannon," he corrected. *"Enchante."* His eyes narrowed. "I understood the concierge to call you Mademoiselle Barton."

She grimaced. "That's Maggie Barton, my

friend and my roommate. Her foster brother was terribly injured in an accident and she flew home this morning.'' She bit her lower lip. ''I probably shouldn't ramble on about it, but she wants me to do something that isn't quite ethical and my conscience is killing me.''

He leaned back, his eyes calm and faintly amused. ''Please,'' he invited with a gesture of one lean hand. ''Often it helps to speak of problems to an uninterested but objective stranger.'' When she hesitated, he chuckled. ''We are strangers, *n'est pas?*''

''Yes. And I don't guess you know anybody in Qawi?''

He lifted his eyebrows expressively.

She shrugged. ''Well, Maggie got a job working for the sheikh there and since she can't take it now, she wanted me to take her place without telling anyone who I was.''

His eyes were twinkling. ''You disapprove?''

''She wasn't really thinking straight, or she wouldn't have suggested it. I don't like telling lies,'' she said flatly. ''And I'm not any good at them, either. Besides, I don't think I can pass for an executive-type businesswoman who's also a widow. I'm not sophisticated and I don't know how to plan parties or welcome visiting dignitaries.

All I know how to do is legal work. I worked for a firm of attorneys in Jacobsville."

He listened attentively, his eyes narrow with speculation and a half smile on his wide, thin mouth. "Amazing," he murmured.

She looked up at him with wide gray eyes. "What is?"

"Never mind." He searched her eyes. "So you think the job is beyond your capabilities?"

"Certainly it is," she said. "I'm going to finish my vacation here and then fly to Amsterdam and go home," she added, making her decision as she spoke.

One dark, elegant eyebrow lifted. "Do you believe in fate, Miss Brannon?"

"I don't know."

"I do. I think you should go to Qawi."

"And live a lie?" she murmured unhappily.

"No. And tell the truth." He uncrossed his legs and leaned forward abruptly. "I know the Sheikh of Qawi. Rather, I know of him," he said unexpectedly. "He is a fair man, and he admires nothing more than honesty. Use your friend's ticket. Take the job."

"He won't give it to me," she interrupted. "He was emphatic about Maggie's qualifications, and one of them, for some reason, was that she'd been married..."

"Tell him the truth, and take the job," he repeated firmly. "He will make allowances. I happen to know that his need of an assistant is personal and immediate. He will not want to waste time trying to find someone else with Madame Barton's qualifications."

"But I'm not qualified," she emphasized.

He smiled. "To meet people?" he chided. "You and I are strangers, yet here we are sharing a holiday trip."

She let a smile touch her soft mouth. "That was only because I almost knocked you down," she pointed out. "I can't really make a habit of it, just to meet people."

He waved a hand. "I think you will make an excellent assistant."

"As I mentioned earlier, I can't speak any other language except Spanish."

"You can learn Arabic."

"And worst of all, I'm not Muslim," she worried.

"Neither is the sheikh." He leaned forward with a grin. "Qawi is unusual as a nation in the mixture of her cultures. There are as many Jews and Christians as there are Muslims, owing to an unusual colonial history. You will feel right at home," he assured her. "And in the past two years, it has become an ally of both the United States and Great

Britain." He grinned wickedly. "Oil contracts are lucrative temptations to democracies. How many friends Qawi has gained because of her new wealth!"

She smiled. "You make this sound very easy," she told him.

"As it is." He frowned as he studied her oval face. She was attractive, but no real beauty. However her features were nice, and she had warm eyes. Her mouth was perfect. He grimaced as he looked at it and mourned for what he could never experience again. Her hair, though, was what fascinated him. It was platinum blond, obviously long, and definitely natural. She reminded him, oh, so much, of Brianne Martin...

She was looking at him, too. She wondered how he'd gotten those scars on his face. There were others on the back of his left hand, the same side as those on his face.

He saw her curiosity and touched his cheek lightly. "An accident, when I was much younger," he said frankly. "There are other scars, better hidden," he added in a harsh undertone.

She smiled self-consciously. "Sorry," she said at once. "I didn't mean to stare. They're not disfiguring, you know," she added easily. "You look like a pirate."

His eyelids flickered. *"Mademoiselle?"*

"You need an eye-patch and a cutlass and a parrot, though," she added. "And one of those sexy white ruffled shirts that leaves half your chest bare."

His delight was in the explosion of brilliance in his black eyes, in the hearty laugh that fell like music on her ears. She had a feeling that he laughed very rarely.

"Oh, and a ship," she continued. "With black sails."

"One of my ancestors was a Riffian Berber," he told her. "Not quite a pirate, but very definitely a revolutionary."

"I just knew it," she said with glee. She searched his dark eyes and felt a thrill in the pit of her stomach that had no counterpart in her memory. Her breath was catching in her throat. No man had ever made her feel so feminine. "Have you ever ridden a camel?" she asked.

"What prompted that question?" he asked.

She indicated a man standing with a small herd of camels at the front of a hotel on the coast, whose parking lot they were just entering. "I really do want to ride a camel before I go home."

"There are no saddles, you know," he said as the driver parked the car and got out to open the door for them.

Gretchen looked at her gray slacks and sandals. "No stirrups, either?"

"No."

She looked longingly at the camels. "They're so pretty. They're like horses on stilts."

"Treachery!" he remonstrated. "To compare a mere beast of burden with something so elegant as our Arabian horses!"

She arched her eyebrows and looked up at him. "Do you ride?"

"Of course I ride." He looked at the camels with distaste. "But not in a suit." An Armani suit, but he wasn't going to mention that.

She caught his sleeve lightly. She didn't touch people often, but she felt safe with him. He wasn't a stranger, even though he should have been. "Please?" she asked. "I don't even want to go far. I just want to know what it's like."

It was like gossamer strands of silk brushing open nerves to have her soft green eyes look at him that way. Her fingers weren't even touching his skin, but he felt their warmth right through the fabric, and his breath caught. Something unfamiliar tautened his tall, fit body.

"Very well," he said abruptly, moving away from that light touch.

She dropped her hand as if he'd burned it. He didn't like to be touched, she noticed. She wouldn't forget again. She grinned at him as they approached the camel master. "Thanks!"

"You'll fall off and break your neck, most likely," he muttered darkly. He spoke to the camel driver in that same odd dialect she didn't understand, smiling and gesturing with his hands as the other man did. They both looked at her, grinning from ear to ear.

"Come along," the tall man told Gretchen, nodding her toward a small wooden block that was standing beside one of the well-groomed tan camels. The single hump was covered by a blanket and there was a tiny braided rope to hold on to.

"I'm not quite sure...ooh!"

The tall man had lifted her right up in his arms. He smiled at her shock as he put her on the camel's back and handed her the single small braided rein. "Wrap your legs around the hump," he instructed, "and hold tight. I've told our friend here to walk her slowly up the hill and back. No galloping," he assured her.

She dug her small camera out of the fanny pack around her waist and handed it down to him. "Would you?"

He grinned. "Of course."

She rode, laughing at the odd side to side gait of the beast. She waved at the grinning motorists who passed her as the camel's owner led the camel up and down by the side of the small paved road. The whole way, the tall man watched them and took photos. He didn't look much like a man of action, and she couldn't really picture him on a camel. He seemed like a businessman, and he was probably as fastidious about dirt and camel hair as he would have been about mud. She'd dreamed of a man of action racing across the desert on a stallion. Her companion, who was charming and good company at least, was no counterpart of the daring sheikh she'd read about in the 1920's novel from which Valentino's movie had been made. It was a little disappointing. She had to stop living in fantasies, she reminded herself, and held on tight to the little rope as she bounced along.

When they returned, and the Moroccan had coaxed the camel onto its knees, the tall man handed him the camera and said something under his breath. He reached up and lifted Gretchen down in his strong arms, pausing to turn toward the camera. "Smile," he instructed, and looked down into her wide, curious eyes. She smiled back, her heart whipping into her throat, her lips parted with lingering pleasure and the beginnings of an odd longing.

"Did you enjoy it?" he asked, hesitating.

"It was wonderful," she said breathlessly. She searched his eyes slowly, aware of the smooth fabric of his jacket, where her nervous hands rested, and the narrow, unblinking scrutiny of those black eyes. She couldn't quite breathe while he held her.

He felt her breath against his chin and again that unfamiliar stirring made him frown. He put her down abruptly and moved away to retrieve the camera. Gretchen stood watching him with nervous discomfort. She felt as if she'd done something very wrong. She had no idea what.

He was back very shortly. He handed her the camera and smiled politely, as if nothing had happened to mar the pleasure of her first camel ride. "The grotto is just down that path. Come along."

She went first, leaving him to follow. There was a stall at the entrance to the Caves of Hercules and she hesitated with her eyes on a small, flat circle of rock with a raised dome and what looked like a fossil on it. Fascinated, she picked it up, finding it silky to the touch.

"Your first souvenir? Allow me," he murmured, paying for it.

"But…"

He held up a hand to silence her protest. "A trifle," he waved away the cost. He nodded toward the cave's entrance. "Go slowly. This is a living cave. You will find limestone walls where, for centuries, men have hewn millstones from them."

She went inside, feeling the cool dampness of

the caves as she walked along the bare ground and mingled with other tourists. There was an opening toward the sea which looked very much like a map of Africa. The walls had circles carved out—the millstones, she thought. She cradled her souvenir in her small hands and took out her camera again, photographing the walls and, when he wasn't looking, her strangely attractive companion. She was enjoying his company as she'd enjoyed little else in her life. And she didn't even know his name!

She moved back toward him. He was watching the waves through the opening in the cavern, his hands deep in his pockets, his expression taciturn and brooding.

He turned as she joined him and the polite smile was back on his face.

"I don't know your name," she said softly.

His eyes twinkled. "Call me...Monsieur Souverain," he said in a deep, soft tone.

"Do you have a first name, or is that some heavily guarded secret?" she teased.

He chuckled. "Philippe," he said smoothly.

"Philippe." She smiled.

The twinkle in his eyes became more pronounced. He pursed his lips. "Come along," he said, turning. "We can go on to Asilah, if you like?"

"I'd like that very much," she said honestly and

then hesitated. "I'm not taking you away from any important business, am I?" she asked, concerned.

He laughed. "I have no important business after today and tomorrow," he assured her. "Perhaps, like you, I am having a holiday."

"I'll bet you don't have many," she said, watching her step as they climbed the narrow, rocky path up to the parking lot.

"Why do you say that?"

"You act like the consummate businessman," she told him without looking up. "I expect you're in town on some huge project that involves all sorts of important people."

"I was," he said. "But the deal rather fell through before I got off the plane. I am working on another, however, which I expect will be even more successful."

She didn't notice that he was watching her covertly as he spoke, and that his eyes were brimming over with humor.

She looked around as they started to get back into the hotel's car, and she caught her breath. "It's nothing like I expected when we left Texas," she confided. "It's so exciting, and the people are all friendly and courteous—it's almost like being at home, except for the way people dress and the sound of Arabic and Berber being spoken." She turned to him with the car door standing open.

"Don't you know anything about Morocco?" he asked gently.

She laughed. "All our television reporters talk about are scandals and political issues and the latest tragedy. They don't tell us one thing about other countries unless somebody important is murdered in one."

"So I have seen," he mused.

She grinned. "That's why Maggie and I came to Morocco, to see what it was really like. And now that we've been properly introduced," she added, smiling as she extended her hand, "I'm very pleased to meet you, Monsieur Souverain."

"I can return the compliment, Gretchen." He brought her hand, palm up, to his hard mouth and looked straight into her eyes as his lips brushed it with a strangely sensuous motion. He made her name sound foreign, mysterious, exciting. The feel of his mouth on her skin made her uneasy, although not in any bad way. Faintly unnerved by the sensations the caress caused in her body, she pulled her fingers away a little too quickly, laughing nervously to cover the action.

He didn't say a word until they were comfortably seated and the car was moving again, but his eyes were even more curious. She looked hunted for a moment, and that would never do. He smiled carelessly. "Would you like to hear something of the history of Tangier?" he asked.

"I'd love to," she replied.

He crossed his long legs. "The Berbers were the first to arrive here," he began, warming to his subject.

They passed cork factories and olive groves along the highway that led down the coast to Asilah, and Gretchen laughed as she watched camels playing in the surf at the ocean's edge.

"They like to swim and sun themselves," Philippe told her pleasantly, "much like tourists on holiday."

"They're very soft, but they aren't as big as I expected them to be. I guess they look different in movies."

"You saw *The Wind and the Lion* with Sean Connery?" he asked at once.

"Why, yes, several times," she confessed.

"The palace of the Raissouli is in Asilah."

She gasped. "He was a real person?"

"A revolutionary," he agreed, "who tried to overthrow the monarchy. He failed," he added dryly.

"My goodness, I thought it was all fiction."

"Most of it was," he told her. "But I also enjoyed it. In my country, foreign films are a large part of our entertainment.''

His country. France, she was certain. She smiled. "I've never been to France," she mused. "I'll bet it's beautiful."

"Beautiful," he agreed, deliberately encouraging her mistaken idea of his background. "And old. Like most of Europe. The kasbah of Tangier dates back to Roman conquest and even earlier."

"I love all of it," she said fervently. "Every cobblestone and villa, every little shop, the people who meander through those narrow walled streets. It's like a fairyland."

His black eyes narrowed. "You enjoy foreign places."

She looked over at him. "I've never even been out of Texas before," she confessed. "Not even to the Mexican border. I've never been...well, anywhere. And to get to see Africa, of all places." Her heart was in her eyes. "I feel as if I'm living a dream."

"Do you know," he murmured absently, "that is exactly how I feel." Then he smiled, and the intensity of his gaze turned to the passing coastline.

Chapter Three

Asilah was bustling with activity. Before 1972, Bojo the guide told them, the whole city was inside the ancient walls. Now there were shops outside as well, and new construction underway. As they searched for a parking space in the crowded city, they saw small donkey-drawn carts carrying people from one side of town to the other, and just outside the kasbah on a tree-lined street near the bay, there were sidewalk cafés. But first the guide indicated that they should go away from the old walled city toward the highway, because that was where the once-weekly open air market was held.

"Market day," Philippe told Gretchen, gently taking her arm to guide her across the busy street which was packed with cars as well as carts. "This will be an adventure."

It was. She saw beautiful fruits and vegetables, herbs and spices, all presented in beautiful order and not one blemish on any of it. There were exotic spices, potions, clothing and hats. There were leather goods and even live chickens and rabbits for sale. Outside the ramshackle order of small tents teeming with people, donkeys and camels lay in the shade waiting for the return trip to their small villages.

"The produce is just beautiful," she exclaimed. "My goodness, this is even prettier than in our supermarkets back home, but it isn't refrigerated."

He chuckled. "Yes, and on this market day, much of it gets sold to city dwellers."

He acquainted her with the various spices and the displays of olives before the guide led them back into the city.

"Are you thirsty?" Philippe asked her.

"I could drink a gallon of water all by myself," she panted, wiping the sweat from her forehead with a tissue from her pocket.

He grinned. "So could I."

He and the guide led her to a small café where he ordered bottled water for her and mint tea for himself. He offered her some tea, but she declined, nervous about trying anything that didn't come out of a bottle.

"You must try the mint tea before you leave Morocco," he told her. "It is famous here."

"I will. Right now cold water sounds better."

"I don't doubt it."

He handed her chilled bottled water and took his mint tea to a small group of tables under a spreading tree near the walls of the old city. Their guide remained behind to speak to a shop owner he knew. "The café owns this small space," Philippe told her, "and patrons pay at the counter and eat here."

"This is very nice," she said, looking around her at comfortably dressed people wandering about. "There are lots of tourists here."

"Yes. The city is the site of an arts festival which is going on even now. The shops in the old walled city are brimming over, and Asilah has put on its brightest face for the festival. It draws people from around Europe and Africa and from all over the world."

"You said the revolutionary's palace was here?" she asked.

He nodded. He sipped his mint tea, finished it, and excused himself to return the china cup and saucer to the stand. She was curious about that, because most of the tourists had disposable containers like hers. Following Philippe with her eyes, she saw the extreme courtesy with which the shop owner treated him. While she was observing that, she noticed something else—foreign men in sunglasses and dark suits standing nearby. They'd parked behind them when they arrived. She wondered why they were here. Whimsically she wondered if they were shadowing some important foreign dignitary who was in disguise. When she got home, she'd have to ask her brother about foreign security. Then she remembered that she was going to Qawi, not home. It made her nervous and a little sad.

Philippe came back and studied her from his great height. "You're worried," he said abruptly.

"Sorry." She pinned a smile to her face as she got to her feet, clutching her half-finished bottle of water. "I was thinking about my new job, if I get it."

"And worrying," he persisted.

She grimaced. "I don't like using a plane ticket in someone else's name and pretending I'm her, even if he does eventually hire me anyway."

He smiled. "I think you have very little to worry about in that respect. As for the plane ticket, the concierge will change it for you, into the right name, and Mustapha or Bojo there—" he indicated their tall driver and guide still lingering at the shop counter "—will even take you to the airport and wait with you."

"They will?"

He grinned at her shocked expression. "Isn't this done in your country?"

"No, it isn't," she said flatly.

"To each his own," he said tolerantly. "You will find life a little different in this part of the world."

"I already have," she said. She laughed gently. "I don't know that it's good for me to be pampered like this. I'm just a very ordinary paralegal."

One eye narrowed. "I think, Gretchen Brannon, that you are not very ordinary at all."

"You don't know much about women from Texas."

"A gap in my education which I hope to correct in the next few days," he said gallantly. With a twinkle in his black eyes, he added in the classic line from an old Charles Boyer movie, "Will you come with me to the kasbah?"

She laughed helplessly. "I really do watch too many movies. I only thought there was one kasbah until the cabdriver at the airport told me what they were."

"Charles Boyer and Humphrey Bogart films," he mused. "They portray a very different Morocco."

"Yes. Those days are long dead."

"The old ways, perhaps. Not the intrigue," he

informed her. He put a hand under her elbow to guide her through the gates of the old city and into the maze of narrow streets and small shops. He leaned down to her ear. "Do you see the man in the beige suit wearing sunglasses? No, don't turn your head!"

She had a flash of vision out of the corner of her eye. "Yes."

"Now, do you notice the gentlemen in dark suits and sunglasses nearby?"

"I saw them earlier...!"

"Bodyguards."

"Really?" She sounded breathless with excitement. "Whose are they? Do they belong to the man in the beige suit?"

He pursed his lips amusedly. "Who knows? Perhaps he works for one of the Saudi princes who have estates outside Tangier."

"The one the guide pointed out, with the heliport and armed guards at the gate?"

"That one. They go sightseeing from time to time. Yesterday I saw the ex-president of Spain in town."

"So did we! I've never met a head of state, former or not."

He kept his eyes carefully on the path ahead and didn't reply.

"Those bodyguards, I guess they have guns?"

"Nine millimeter Uzis and they know how to use them."

She gasped. "Good Lord. I hope nobody attacks him."

"Nobody knows him," he said lazily. "Heads of state from the Middle Eastern countries wander around here all the time and are never noticed. They blend in."

"If you notice the Sheikh of Qawi, how about pointing him out to me?" she asked facetiously. "Maybe I can throw myself on his mercy before I arrive in his capital city like an unclaimed parcel."

He put on his own sunglasses and grinned. "I can promise you, his own subjects wouldn't know him in a European suit."

"Is he...perverse?" she asked bluntly, worried in spite of Maggie's assurances.

He stopped dead and looked down at her. His eyes, behind the dark lenses, were concealed. "What?" he asked icily.

She bit her lower lip. "My friend, Maggie, said that there were rumors about him and young women. She said they weren't true and that he started them himself."

"He did," he said quietly. "I can promise you that you will be in no danger from him. In fact," he added thoughtfully, "I think you may find yourself pampered as you never expected to be, under his protection.''

She drew in a breath. ''I hope you're right!'' she said fervently. ''Oh, look at those shawls!''

She rushed forward to a display over the doorway of a shop. There was a black shawl with pear-shaped fringe work that took her breath.

''A Moroccan scarf, like those the women wear around their heads when they go out in public,'' he said. ''In Qawi, we call a head covering a *hijab*. Do you fancy it?''

''I suppose it's very expensive,'' she said, glaring up at him. ''But you're not buying it. If I can afford it, I'll buy it for myself.''

He grinned. ''Ah, that American independence asserts itself! Very well.'' He spoke to the man in that gutteral tongue she still didn't recognize and laughed as he glanced down at her. ''It is fifty-six dirhams,'' he told her.

''Fifty-six…!''

''Seven American dollars,'' he translated.

She let out her breath and smiled. ''I'll take it!''

He helped her find the coins to pay for it and let the man package it for her. He put the parcel under his arm and led her through the maze of other shops where she bargained with delight for a small pair of silver earrings and a worked silver and turquoise bracelet.

"There," he said as they went down a long cobblestoned path, "is the palace of the Raissouli."

It took her breath away. The tiles, in white and many shades of vibrant blue, were combined in the most beautiful mosaic pattern she could have imagined inside the white, white walls of the exterior. There was little inside to see, but she touched the ceramic tiles with utter fascination.

"All the tile work is geometric," she murmured.

"Worshipers of Islam are forbidden from representing anything human or animal in the patterns," he explained. "Thus the geometric designs."

"They're so beautiful." She sighed with pleasure. "When I think of our concrete and steel and brick buildings back home..."

"But you have wooden ones as well," he reminded her.

"Yes, old Victorian homes with exquisite gingerbread woodwork. I've seen those. In fact, our ranch house is built like that. It isn't luxurious or anything, but it's rather pretty when it's freshly painted."

He studied the gleam of her platinum hair as they went back out into the sunlight and back out the gates of the old city and onto the streets. "Do you ever wear your hair down, Gretchen?" he asked softly.

"It's very fine and flyaway," she said with a smile. "Besides, it gets in my face in the wind, especially the sort they have here in Morocco. It blows constantly."

"How long is it?"

She searched his curious eyes. "It comes down a little past my waist. Why?"

"I know another woman, also an American, with hair much like yours." He grimaced. "She cut hers. I imagine her husband encouraged her," he added darkly. "He knows how much I admire long hair."

Her eyebrows arched. "Her husband?"

He glared. "They have a son, almost two years old."

"She turned you down, I gather?"

His chin went up. "I would not offer marriage," he said evasively. "He did."

"Why, you rake," she teased.

He didn't smile. If anything, he looked grim and introspective.

"Sorry," she said at once. "I suppose she meant something to you?"

"She was my world," he said abruptly. "But there again, fate robbed me." He glanced beyond her and frowned.

She turned, in time to see the man in the beige suit now standing with the bodyguards. One of the two men in black suits on the side of the street was making an urgent gesture with one hand. The man in the beige suit motioned to Philippe.

"We must go at once," he said, propelling her down the walkway to where their guide was waiting with the black-suited men. He was quite suddenly someone else, someone who exercised authority and expected instant obedience. When they reached the black-suited men, they were standing with the one in the beige suit—the man Philippe had described as an employee of a Saudi prince. But the man wasn't behaving like royalty at all. In fact, he was acting in a totally subservient manner, almost pleading from the tone of his voice.

Philippe snapped out questions and then orders in a language that sounded different from the one he'd used in these shops. He glanced down at Gretchen with concern and guided her back toward the car, with their guide in front and the other three men behind and to the side of them.

Gretchen didn't speak. She had a sense of urgency and danger which made her move quickly and keep quiet. She felt Philippe's quick, approving gaze as they made their way back to the car and got inside. The suited men got into the car behind them, another Mercedes she noticed, and they pulled out into the street and quickly back onto the highway that led to Tangier.

In scant minutes, she realized that they were gaining speed and that a third car was apparently in hot pursuit.

She glanced at Philippe with visible apprehension. He had pulled a cell phone from his pocket and was speaking into it rapidly in a foreign tongue. The car behind them, apparently following orders, suddenly whirled and blocked the narrow road so that the pursuing car had to swerve or hit them. As they raced away, the sound of rapid gunfire echoed behind them. Gretchen's hands clenched so hard on her plastic bottle of drinking water that she almost burst it.

"It is all right," Philippe said in a soft, comforting tone, his face hard and somber. "We are perfectly safe. You react well to a crisis," he added with gentle praise.

"That was gunfire!" she said breathlessly.

"It was not meant for us," he said nonchalantly. "We have only helped the young man in the beige suit avert a kidnapping attempt. I assure you, the Moroccan authorities are even now on the way to apprehend the perpetrators."

"But they were armed," she persisted.

He waved a hand. "Armed, but hardly in the class of Ahmed and Bruno."

"Who are they?"

He chuckled. "Bodyguards."

"Oh, yes. The prince's bodyguards."

He lifted an eyebrow and smiled at some private joke. He slid back his sleeve and checked his watch. It was thin and gold, expensive-looking. "I regret having to cut short our sight-seeing tour, but we would have had to leave soon, just the same. I have a rather important business meeting later this afternoon." He lifted his dark head and searched her eyes. "Will you have dinner with me this evening?"

Her heart skipped and she smiled whimsically. "If you…I mean, I really would like that."

"*Bien.* I will call for you at a quarter till eight."

"All right." She wasn't used to having dinner so late, but the hotel didn't serve meals until that hour. She was already hungry. Perhaps she could find something to nibble on in the small refrigerator in her room.

"Did you have breakfast?"

She hesitated. "Well, yes."

He smiled warmly. "But no lunch. You do know that the hotel serves a marvelous little buffet beside the swimming pool around 3:00 p.m.?"

She sighed with relief and smiled back. "I do now. You see, the menus are all in French and I've had to have waiters translate them for me."

"I will do that for you this evening." He pulled out his phone again, pushed in numbers and spoke into it rapidly. The reply came at once. He listened, said something else, and put it away with a sigh. "The would-be kidnappers are in custody."

"I've never seen anything like that in my life," she said on a heavy breath.

"Sadly, I see it far too often," he said absently. He said something to the driver, who nodded. He leaned back again and crossed his legs. "I must have Bojo drop me off at the embassy," he told her. "But he will drive you back to the hotel and escort you inside. I have instructed him to make the concierge aware of our...adventure...this morning, and to look out for you."

She felt as if he were wrapping her up in soft cotton, like a treasure. She barely knew him, yet he wasn't a stranger. "Thank you," she said, feeling that the words were hopelessly inadequate to express what she really felt.

"The entire incident was my fault," he muttered darkly. "I was careless."

"I don't understand. We were only sightseers."

They approached a group of imposing buildings in the middle of the city and the driver pulled up to the curb and stopped.

"I must go." Philippe took her hand to his lips and kissed it lightly just above the knuckles, with his black eyes holding hers the whole time. "Don't brood," he added gently. "You are safer right this moment than you have ever been in your life." He turned his head and said something sharp in that gutteral language. Their driver chuckled and replied with a wave of his hand.

Philippe left the car without a backward glance, but as the driver pulled away from the curb, Gretchen noticed that the black car with the two bodyguards slid quickly to the curb in the wake of hers and the two dark-suited men got out and followed close behind Philippe.

She frowned, wondering why they were following him instead of the Saudi prince. "Those bodyguards..." she began.

"Mademoiselle must not worry," the driver said easily. "Monsieur is in good hands."

"But aren't those men supposed to be the Saudi prince's bodyguards?"

He hesitated. "They are not in the employ of the prince," he said finally. "They are often called upon to escort visiting dignitaries. And important businessmen," he added hastily and smiled.

"I see. Thank you." She smiled and leaned her head back against the seat, relieved and still a little puzzled. Now that she had a friend in Morocco, she didn't want to lose him so quickly.

Bojo got out of the hotel's Mercedes, which he had driven, and escorted Gretchen in to the concierge. He seemed different now, very focused and intent as he related, in the language she didn't understand, what had happened. She noticed that while he was wearing the long striped, hooded robe favored by many Moroccan men, that underneath it he was wearing a suit. She studied him unobtrusively, noting the expensive watch on his own wrist and a diamond-studded ring on his left middle finger. He didn't look like a hotel guide at all. But then he turned back to her, motioned to one of the bellboys and had her escorted up to her room, all with reassuring smiles and consideration. She wondered if she'd ever get used to all this pampering.

She looked at herself in the mirror and noticed a fine layer of yellow sand. The wind seemed to blow all the time, and she'd noticed that none of the cars seemed to have or use air conditioning, because the windows were always open. The sand came into the cabs and, apparently, everywhere else. She took a quick shower, careful not to use more water than she had to. Water in a desert country must be precious.

Her wardrobe was severely limited by Maggie's insistence on only one carry-on piece of luggage. She put on a pair of white slacks with a patterned white-and-purple silk blouse and sandals and grimaced at the white Mexican peasant crinkle-cloth dress hanging in the bathroom, which was all she had to wear to dinner. Perhaps she could wear her hair long and put on her single strand of cultured pearls and their matching earrings and pass. She felt uncomfortable at the idea of disgracing Philippe, who would probably turn up in a dinner jacket and be embarrassed by her.

She went down to the buffet luncheon with apprehension, which was lessened when she saw other tourists in bathing suits filling up china plates. The waiter grinned and her and she grinned back. She realized that many of their visitors would be similarly limited in wardrobe and she stopped worrying.

She had proscuitto and melon with tiny pastries of stuffed pigeon and wondered what people back in Jacobsville would think of the entrée. She sipped water "with gas" as the waiter called sparkling water and felt like a Sybarite on holiday. The sun was warm, the grounds exquisitely beautiful and full of blooming roses and other flowers. The sounds of carefree bathers fell softly on her ears as she curled up drowsily by herself in one of two canopied swings behind the row of padded chaise lounges. Before she knew it, she was asleep.

She was dreaming. She was being rocked in a boat while the breeze stirred a loose strand of hair at her throat. Her cheek was resting on a soft pillow that seemed to beat rhythmically. She sighed and stretched, and the pillow made an odd sound.

She opened her eyes and looked up into a scarred dark face with black eyes that held an odd expression. Her cheek was against his shoulder, and she was cradled across his long legs in the swing. For long seconds, they simply stared at each other in the fading sunlight.

"How fortunate that you went to sleep out of the sun's reach," he said in a voice that was more heavily accented than she'd heard it before. "Sunburn can be lethal in this climate."

"Lunch was delicious and I got drowsy," she said in a hushed tone.

One of his hands was at her throat. He moved it in a faint caress, looking down at her soft mouth for an instant before he lifted his gaze beyond her to the sea. "I sleep very little," he said quietly. "Mine brings nightmares."

"About what?" she asked, intrigued by the familiarity of being held close to him when she should be nervous and wary. He was a stranger. He should have been a stranger...

He spread her fingers against the silky fabric of his jacket and smoothed over her short nails. "War," he said quietly. "Death. The screams of the innocent in the darkness of terror."

She stared up at him uncomprehendingly, with

wide, curious eyes. "Aren't you from France?" she asked hesitantly.

His black eyes slid down to search hers. "No."

"Then, where…?"

The hand at her throat moved, so that his thumb pressed the words back against her lips. "It is too soon, Gretchen," he said gently. "Much too soon for truth. Let us live in a world of utter fantasy for a few days and let tomorrow wait for answers."

She smiled hesitantly. "What sort of fantasy do you have in mind?"

He traced her mouth tenderly. "A very innocent sort," he said with an oddly harsh laugh. "The only sort I am capable of."

"I don't understand."

"I know. Perhaps it is as well that you don't." He smiled down at her, cradled in his arms like a kitten. She smelled of orchids. He traced her cheek with its faint flush and her straight nose, and then her thin eyebrows as if he were sketching her. "How old are you?"

"Twenty-three," she said honestly.

His forefinger eased between her parted lips, sensuously tracing the upper lip and then the lower one, enjoying her reactions. Her breath was jerky against his skin. Her eyes were dilating. He felt her body stir involuntarily and cursed himself and his fate.

"What are you like in passion?" he asked roughly. "Are you submissive, or do you like to bite and claw...?"

Her scarlet blush interrupted him. He scowled down at her horrified expression just before she struggled away from him and moved a foot away on the swing, trying to catch her breath.

"I don't know...what sort of women you're used to," she choked, avoiding his intent scrutiny, "but I don't do that kind of thing!"

His arm was across the back of the swing. His narrow black eyes watched her, intrigued. "What sort of thing?"

"Sleep around," she said flatly and glared at him. "Least of all with a man I've only just met. So if that's why you've been so nice to me, well, you'd better find a more modern woman. If I ever go to bed with a man, it'll be my husband and nobody else. Period."

The harshness went out of him at once. He looked at her with curiosity and, then, with utter delight. He smiled and then he laughed.

"Go ahead," she invited warily. "Call me a prude. Say I'm living in the last century. I don't care. I've heard it all before."

"The small, still voice of reason in a mad world," he said under his breath. "I knew that you were unique among your countrywomen," he added huskily.

"I'm a throwback to Victorian times," she agreed.

He took her hand in his and held it gently. "I don't want a sexual interlude with you, Gretchen," he said quietly.

She hesitated. "You don't?"

He looked at her small hand and hated himself for the curse that denied him a man's expectations. He smoothed his fingers over hers while he considered his options. He could send her home at once. It would be the best thing for her. But she opened his heart. She made him want to live. She made him laugh and smile and look at the world as a place of fascination and delight. He hadn't felt that way for a long time. For two years, in fact. He hadn't ever expected to feel that way again. And if it was like this, so quickly, how would it be as time passed and they got to know each other?

His features twisted. Yes, how would it be when she knew his horrible secret, when the truth came out. Would she look at him with pity, or with contempt and disgust? Could he bear to see that, in her soft green eyes?

He looked at her with torment in his face.

"Oh, don't look like that," she said with concern. "Whatever's wrong, it will all come right one

day. Really it will. You have to look for miracles
or they don't happen, Philippe.''

"How do you know that something is wrong?"
he asked at once.

She frowned. "I don't know. But something is.''

His breath caught in his throat. His fingers tightened on hers. He looked into her eyes and knew
at that moment that he wasn't going to be able to
let her go.

Chapter Four

"It isn't something I've said, is it?" Gretchen asked, breaking into his thoughts. "I know that I'm very opinionated. I didn't mean to be rude..."

He brought her fingers to his lips and then released them. "It isn't anything you've said. In fact, I quite admire your attitude," he added with a smile. "Muslim women value their virtue. But it is a rather unusual trait in this day and age."

"That's what everyone says, all right," she agreed whimsically. She averted her eyes. "My parents were very strict and deeply religious." She toyed with a button on her shirt. "I suppose you're Muslim?"

"No," he said unexpectedly.

That brought her face up. She searched his eyes curiously.

"I am a Christian," he said unexpectedly, and without explanation. "And so are many of my people. We are almost equally divided between Muslim, Christian and Jew. It makes for interesting politics," he added with a grin.

"I'm surprised at how much I don't know about this part of the world," she told him. "I thought everybody was Arab, and Muslim. But I've learned already that many of the people who were born in Morocco are Berbers, not Arabs."

"A people very proud of their ancient heritage," he agreed. "The Berber language is not a written one, either. It is passed down from generation to generation verbally, and its history is woven into the carpets they sell, story by story."

"I'd love to see them," she said.

"Tomorrow," he promised. "I'll have Bojo take us on a walking tour of the city."

"I've already been, but I didn't want to look at carpets," she said sadly. "I didn't realize what I was missing."

He chuckled. "Something to anticipate," he said. "Now, I still have some telephone calls to make, so I must leave you. I'll be along for you just before eight."

"I only have one dress with me," she told him. "It's a lacy white Mexican dress..."

He guessed her thoughts from the worry on her

face. "And you think I may be ashamed of you, because you aren't wearing something very expensive?"

"Yes," she said honestly.

He smiled. "I'm sure that whatever you wear will be charming," he said gently. "I look forward to tonight."

He left her there on the swing and she watched his elegant back as he walked away. One thing this country had already impressed on her was the grace of movement that these people seemed to share with Arabs. Nobody ever seemed to hurry. It was a wonderful slow pace that suited the easy manner of life and business, unrushed, unharried. She wondered whimsically if anyone here ever got ulcers. She really doubted it.

She dressed with more care than ever that evening. It had been months since Daryl had taken her out and pretended to be in love with her. She thought of him with mingled shame and self-contempt. She'd been easy prey for him, in love for the first time in her life and flattered that such a handsome young man should be so interested in her. He'd even come to sit with her at the hospital during the last terrible days when her mother was dying.

Only after the funeral had she understood his

interest. He stopped by the ranch after work and offered to marry her and manage her inheritance for her. When she explained that there was no inheritance, he'd looked shocked and then angry. Muttering something about a waste of time, he'd walked away and never looked back. Her brother, Marc, had tried to warn her about him, but she'd only gotten angry and refused to listen. It was the first time a man had made her feel special and loved. What hurt was that she'd been naïve enough to believe him. But, then, her mother had been so possessive and dependent on her that she rarely got to date anyone while she was in her teens and early twenties. Even then it was mostly blind dates that were one-time occurrences. Marc had commented once that she needed to assert herself more with their mother, despite her illness, but Gretchen's soft heart had been her undoing. When she asked for more freedom, her mother agreed, and then cried and cried about being left alone. Gretchen settled for those rare blind dates until Daryl came along.

She'd met him at the law office where she worked. He'd had Mr. Kemp do some legal work for him and in the course of talking to Gretchen, he'd learned that her mother was terminal and that she lived on a large ranch. Suddenly, he was around when she went to lunch at the local café, and she ran into him often at the supermarket. He asked her to go with him to Houston to a ballet, but she told him her circumstances. He'd laughed and said they could have a picnic in her house and her mother could join them.

Gretchen had been floating on air. Not only did he charm her, but he charmed her mother. He really did make her remaining few weeks happy and cheerful. Gretchen treasured her few stolen minutes with him, thrilling to his kisses and caresses. He'd proposed the week her mother died, and she'd had at least that future happiness to anticipate while she mourned the only parent she had left.

Then, like all dreams, it had ended abruptly. The shame and humiliation she felt was only heightened by Daryl's very public avoidance of her after the funeral. People felt sorry for her, but she didn't want pity. She wanted escape. Then Maggie had phoned and asked if she'd like to go to Morocco...

She came out of her depressing thoughts and back to the present. She looked at herself in the mirror. With her long blond hair loose and faintly waving down her back, and the white dress flowing around her slender curves, with pearls at her ears and neck, she looked different. She wasn't pretty, but she wasn't ugly, either. She felt vulnerable, too. She hoped her new friend meant what he said about not wanting a passionate affair, because for the first time, she might be at the mercy of her own repressed needs. He was far more attractive than Daryl had ever been, and he aroused a fiercer hunger in her than even Daryl had. She could tell already that Philippe was sophisticated. Probably, he'd left a trail of broken hearts and affairs behind him. She had to make sure she didn't end up as one of them. She'd had enough grief lately.

Promptly at a quarter until eight, there was a knock on the door. She opened it, to find Philippe in a beautifully tailored dark suit with a white shirt and patterned blue silk tie. He looked elegant and rakish, like a photo in a fashion magazine, and she felt inhibited and tawdry by comparison in her chain-store dress and shoes.

His black eyes fixed on her long mane of hair and he seemed mesmerized. Slowly, his hand lifted to it, smoothing down it, savoring the feel and scent of it. His indrawn breath was audible. "And you hide it in a braid," he murmured deeply. "What a waste."

She smiled self-consciously. "It worries me to death when I wear it like this."

"But you did it, for me, yes?"

She moved restlessly. "Yes."

He tilted her chin up and searched her eyes. His thumb moved over her chin. "We are strangers, and yet we have known each other for a thousand years," he said under his breath.

Her heart bumped in her chest. "How very odd," she replied in a hushed tone. "I was thinking that, only this afternoon."

He nodded. "It is, perhaps, the most cruel cut of fate," he said enigmatically as he removed his hand. "Come along. I understand they have belly dancers from Argentina this evening," he added with a wicked smile.

She moved a little closer to his side. "Decadent man."

"I'm not decadent. I appreciate beauty." He took her arm just below where the black shawl she'd bought reached with its fringe. "Believe me, I find you far more intriguing than a dancer, no matter how adept."

"Thank you."

"It isn't flattery," he said as they walked down the carpeted hall past the curtained windows that looked down on the open patio below. "I know you well enough already to know that you loathe insincerity as much as I do."

She smiled. That was reassuring. They went down in the elevator and walked down the steps that led into the courtyard, where a central fountain was surrounded by beautiful mosaic tile. Tables with white linen tablecloths and napkins and pink china were set with silver utensils and crystal glasses. Several couples were already seated, and a beautiful dark-haired woman in a white dress with lavish colored embroidery was sitting on a stage with her accompanist, both with guitars in their hands.

"Tonight's entertainment," he informed her. "She is from the Yucatan Peninsula in Mexico, and she sings like an angel."

"Do you know her?"

He shook his head. "No, but I came here from Madrid. She was appearing in a hotel there, too."

"Madrid?"

They paused while a white-jacked waiter in a burgundy fez led them to a table. Philippe seated Gretchen and then himself. The waiter left menus and departed. "I do business all over the world," he told her with a gentle smile. "You might call me an ambassador, of sorts."

"That explains the bodyguards, I guess." He looked puzzled and she shrugged. "I saw them follow you into that building this afternoon and asked Bojo about them. He said that they often watch out for businessmen as well as visiting dignitaries."

He let out an odd sigh. "Yes, they do."

"I enjoyed this afternoon very much," she said abruptly. "It was kind of you to offer to go with me. It's lonely now that Maggie's gone. I suppose she's in Brussels now, waiting for her flight back to the States."

"Have you ever been to Brussels?" he asked curiously.

"Yes. Maggie and I flew from Brussels to Casablanca and then here. I'm going back through Amsterdam on my way home..." She hesitated. Her eyes lifted to his. Suddenly the thought of home was unpleasant. "Well, not now, of course," she added slowly. "I'll be going to Qawi instead." She looked down at her neatly folded pink napkin. "Philippe, I don't suppose you ever get to Qawi?"

"In fact," he said slowly, "I spend a great deal of time in Qawi. I do business with the ruling sheikh. Quite a lot of business."

Her eyes lifted and dreams danced in them. It really was like a fantasy, as if she'd given up ordinary surroundings and had been caught up in mystery and joy. It was all there, in her face, the delight she felt.

He smiled at her, his black eyes searching her excited expression. "And now, Qawi seems less frightening to you, does it not?" he asked softly. "As you see, we won't say *adieu* when you leave Tangier. We will say *au revoir*."

"I'm glad."

His long fingers touched the back of hers where her hand lay on the table beside her glass. "So am

I. Although," he added broodingly, "I am not doing you a favor to let you go there."

"Why not?"

"You may discover that appearances can be very deceptive."

Her eyes sparkled. "Don't tell me. You're really an international jewel thief or a spy on holiday."

He burst out laughing. "No," he said. "I can assure you that isn't the case."

She studied his hand. It was his left one, and there were scars on the back of it, white lines against his olive complexion. She touched them lightly. "From the accident?"

His whole body clenched at the memory of the injuries. "Yes," he said reluctantly, withdrawing his hand.

"That was clumsy," she said, grimacing. "Sorry. I didn't mean to pry."

He stared at her with conflicting emotions. "You will have to know before you leave Tangier," he said quite calmly. "But I prefer to put it off for a few days. Honesty can be a brutal thing."

"Then you're an ax murderer," she said thoughtfully, nodding. "I understand. You don't want to shatter my illusions of you as some elegant scoundrel."

He laughed again, caught off guard. "You remind me of her, so much," he said without thinking. "The first thing that attracted me to her was a sense of humor that made me laugh at myself, something I was never able to do before."

"She?"

He shifted, as if he hadn't meant to say that. "A woman I knew," he hedged. "A blonde, like you, with a very open personality. I thought she was one of a kind. I am delighted to find that the earth contains another woman similar to her."

"Maggie thinks I'm a certifiable lunatic."

"You're refreshing," he said, leaning back in his chair to study her. "You might be surprised at how many people say only what is expected of them, out of fear of giving offense. I abhor being toadied to," he added quite fiercely, and his eyes blazed for an instant.

He must be, Gretchen decided, someone very important. She wanted to ask him about his life, his background, his work. She was curious about him. But he seemed not to like discussing his past.

She glanced at her menu and grimaced. "French. Everywhere we go, everything's written in French," she moaned.

He laughed softly. "I must make it my business to teach you to read a menu. Here." He shared his menu with her, pronounced each entry and made her pronounce it after him, and then explained what it was. She started with an appetizer of proscuitto and melon, followed by a main dish of lamb done in a Moroccan sauce. He ordered fish and a bottle of white wine.

"I've never had wine before," she said, watching his eyebrows go up.

"Would you prefer something else?"

She lifted a shoulder. "I suppose I should know something about wines. If the sheikh isn't Muslim, he probably has a wine cellar and will expect me to know all sorts of things about wines."

He pursed his lips. "Probably," he murmured. "But one can rarely go wrong with a good white wine, like a Riesling or a Chardonnay. Although I prefer an Alsace wine, like a Gewurztraminer. It is an acquired taste."

She shook her head. "I'll never learn."

"Of course you will. Each night, we'll sample a different wine from the list. By the time you leave Morocco, you'll be knowledgeable."

She smiled. "You're very sophisticated."

"I was educated in Europe," he told her. "One matures rapidly in a sophisticated environment." His black eyes narrowed. "But I wasn't born to wealth, and I never forget my beginnings. Poverty is the true plague of the twenty-first century, Gretchen. And greed is its blood brother."

"Do you feel that way, too?" she asked softly.

He chuckled as the waiter returned and took

their order. When the wine came, he taught her how to taste and savor it. "This is a Riesling," he said. "Not too heavy, not too light."

"Just right," she mused, and liked the way it tasted. "We had a little grapevine, but the foreman ran over it with a tractor."

"Barbarian," he said.

She chuckled. "That's what I used to call him," she murmured. "Conner the Barbarian. Not one flower in the yard was safe if he ever got on the tractor. He's a great horseman, but he has a knack for running lawnmowers over flower beds and into trees."

He chuckled, too, at the imagery. "And this is the man you trust to keep the ranch for you?"

"Oh, but he's great with horses and cattle," she told him defensively.

"And I suppose you adore him?"

"I had a terrific crush on him in my teens," she agreed. "But I grew out of it."

His eyes narrowed. He didn't speak again until their salads were delivered, along with coffee for Gretchen and sparkling water for her companion.

"You like flowers, then," he continued.

"I love them," she said dreamily. "I grow prize tea roses and an assortment of flowering shrubs."

He toyed with his salad. "My father has a mania for orchids," he told her. "He calls them his 'grandchildren' and gives them all names.'' He smiled affectionately, lost in thought. ''When I was a child, I was jealous of them. He actually had a servant taken to jail for forgetting to water a sick one, which later died. A very vindictive man, my father.''

She chuckled. ''I can imagine how he felt. I have a special fondness for sick roses. I seem to have the touch for making them bloom again.''

He studied her intently. ''Some sicknesses, alas, cannot be cured by even the most loving of hands,'' he said absently, and bitterness made harsh lines in his face.

He was a man of many contrasts. She watched his long-fingered hands move and was fascinated by their dexterity and grace.

He caught her scrutiny and tensed. ''You find the scars distasteful.''

She looked up at once. ''Good Lord, no,'' she said at once, and with obvious sincerity. ''I was watching how you use your hands. Everyone in this part of the world seems to move gracefully, especially the men. It isn't like that back home.''

He relaxed and finished his salad. It was his own guilt at deceiving her, he thought, that was bringing on these bad moods. He had to stop it. What was, was. Nothing in the world could ever change it.

"We move as we live, unhurriedly," he said simply.

"I'll bet you don't have half the rate of vascular problems that we have in the States," she remarked.

"That is most likely true." He finished a last bite of salad and pushed the bowl from him. His dark eyes searched hers. "You go to a country vastly different from your own, much less sophisticated than Morocco. Many modern conveniences do not exist there, and even electricity is a recent addition. The people of Qawi were largely nomadic until the early part of this century. When it was parceled out among the Europeans, the people resisted and many families were decimated. It will require a great deal of tolerance for you to adjust to such archaic surroundings."

She put down her own fork. "Do you think I should go home?" she asked bluntly.

He wanted to say yes. He wanted to tell her to run, now, while she still could. But he looked into her eyes and felt as if part of him were sitting across the table. He couldn't make the words come out.

"I know it's a risk," she said, glad that he hadn't said anything immediately. "But I already love Morocco. I think I'm going to be very much at home in Qawi, if the sheikh is patient with my ignorance about local customs."

His dark eyes narrowed. "I think you will find him patient, in all things."

"I hope so," she added fervently. "It's like a leap of faith," she added slowly. "A step into the unknown. Maggie said that I was vegetating in Texas, and I think she was right. I've never been anywhere or done anything adventurous in my life. I never realized the world was so big and its people so diverse. I'll never forget any of this, whatever happens."

"Nor will I," he said quietly, and it sounded as if the words were torn from him. He was holding his wineglass so tightly that Gretchen wondered if the stem was going to snap. She wondered what was making him so broody, if it was his usual manner.

The entertainer sat down on the small platform with her accompanist and began to sing a poignant love song in Spanish. Gretchen sighed and closed her eyes, to enjoy it even better.

"Do you understand the words?" Philippe asked.

"Yes." Her eyes opened and looked into his. "It's a song about a man and woman who fall madly in love but can't marry because he's going off to war. They're saying goodbye. It's very sad."

He smiled. "You understand Spanish."

"Yes. I speak it badly, but I can read it and understand it if it isn't spoken too rapidly."

"It is one of my favorite languages as well."

His hand slid across the table and his fingers linked slowly with hers while he turned his attention back to the singer. Gretchen stopped listening to the beautiful song. Philippe's lean, warm fingers holding hers pushed away her reason. She closed her eyes again and gave in to the sensual delight of his touch.

The program was only a short one, and all too soon, the singer took her bows and left the microphone. When Gretchen came back to reality, Philippe had let go of her hand and was getting ready to pay their bill with a credit card—a gold credit card, she noted, reinforcing her opinion of his station in life. He was obviously a wealthy man, that was evident from his clothing. She wondered if he might think she was playing up to him because he had money. She was certain he'd experienced that sort of woman.

He gave the card to the waiter and tucked a large tip under the lip of his plate for the man.

She hadn't considered it, but she was certain now that he was going to escort her back to her room and leave her. He hadn't said anything about his plans for the next day, but they probably wouldn't include her. She had a poor batting average with men as a rule. She didn't know how to flirt, she wasn't a brilliant conversationalist, and she was only passably attractive. It depressed her to think that she'd assumed far too much after Philippe had found her in the swing. His attention had made her giddy with hope, but he looked as if he was carrying a heavy burden, and his eyes didn't meet hers after the waiter returned his card.

He pulled out her chair with that same old-world courtesy that seemed such a part of him and held her elbow as he escorted her up the small row of steps that led to the lobby.

"I must go out," he said without looking at her. "I have a business engagement this evening which must be honored."

"I understand. It was a wonderful day. Thank you. Maybe I'll see you around the hotel..."

He stopped at once, drawing her out of the pattern of traffic, and stood looking down at her with a dark scowl. "Are you tired of my company so soon?"

Her face mirrored her surprise. "I...I thought perhaps you were tired of mine," she faltered.

He relaxed. "Would that I were," he said under his breath. "I would be doing you a favor."

"Can't you tell me what's bothering you?" she asked boldly.

"No." He glanced at his watch. "Tomorrow, we'll take Bojo and go to the carpet showroom. But not early. I have a breakfast meeting as well. Shall we say ten o'clock, in the lobby?"

"Ten o'clock," she said with helpless eagerness. "I'll be waiting."

He smiled gently. "Are you always so enthusiastic about things?"

"I'm afraid so," she said sheepishly. "It comes from having so little. We were very poor when Marc and I were growing up, so we learned not to expect much. We tend to appreciate things more than ordinary people, I guess. We lived in hard times."

His black eyes narrowed. "I, also, grew up in abject poverty. It is why I must do what I can to help my people escape it. Education is the key, Gretchen. There must be good schools, good teachers, and all the latest technology in them, especially computers."

She smiled. "So that you can compete in the world market," she guessed.

He nodded. "Exactly. I never want to watch another child starve to death as long as I live."

Her breath caught. She was getting a painful picture of his youth.

"Such compassion in those soft eyes," he murmured quietly. "Lucky Qawi, to attract such a gentle spirit."

"That's just the thing," she pointed out. "They're expecting Maggie, who's sophisticated and well-traveled and a born organizer."

"Organization can be learned. I think that the sheikh will have a delightful time...teaching you."

"Does he have a harem?" she asked worriedly.

He burst out laughing. "No. He is a modern ruler."

"Oh, thank goodness!"

"So you have no desire to grace his bed, then?" he teased.

She flushed. "Stop that. I'm going to be a social secretary, not a scandal in high heels."

He nodded. "So you are." He glanced up and looked at the concierge, who looked back and made a gesture, as if some private, silent conversation had just taken place. "Don't leave the hotel alone," he reminded her.

"Not at night," she promised.

"Nor in the daytime, either," he emphasized. "I must leave you at the elevator. Bojo is waiting for me in the hotel limousine." He lifted her soft hand to his mouth and lightly brushed the knuckles with his lips. She felt a pleasant tingle all over her body as she met his eyes. "Until tomorrow."

"Yes," she said breathlessly. "Tomorrow."

He gave her a warm smile and walked away, elegant as always. She watched him go with a long sigh. In such a small amount of time, her life had been turned on its edge. She hoped she wasn't going to live to regret spending her holiday with a man who knew more about women than she knew about Texas. But her pleasure in his company was impossible to deny, whatever happened.

She went up to her room in the elevator and undressed. It was early, but she went to bed anyway. Tomorrow would come more quickly if she went to sleep now, and she wanted it with all her heart. She gave a thought to poor Maggie, who must be at least halfway home by now.

She turned out the lights and closed her eyes, pillowing her cheek on the hand that Philippe's firm mouth had kissed so tenderly.

Chapter Five

It had been a mistake to go to bed early, Gretchen decided, because she woke at five the next morning and couldn't go back to sleep. She got up, dressed in neat white slacks and a pink knit shell with a white cotton jacket, donned socks and sneakers, snapped her fanny pack into place and paced the room and watched television until she could go down to the elaborate breakfast buffet.

She knew that Philippe wouldn't be there, because he'd already told her that he had a breakfast meeting, but this was the table where she sat with him the night before and listened to the talented singer. It was the next best thing to being with him.

She loved the small gurgling fountain and the beautiful inlaid tile that hallmarked the architecture. She remembered the palace in Asilah and the beautiful shades of blue ceramic tile that had graced it. She would never forget that, or her ride on the camel, with Philippe alternately taking photographs and laughing at her delight. It amazed her that a man she'd known for such a short time had become such a vital part of her life. She had to try not to let herself go crazy over him. Her job was in Qawi, and inevitably she was going to have to leave here, and Philippe.

He'd said he wasn't from France. She wondered where he called home. It was some comfort that he had business interests in Qawi, though, and she would at least see him again from time to time. And when she got her photographs developed, she would have some souvenirs of their time together. She picked at her yellow melon listlessly. She didn't want to look ahead to a time when Philippe would be out of her life.

As she looked around at the fresh flowers on the tables, she remembered how her mother had loved them. She still felt her recent loss, as she was certain Marc did. She hadn't seen him since after the funeral, when she'd had to stop him from going after Daryl with both fists when he heard what the man had done. For a conservative law-enforcement type, her older brother was amazingly uninhibited when it came to expressing opinions. He'd used words she'd never heard to describe her errant ex-fiancé.

She toyed with her bread knife, wondering what her brother would think of the elegant, sophisticated man she'd attracted here. He'd be suspicious, she decided, as she should be. It was odd for such a man to take an interest in an innocent like Gretchen. She'd better remember that and watch her step. He might really be some international scoundrel looking for a convenient "cover," if that was what they called it. She didn't look at all suspicious, and she couldn't discount the idea that he might be only using her for reasons of his own. She was helpless to stop herself from seeing him, just the same, whatever his motives. She'd been alone a long time. Too long.

The thought that he might like her for herself she discounted at once. She felt absolutely miserable when she considered her lack of looks and sophistication. Maggie would have been Philippe's ideal sort of woman. She hoped her poor friend was going to be able to cope with a blind Cord Romero. From what she remembered of him, he was hell on two legs with both eyes working. Blind, he'd be a handful even for a veteran nurse.

The waiter poured coffee into her cup and asked if she was hungry. With a shy smile, she went to the table and filled a plate with fruit and rolls, never one for the traditional sort of breakfast.

Ten o'clock would never come, she decided. She'd spent the next two hours alternately pacing her room, redoing her hair, reading the hotel menu, watching the news on the one English language channel on the television, and staring out the window at the harbor far in the distance. There wasn't a screen on the window, so when she opened the slanted wooden shutters, she could smell the exotic scents of Tangier on the endless breeze that came off the water. Somewhere far across that expanse was the Rock of Gilbraltar and, further, Spain. But there was a faint mist or fog, and she couldn't make out land.

The abrupt knock on the door startled her. She didn't need to check her watch to know the time, because Philippe seemed always to be early.

She opened the door, and there he was. He was wearing white slacks with a red knit shirt and a white jacket over it. He looked elegantly casual, and she decided that he probably didn't have any really casual clothes, like blue jeans and chambray shirts. He was a very citified sort of man. He'd make a strange contrast to people like her male acquaintances back home, who went around in denim and boots and spent their days pitching hay and working cattle. She remembered her brother breaking horses in the corral, after the sudden death of their father, and sticking like glue to a bronc.

"You look very nice, *mademoiselle,*" he teased with a gentle smile, interrupting her chaotic thoughts.

"I was just thinking the same about you," she said, fumbling to lock and close the door. "I guess you've never ridden a wild horse in your life," she added wistfully and with a sad little glance at him.

His expression was hard to read. "Why do you say that?" he asked with studied carelessness.

"Just that you dress so well," she said, smiling apologetically. "My boss is the only man I know who dresses up and he's a lawyer. All the men around Jacobsville wear denim—you know," she added when he frowned curiously, "jeans and work shirts and dirty boots."

"Ah," he said after a minute. "Cowboys."

"That's right." She fell into pace beside him as they walked down the long hall with its Moroccan motif. "I don't think I've even seen our foreman in a suit."

The reference piqued him, for some reason. It sounded as if she thought him a fashion plate, a man without physical skills. "Do you ride?" he asked.

She smiled. "I used to. Like a monkey," she said with a chuckle. "My brother Marc put me on my first pony when I was about three, to my mother's horror. I took to it at once. I had a beautiful Belgian mare of my own, once, and I loved to ride," she added.

He pursed his lips and stared at the elevator. "I believe the sheikh has a nice stable of purebred Arabians," he murmured.

"I don't suppose he might let me ride one?" she asked wistfully.

"Most of his Arabians are stallions, used for breeding only, and dangerous to handle," he said evasively. "Besides the blood stock, he has mares and geldings that could be used for that purpose, of course."

"Of course." She looked sad, remembering the horses they'd had to sell because they could no longer afford to keep them—including her lovely Belgian mare.

Philippe noticed and stared at her curiously. "You love horses, yet speaking of them makes you sad. Why?"

He was far too perceptive. She smiled. "Oh, I was thinking about the ranch," she said with deliberate carelessness. "Our horses were used for working cattle. They were mostly quarter horses."

"I have heard of your famous Texas quarter horses," he remarked.

"You never have told me where you come from," she pointed out.

"First things first." He helped her into the elevator and pressed the button for the ground floor. "Today, we enjoy the sights."

It was an adventure following Bojo and Philippe around the Socco. Bojo knew all the local merchants and where to get the best prices. She sat in the carpet shop fascinated as the clerk explained the diversity of Berber designs and patterns to her. They were a little like hieroglyphics, she thought as she studied them up close. There was a huge selection, and not only of wool carpets. There were silk and cotton ones as well. She fell in love with a lime-green cotton Berber rug with figures on it.

Despite her protests, Philippe bought it for her and, having her write down the ranch address for him, gave it to the merchant and had it sent to her home. She told him that her housekeeper, Katie, and her husband would get the mail in her absence from the ranch. Along with the foreman, they ran things smoothly for Marc since he was away so much.

"And now you have a true souvenir of Morocco," Philippe teased as they walked back down the narrow alleys that were sided by high adobe walls. "Look here," he added abruptly and pulled her into a small alley that ended at a wrought-iron gate. Behind it was a beautiful garden in full bloom. "This is one of many vacation homes in Tangier where foreign people come to vacation." He mentioned the name of a famous opera star and heard her intake of breath. "You like him?" he asked, surprised.

"Oh, I love opera," she said genuinely.

He smiled. "I love it, too. Music is one of the few pleasures I have left," he added with such solemnity that she looked up in surprise.

"What's happened to make you so bitter?" she asked softly.

His face hardened. "Nothing that should concern you, *mademoiselle,*" he said in a crisply formal tone.

"I wasn't trying to pry," she said gently. "I'm sorry," she added as she turned away and walked back the way they'd come. Obviously she'd hit a nerve there. He was a very private person. She'd have to remember that, and not be too inquisitive. Whatever it was must be painful.

He hated the very thought of what he must eventually tell her. He hated being reminded of his deficiencies, especially by this woman. In such a very short time, he'd become accustomed to her. He had no idea how she might react to his secret past, and he didn't want to have to think about it just yet.

He let her lead the way back to Bojo, who took a long look at Philippe's somber face and suggested lunch.

They left the Socco and went to a nearby restaurant where Gretchen felt too uncomfortable to eat more than a salad. Philippe spoke hardly a word while he picked at his food. While they were eating, Bojo's cell phone rang. He answered it, frowned, and spoke briskly before he hung up abruptly. He and Philippe spoke somberly in a language she didn't recognize. Now, they were both brooding.

She was certain that Philippe planned to escort her right to the hotel after lunch, and he did just that.

"Don't leave the hotel under any circumstances," he told her firmly as they stood in the lobby. "And don't believe anyone who tells you I want to see you. If such a message comes, it won't be from me. You must promise this."

Judging by his grim expression, something was very wrong. She remembered the men in the black sedan and the gunshots, and she was worried for him. "I don't suppose you'd like to tell me what's happened to make you this concerned?" she asked.

He ignored the question. "I should have put you

on a plane back to the United States at once," he said curtly. "Now, there is no such possibility. Your safety is linked to mine, and I am in very grave danger. I regret this more than I can tell you."

Her eyes widened. He looked like a taut rope. She'd have given anything to wipe away that fierce uneasiness. "You mean you really are an international jewel thief?" she asked with a wicked twinkle in her eyes. "How exciting! Who's chasing us? Interpol?"

He laughed despite his fears. "No. Not Interpol." The smile faded. "Gretchen, I want you to be afraid. It may save your young life."

"Sorry, but I'm not afraid of much. I grew up on a ranch and I work for a criminal lawyer. Do I get a trenchcoat and a gun?" she persisted. Then she frowned. "On second thought, we might skip the gun, Marc says he's rarely seen a worse shot…Philippe!"

He caught her by both shoulders and shook her gently. "I know you mean well, but this is no time for humor. Be serious!" he said with intimidating authority in his tone.

The hard, strong touch of his hands was electric. She stared up at him with parted lips and sparkling green eyes. It felt as if her body had been struck by lightning. She could feel the heat of his body, almost taste the mint that clung to his hard lips. She'd never felt such an intense reaction to a man, and it made her reckless. Her hands went to his chest and pressed there as she lifted her face and looked up into stormy, wild black eyes that hypnotized her.

"Heavens, you're strong!" she murmured absently. Her hands were on his arms now, too, and her fingers contracted on the firm muscles there, as if to punctuate the words. He was incredibly handsome. She actually moved closer without realizing it.

He felt the barest brush of her breasts against his shirtfront in the opening of his jacket and he caught his breath. His eyes went down to her breasts, and the look on his face made her shameless. She took one more step and felt his legs brush hers. For the first time in her life, she was overwhelmed by absolute physical need.

When she moved, something happened to him...something...devastating!

A sound like a harsh groan passed his lips. He shivered. His eyes widened as if in horror as they met her uplifted, dazed ones. He cursed under his breath and pushed her away so quickly that she wobbled before she caught her balance.

"Did I do something wrong?" she asked with evident concern and a little embarrassment.

He took a raspy breath. One of his hands clenched at his side. He couldn't breathe. He couldn't even form words. There was a red-hot ache in his lower belly, in his hard thighs. This was...impossible!

"I must...go! At once!" His face was like stone as his eyes glittered down at her. "Remember what I told you. Stay inside!" It sounded more like a command than a request, and in a tone that made her skin chill.

He left abruptly and without a backward glance, motioning imperiously to Bojo, who followed him quickly out of the hotel.

Gretchen managed to get into the elevator and went at once to her room, grateful that the little scene hadn't been witnessed. The concierge had been on the phone and the lobby had been empty. Philippe had literally thrown her away, as if she disgusted him. She groaned out loud and leaned her forehead against the cold metal of the elevator. Now she'd offended him by being forward, and he'd never come near her again. She should go to her room and pack, leave for Qawi, forget that she'd ever been in Tangier!

Philippe made it into the waiting limousine and had Bojo take him back to his own hotel, further along the street. He went straight to his room, into the bathroom, closed the door, turned on the shower, and stripped. For the first time in years, he forced himself to look in the mirror at his nude body.

He gritted his teeth as he stared at the damage the land mine had done to him. The scars were no more than white lines against his olive skin now. There, on his lower abdomen, were the worst ones. These he could show to no one, to no woman, ever. But the doctors had told him that he would never again function as a man, and for the first time in all those years, he questioned what he'd accepted as truth.

He closed his eyes and pictured Gretchen's body, her silky innocent body, pressed against him with no fabric between them. Again, he felt the strange new stirring of his body. He opened his eyes and looked in the mirror. As he watched, the thoughts he pictured…aroused him.

"Mon Dieu!" he gasped reverently at the sheer power of the arousal.

Nine years. Nine long, endless, agonizing years of impotence that everyone said was permanent. And he was aroused by a virgin. Not only that, but the one woman on the planet that he couldn't seduce.

Irony of ironies, he thought. Now there was a tiny possibility that he could still be a man, and it was no use, no use at all. He could never dishonor a virgin, even for this motive. And even if he could be aroused, there would be no guarantee that he could maintain it long enough for a true sexual encounter with a woman. Over the years, there had been fleeting phantom darts of pleasure, but with no woman had he achieved even this reaction. His eyes narrowed. But, of course, he hadn't tried to achieve it. He'd believed the doctors, and he'd never so much as touched a woman in those nine long years. He'd never tested the truth. And now that he had, now what? Even if he gave in to his hunger for her and kept her with him, she would be in danger here in Morocco from his enemies.

What Bojo had just learned made him furious. His worst enemy had just been released from a Moscow jail and given his freedom. Several of the man's old mercenary buddies had simultaneously disappeared. It wasn't much of a leap to the certainty that retribution was in the planning stages. He had to get out of Morocco soon, and get Gretchen out as well. She had already become the weak link in the chain, because she attracted him. The man who had her could name his price, whatever it might be. He would do anything to save her. And it wasn't just because she reminded him so much of Brianne...

He had only two courses of action. He could tell

Gretchen the truth and let her make the decision. Or he could make it for her and send her home before she got into even more danger, or raised hopes that would never come to fruition. She'd been badly hurt emotionally. He didn't want to be the cause of any more grief for her. On the other hand, he had to know if she had the power to make him whole again. Surely that wasn't so much to ask of fate. All he wanted was a taste of life again. He must know. Whatever the cost to either of them. He could protect her. After all, letting her go home would put her even more at risk. Besides, he didn't want her around that man she'd been infatuated with. Not now.

With that determined, he stepped into the shower and bathed.

Gretchen had packed as soon as she reached her hotel room, in a fever of humiliated self-contempt. But she came to her senses even as the suitcase was open on her bed. How could she leave Philippe now, just when they were growing closer? She had no real desire to leave, despite Philippe's very strange behavior. She couldn't understand why he'd been so protective of her and then had pushed her away with something like disgust when she was a little forward with him. Surely no man in his right mind would ward off the advances of a young, moderately attractive woman. Certainly Philippe wouldn't. He was sophisticated and obviously experienced. She wished she knew what she'd done wrong.

She'd never behaved so brazenly before. He was a foreigner, though, and might be used to a more submissive sort of woman altogether. She looked for an excuse not to leave, and decided that she couldn't leave without seeing him again, at least without trying to understand what she'd done that had offended him. She put away the suitcase and spent the rest of the day at the pool.

The next morning, she dragged downstairs to breakfast a few minutes later than usual, hoping nobody would notice the dark circles under her eyes from lack of sleep. She'd been awake most of the night, thinking up ways to bring the subject out in the open with Philippe. If he came back, that was. If he didn't...well, she'd just have to go on with her life. She would go to Qawi, she decided, and start over again in a new direction. But she prayed she would see Philippe again.

She forced herself to think about filling her plate instead of brooding over her Philippe. Like these fascinating people, she had to learn that life lived itself and couldn't be controlled by anyone. Hearts broke. She knew that better than many people. She shouldn't have expected so much from a casual encounter, anyway. She forced herself to smile at the waiters and put on a happy face for them. No sense making everybody else miserable because she was.

As she sat at her lonely table, picking at her food, she looked up and there was Philippe with a huge bouquet of white roses. He searched her eyes quietly for a long moment before he bent and placed the bouquet in front of her on the white linen tablecloth.

"Forgive me," he said quietly.

She looked up into his dark eyes and he knew at once that she hadn't slept. Neither had he. His conscience had tortured him.

He sat down across from her and caught her cool fingers tightly in his warm, strong hands. "I never meant to be so rude to you," he said quietly. "Or to hurt you."

Her green eyes were like new leaves. "You aren't mad at me?"

His eyes closed. "I never was!" he whispered, and brought her palm to his lips to kiss it hungrily. "It wasn't anger, Gretchen!"

Her heart jumped at the fervor of his mouth on her skin. Her heart began to race wildly. It wasn't one-sided. He was attracted to her! She studied his tanned face intently, her own coloring with excitement as she looked at him. "I'm so glad! I thought

I'd made you uncomfortable. By being too forward,'' she added quickly.

His eyebrows arched. "Forward?"

She lowered her gaze to their clasped fingers. "I practically threw myself at you, and you don't like me to touch you, anyway. I knew that and I should have...why are you laughing?"

He was almost doubled over. He kissed her palm hungrily and gave her hand back, signaling a waiter for coffee. Life was beautiful. He felt years younger and alive and every inch a man. He looked at this woman, so unaware of her charms, and smiled with his whole heart. He looked unspeakably handsome to Gretchen's eyes, even with those white scars down his left cheek. They were hardly noticeable at all except when he smiled or frowned.

"I love for you to touch me," he said huskily when the waiter had poured his coffee and warmed Gretchen's. "In fact, I've never enjoyed anything more."

She stared at him with delight. "Really?"

"Really." He leaned back in his chair, toying with the handle of his cup while he studied her. "I'll tell you all about it one day. This is much too soon. What would you like to do today?"

Her face brightened. "Anything you would."

He chuckled softly at her enthusiasm. "Anything?" he teased softly.

She leaned forward, glancing around them with exaggerated wariness. "We could hijack two camels and start a travel agency."

He burst out laughing. "What a thought! And do you think I could ride a camel?"

She hesitated. "Well..." She didn't want to come right out and say she thought he was too fastidious for anything so rough.

He cocked a black eyebrow and grinned at her. "One day," he mused, "you may discover that I have hidden abilities. But for now, suppose we go and see the Forbes Museum? The house, actually a palace, is now on the market, but I believe we can have a look around. Malcolm Forbes had a grand party there some years ago, which was widely reported on television."

"I know, I saw the stories! That house?" she exclaimed. "Oh, I'd love to see it!" Actually, she'd love to have his company all day, but she wasn't going to risk embarrassing herself again.

He grinned. "Then finish your breakfast and we'll go."

She dipped her fork into her bowl of fruit with renewed pleasure. It seemed that dreams really did come true. Her eyes fell on the roses and she traced their soft petals with her free hand. "Thank you for these," she said softly. "I love flowers."

"So I noticed." He gestured to the waiter, said

something to him in an abrupt, commanding tone, and waved him away with the bouquet.

"Where is he taking my roses?" she asked, equally shocked by her companion's tone of authority and the man's quick obedience.

"He's putting them into a vase, which one of the maids will deliver to your room," he said softly. "I like the idea of my flowers watching over you as you sleep."

Her cheeks colored delicately as she looked into his eyes, and her breath left her audibly.

She was easily flattered, he noticed, and it disturbed him. Perhaps she was on the rebound from her betraying fiancé, or just reeling from her first real taste of attraction. Whatever motivated her, she kindled flames in him that he hadn't felt for nine years. He wanted her. Nothing was more important than that, for the moment.

They went through the museum in the Forbes mansion on the sea, and walked through the grounds. Philippe held her hand and made her feel like a closely guarded treasure. But wherever they went, Bojo went along, and so did the two bodyguards she'd seen in Asilah. This time, there was no Saudi prince around, either. Her companion was becoming a bigger mystery than ever, but she was helpless to deny herself his company. She was falling in love, for the first time in her life.

Chapter Six

Philippe seemed to enjoy Gretchen's company as much as she enjoyed his, because he found all sorts of activities for them to share. For the next four days, without making it obvious, Philippe made sure that Gretchen was under surveillance for every step she took, even when he wasn't with her. She spent a great deal of time in the garden and the swimming pool when he wasn't escorting her around the city. He did have business meetings with foreign officials about business back home, and these took up a great deal of his time. But he managed at least one meal a day, sometimes two, with Gretchen. The more he learned about her, the more he liked her. She was consistently honest with him, and the fact that she didn't know who he was made him confident that she wasn't playing up to him deliberately. It was refreshing to be taken at face value. Then he remembered Brianne's unexpected compassion, and reality came crashing down on him. It was dishonest, to let Gretchen hope for a normal relationship with him, when he knew he could never give her one. But he was beginning to have doubts even about that.

As the days passed, he learned that his initial physical reaction to her was no fluke. Every time he touched her, he became aroused, to his consternation and delight. She was too innocent to realize it. And, of course, he didn't let her close enough to risk that. He held hands with her, but he didn't dare go a step closer, to her obvious disappointment. He enjoyed her impish flirting, her jubilant company, her obvious attraction to him. He couldn't risk making her run from him yet. Not until he was certain she wouldn't want to. She was becoming essential to him.

Several days later, Gretchen was sitting by the pool in her red bathing suit with her sunglasses on when a shadow loomed over her. She opened her eyes, and there was Philippe, elegant in a business suit and looking far more somber than ever before.

She took off her dark glasses and blushed at the look he gave her scantily covered body. His eyes narrowed on her full, firm breasts before they traced a path over her flat stomach and narrow hips down her long, elegant legs to her pretty feet. He caught his breath at the delicious surge of pleasure that rippled over him. The sensations she evoked were new and exciting to a man who'd been dead from the waist down for so many years. He was becoming addicted to these little spurts of pleasure when he was with her. He was also becoming curious about whether or not he could prolong and maintain that state of arousal in bed, a curiosity he didn't dare indulge. Not just yet.

"Come with me, Gretchen," he said after a minute, and with a gentle smile. "I've put this off as long as I can. We must speak."

He leaned down and caught one of her hands, pulling her up with him. He retrieved her cover-up from the foot of the chair and handed it to her. She slid into it and let him lead her up a bank of marble steps to a patio high above the pool, shaded by tall trees. They sat down at one of the marble-topped tables in white wrought-iron chairs. When the bartender came to take their order, Philippe ordered a mixed drink with rum for both of them.

She knew that her time in Morocco was almost up, and she would have to go on to Qawi while Philippe went home—wherever home was. The thought of leaving him made her empty. In such a short time, he'd become necessary to her happiness.

His somber expression made her uneasy. "I don't drink," she began.

"You will when you hear what I have to tell you," he said with grim humor. He took out a thin Turkish cigar from his pocket and asked, "You will permit?" At her nod, he lit it, and blew out a cloud of smoke. It was the first time she'd seen him do it. He was obviously uncomfortable.

He didn't speak until the waiter brought their drinks, was paid, and went away. "A piña colada," he told her. "With only a touch of rum. Try it."

She did, wrinkling her nose at the bitter taste of the alcohol.

He smiled. "It tastes better, the more you drink," he said dryly, and took a long swallow of his.

"What do you want to talk about?" she asked.

"About myself," he said, leaning back in the chair. "It's past time I was honest with you." His face hardened. "Regardless of my own inclination, I don't want to give you false hope about a relationship with me."

She flushed. "Philippe...!"

He held up a hand. "This is harder for me than you can possibly imagine," he bit off. "Please, let me finish before you speak. Nine years ago, while

I was in Palestine on a business trip, I stepped on a land mine left over from one of the regional conflicts,'' he said, avoiding her shocked eyes. "Since then, I have not been…a man.'' That wasn't quite true, but he didn't dare share his suspicions with her at this point. She barely knew him. He would have to win her trust before he ventured into anything more physical with her. Besides that, he confessed silently, he wanted to see how she would react to a man whom she thought was totally impotent.

Gretchen felt her dreams collapsing. She began to make connections. The scars on his left hand. Her eyes went to them blindly and then to the others on the left side of his face. An accident. Yes. An accident that had destroyed him as a man. She took a huge swallow of the drink, choked and almost strangled. Her heart was breaking…

His eyes were on his glass, not on her. Well, what had he expected, he asked himself bitterly. He remembered Brianne's kind but pitying reaction and closed his eyes, shuddering with self-contempt.

Then, suddenly, he felt something cool and tender against his hand, against the scars. He opened his eyes, and saw her fingers caress over them, her wide green eyes full of compassion as they met his shocked ones.

"I wondered why you weren't married," she said slowly. "I mean, you must know that you're very handsome, and very sophisticated, and charming. I wondered why you'd even look twice at someone as plain and dull as me."

"Dull? Plain?" he asked, genuinely surprised.

She shrugged. "I'm not much of a bargain. So I thought maybe you were taking me around with you because you were just lonely and I was handy." She grimaced. "It was the only way I could explain why you kept seeing me at all."

He let out a long breath. He was right about her. She wasn't running. She had courage. His lean fingers turned and caught hers tightly. "You have a low self-image."

"So do you," she told him bluntly, surprising him. "And you shouldn't. I know men set great store by physical prowess, but you should remember that you're talking to someone who knows nothing about sensual pleasure. Daryl fondled me once or twice and I tolerated it, but I didn't really like it. That's the only real experience of men I have. So maybe I'm frigid anyway. Even if I'm not, how can I miss what I've never even had?" She searched his turbulent eyes. "I like you, very much," she said shyly, and managed to smile even through her embarrassment. "So...so does it matter? About your...wounds, I mean?"

He leaned back in his chair with an expulsion of breath and let go of her hand. He finished his drink almost in one go, and sat gaping at her. He was absolutely lost for words.

She winced at his reaction. "Don't tell me," she sighed. "I've put my foot in my mouth again, haven't I? I make things worse every time I talk to you."

"I've never known anyone like you, Gretchen," he said on a heavy breath. His eyes narrowed on hers and he looked suddenly years beyond her in maturity, in sophistication. There was an odd sort of arrogance in his lean face as he studied her boldly. "So you find my...condition...undaunting?"

She smiled gently. "You'd still be you, even if you were missing arms or legs," she pointed out. "I enjoy being with you. I feel...safe."

He laughed hollowly. "As you are," he said bitterly.

"No! Not that sort of safe," she corrected, frowning as she searched for the words. "I'm not afraid of anything when I'm with you." She averted her eyes. "Although I must admit that I was terrified you were going to try and seduce me."

"Were you? Why?"

She stared down at the intricate pattern of tiles under her feet. "Because you could."

There was no sound from the other side of the table for so long that her eyes came up. He was sitting like a statue, staring at her. "I begin to wonder about that," he said almost to himself. His eyes narrowed. "I didn't expect this reaction from you. I must confess I thought your first impulse would be to get on the next plane back to the States and put me right out of your mind."

"Back to my boring job and my boring life?" She laughed softly as she pushed her drink around on the surface of the table. "I don't really have anything to go back to in Texas. Loneliness is portable." She traced a pattern in the vapor on the chilled glass. "You said you do get to Qawi, from time to time," she added, glancing at him quickly.

He leaned back and crossed his long legs. Now was the time for total honesty. She'd earned that from him. "Yes. I live there," he said conversationally.

She blinked. "You didn't say that before!"

"I didn't know you before," he continued quietly. "I wanted to see whether or not you were willing to tell me who you were. I knew that you weren't Maggie Barton, you see," he added with a slow smile.

"But, how?"

He shrugged. "I have a photograph of her in my desk," he said. "Along with her résumé." He met her searching gaze and sat leaning back in his chair, his black eyes glittering faintly, while he waited with damning patience for her to put the final puzzle together.

Her eyes widened. She was remembering all the things she'd heard about the ruler of Qawi—his age, his unmarried status, his strange reputation...

Her breath sighed out in a fearful rush as she realized who Philippe was. Those bodyguards were his. Bojo wasn't a guide at all, he was actually one of the bodyguards. Philippe wasn't a foreign businessman or an ambassador. He was the ruling sheikh of Qawi. He was her new boss!

He chuckled at her wide-eyed stare. "So you finally put two and two together and make four, Gretchen?" he teased gently. "You were honest with me from the outset. I knew almost before the end of our first day together that I could trust you with my life."

"But, I've been horribly rude and unprofessional!" she began.

"You delight me," he replied softly. "You have the courage of a hunting falcon, and you never tell lies. If I were the man I had been only nine years ago, you would already be mine in every sense of the word."

"Me?"

"You." He pushed his glass aside and leaned forward. His eyes narrowed. "Gretchen, it wasn't only to be a social secretary that I insisted on hiring an experienced American woman. Now that you know the truth about me, perhaps you can understand my fear of gossip. A ruler in my position cannot afford to let his weaknesses show, especially one of this magnitude. I had an ulterior motive for the job, and I have it still," he added grimly. "You may not be able to accept the conditions that apply. But in all good conscience, I must outline them for you."

"What would I have to do?" she asked simply, still reeling from the confession, which meant an end to all her hopes. Not only was he incapable of intimacy, but he was the equivalent of a king. She was a poor working girl from Texas. There was no possibility of anything closer than friendship entering their fragile relationship. She was devastated to realize how disappointed she was. And even so, she couldn't bear the thought of never seeing him again, even if her part in his life was a very minor one.

"You would have to be found in compromising situations with me. Only in front of your female servants, however," he stressed curtly. "It would never occur to me to have you seen by any of the men in my personal guard or my circle of friends. You would be the only occupant of my harem, playing a part.''

Her body tingled all over. ''Pretending to be your lover,'' Gretchen said on a rush of breath, with sparkling green eyes and a faint rush of color.

''Yes.''

She felt deliciously hot all over. The thought of his mouth on hers made her knees weak. He wanted pretence. She wanted him, and was only just realizing it. Impossible or not, he attracted her fiercely. All sorts of shocking, exciting images formed in her mind. ''I have no idea how someone in a harem behaves,'' she began slowly.

''Nor have I, despite the lurid depictions in motion pictures,'' he said, with the first touch of amusement since the conversation had begun. ''We will have to learn together.''

Some of the uncertainty left her expression. She grinned back at him with evident pleasure. ''I see. We're both beginners and we start even?''

''A very nice way to put it,'' he agreed. His dark eyes were soft. ''At least your virtue would be completely safe with me.'' He hoped. He didn't dare tell her what her touch did to him, or what it could ultimately mean. He didn't want to frighten her off.

"How far would this pretense have to go, exactly?" she wondered aloud.

"It would have to be convincing," he said. "That is all."

She lowered her eyes demurely. "You'd kiss me and...so forth?"

He lifted an eyebrow. "Yes. Especially and...so forth," he teased.

She smiled impishly. "And I'd get to have meals with you, I suppose?"

He nodded.

"And we'd go places together...oh, no, we wouldn't," she added, remembering a fiction novel she'd once read about his part of the world. "Women don't go out in public with men."

"I govern Qawi," he pointed out. "Women have the vote and they are independent of men financially. Those Muslim women who wear the *aba* and the *hijab* make that decision for themselves without coercion from the government. I have women ministers in my cabinet and many of the new corporations opening branches in Qawi employ female executives. As for my private life— I am sheikh. I make my own rules. We could go out anywhere you like. We could even go sailing," he added. "I have a yacht."

She was more excited than he'd ever seen her. "I love ships."

"Have you ever been on one?" he queried.

She laughed. "Well, not yet. But it looks very exciting."

"Then we will have a cruise." He frowned slightly at her animated features. "It doesn't... bother you, the thought of being handled so intimately by a man in my...condition?"

"Oh, no," she said softly, thinking how fine and strong his hands looked. She remembered being held by him in the swing on the lawn and she tingled with pleasure. "I think it would be madly exciting, And to be the only woman in the whole harem...!" Her eyes danced as she glanced at him. "Think what a reputation I'd have in the household! They'd think I was worth ten other women!"

His body tautened deliciously and he chuckled. "You find me attractive?" he asked slowly.

She swallowed and lifted her drink to her lips. "Very," she said huskily.

He felt the world stop and start again in the few seconds he spent looking into her warm, soft green eyes. He couldn't have imagined her reaction to his proposition. He felt almost whole again.

He reached across the table and possessed her free hand, entangling his fingers tightly with hers. "The one thing I can promise you is satisfaction," he said quietly, his eyes kindling with soft flames. "Even if not in the conventional manner."

She smiled, looking faintly confused. "Yes, I think it will be a very satisfying job, at that."

She hadn't a clue what he was referring to. That was exciting as well. His lips parted. He glanced down and noticed the long-forgotten cigar lying on the tiles, extinguished. He let go of her hand and reached down to lift it, placing it gently in the ashtray on the table.

"I hope you don't mind leaving Tangier in the morning," he said suddenly.

Her heart jumped. "So soon? But, why?"

"You remember the phone call Bojo received just before I left you so abruptly a few days ago?" he asked, deadly serious now.

She nodded, waiting.

"It was one of Bojo's contacts. My worst enemy has bought his way out of a Russian jail and is probably even now planning an attack on me. In fact, it was very likely his men who attempted to kidnap me in Asilah the other day, although I cannot prove it."

"Why?" she asked.

"Who do you think gave the evidence that put him in jail?" he mused. "I implicated him in an attack on an oil platform and an ecological disaster in one of the Soviet states. He lost everything he had. Now he thirsts for revenge, and not only against me. I have doubled the security around us for the past four days, but it is only a matter of time until Kurt Brauer tracks us here. We must leave Morocco and fly on to Qawi, where I have enough people to protect you.''

"You really think this Brauer man would hurt me?" she asked, aghast.

"Certainly," he said simply. "He would hurt anyone connected to me, even in the most casual way, if he could. It is his manner.''

"Do you have many enemies like that one?"

He smiled, and his eyes were genuinely affectionate. "Not many," he said on a chuckle. "Fortunately for both of us." He hesitated, watching her. "You may regret having said yes to this job, Gretchen. If the nature of it makes you uncomfortable, you can back out if you want to, but do it quickly. Once you go to Qawi," he added firmly, and with an odd sort of possession in his tone and his searching gaze, "you stay.''

She thought of lying in his arms and letting him touch her as a lover would. Her heart raced. "I don't want to back out," she said at once, and with obvious sincerity. "And I'm not afraid of your enemies. I'll stand with you, no matter what."

His heart swelled at her fervent tone. He smiled slowly. "I knew you had courage," he said softly. "Then, so be it. We leave the future in the hands of fate.''

"In the hands of fate," she agreed, and she smiled back, feeling that the truly great adventure of her life was underway.

Gretchen was waiting in the lobby the next morning when her new boss came by with Bojo to take her to the airport.

"Something just occurred to me," she said as they went out and got into the hotel's limousine, driven this time by a smiling Mustapha.

"What?" he asked as he slid into the back seat with her, leaving Bojo to occupy the passenger seat in front.

"Philippe is really your name, isn't it?"

He chuckled. "In fact, it's one of several. But I'm known by it abroad."

"Philippe," she said, making it sound like a verbal caress. She smiled. Her lips pursed. "And the Souverain part?"

His perfect white teeth showed against his olive complexion. "French for sovereign—which I am," he added facetiously. "And I do have French blood, as well as Turkish and Arab. My real surname is Sabon. I thought it better to keep my identity secret until I knew you better."

She laughed. "I was so naïve."

"You were, and are, an absolute delight," he corrected. "You made me ashamed of the masquerade, especially when you were so honest about yourself, right from the start.''

''I hate lies,'' she said simply.

''So do I, but one must occasionally employ small ones,'' he returned. He studied her faintly sunburned face. She was wearing a long-sleeved silk blouse over a green-patterned sundress that brought out the emerald sparkle of her eyes. ''Aren't you hot in that?'' he asked suddenly, indicating the long sleeves.

''Yes, I am, but the travel brochures said people here would pinch bare arms.''

He shook his head. ''Don't read travel brochures. Ask a native.''

''Are you a native of Morocco?'' she asked, puzzled by his wording.

''I've never been sure about my birthplace,'' he remarked quietly, studying her. ''Much of my early life is a blur.''

''Why?''she asked, puzzled.

''I grew up as a ragged little street beggar in Baghdad,'' he said with ill-concealed bitterness in his dark eyes. ''I was starving when my father came to Iraq, allegedly on a state visit, and tracked me to an old nurse who was keeping me,'' he hesitated, ''who was using me,'' he corrected bitterly, ''to beg for food. The nurse had been a servant of my mother's who ran away with me when my mother vanished. She was afraid that my father might kill me for my mother's sins."

"What did your mother do that was so terrible?" she asked.

He took her soft hand in his and held it tight in his, making her tingle with pleasure. "She slept with at least two of the palace guards," he said through his teeth. "At that time in our history, the penalty for adultery by a Muslim woman was death. She fled the country."

"I suppose your father had a harem?" she asked with faint distaste.

"My father is Christian," he said, surprising her. "He had one wife, and despite their different religions, he was faithful to her. A Muslim woman is not permitted to marry outside her faith. But, then, my mother was apparently unconcerned with questions of religion, or morality. More than once, my father and I have agonized over whether I am actually his son. Neither of us has had the courage to have blood tests done," he added with bitter mockery.

"I'm sorry. I was making assumptions."

He turned toward her. "I have noticed that about Americans," he said softly. "As a nation, you seem to be obsessed with sex."

"Don't look at me," she murmured dryly. "I don't indulge."

"I know." He brought her moist palm to his lips and stared into her eyes. "It excites me to know. Purity is a valuable commodity in this part of the world, for both men and women. We find your Western idea of morality corrupt."

She crept an inch closer to him, wary of the two men in the front seat who were talking together spiritedly, oblivious to their passengers.

He turned, so that his knee touched her legs in the long skirt of the sundress. His eyes searched hers. "You have an...odd effect on me," he whispered tautly.

Her eyes fell to his firm, beautifully chiseled thin lips. "Is that why you pushed me away?" she asked softly.

His lean hand slid into the coil of blond hair at her nape and drew her ear to his lips. "I pushed you away because you aroused me, quite noticeably," he whispered bluntly, his voice rough with emotion. "It had been nine years since I...felt such an intense reaction to a woman."

Her lips parted. She felt her body swelling, felt her heart beating. She wondered if he could hear it, because it was so loud. Unconsciously, one of her hands was pressing against his white shirt under his jacket and her nails curled into the fabric, feeling a cushy softness under it. He wanted her— he wanted her!

He made a sound deep in his throat and his hand at her neck bruised for a few seconds. He drew back so that he could see into her green eyes. He watched them dilate, felt her jerky warm breath at his lips, watched her bodice shake with each hard pulse of her heartbeat. Two little peaks formed in the silky fabric, outlined by the sheer white cotton blouse over it.

She stared back at him with barely contained desire and fierce pride that she could do something other women couldn't. She was all but shivering with delicious new sensations.

His thumb was under her ear, against her throat, feeling that frantic pulse in her neck. "He fondled you, you said," he murmured.

It took a minute for her to realize what he was saying. "Through my blouse," she whispered shakily. "Not under it. Not ever. I hated it when he handled me." Her nails curled harder into his broad, muscular chest. She knew he would be hairy under it. She could feel the thick, soft cushion under the fabric. "I would…love…letting you touch me…!"

He dragged her face into his throat and shuddered, holding her there while he fought for control. His body was throbbing. Throbbing! He couldn't breathe. His hand contracted behind her head and pressed her cheek to his chest, where her fingers curled into him.

She made a tiny little sound in her throat and he groaned audibly at her ear. Damn the men in the front seat, damn the limousine, damn the people in the street milling around the car with its open windows... He wanted her!

"Sit up. Right now!" he said through his teeth and dragged her away, putting her firmly back in her own seat while he looked deliberately out the other window, his fist clenched by his side.

She was reeling. But this time she knew he hadn't pushed her away because he didn't like her to touch him. She looked at him deliberately below his belt, where his jacket had fallen open. She might be innocent, but she knew from her reading how an aroused man looked. And he was violently aroused. It made her sing with pleasure to know that she'd done that to him, when no other woman had managed it in nine years.

Then doubt crept in and she wondered if he'd manufactured that story about being impotent. She thought about it and decided that he couldn't have. The shock and newness of his improved condition was making him wild. She could see it in the fierce clench of his hand, and she felt proud of her femininity. She'd felt inadequate since Daryl. Now she knew that it wasn't because she was somehow lacking in physical attraction. Philippe wanted her. He really wanted her!

She thought about lying in his arms with her body bare to his eyes, his hands, his mouth... It would be heaven to let him touch her.

She reached down between them to his clenched fist and covered it with light, cool, caressing fingers. He captured it at once, levering his fingers in between hers as he turned his head and looked at her with an expression that could have melted metal. She drew in her breath sharply and his hand contracted.

She knew at that moment that she loved him...

Chapter Seven

The minute Gretchen and Philippe arrived at the airport with Mustapha and Bojo, the atmosphere changed entirely. They were met at the entrance by three more men in suits, very big men with bulging jackets who surrounded them at a signal from Bojo and escorted them through the crowded terminal and out to the tarmac where a Learjet was waiting. One of the men looked more like a professional wrestler than a bodyguard, right down to the jet-black hair caught in a ponytail. He didn't speak at all, but at a sharp word and a gesture from Philippe, he immediately became part of Gretchen's shadow.

Two uniformed men met Philippe with deep bows and spoke in respectful tones. Philippe spoke in turn, obviously giving orders. He took Gretchen by the arm and led her up the steps and into the cabin of the spacious little jet. They were followed by the bodyguards and Bojo, all of whom took seats at tables a good little distance behind Philippe's.

The private jet was fascinating to Gretchen, who'd never been inside one. It had comfortable seats, tables, a uniformed flight attendant and every sort of electronic gadget Gretchen could have imagined.

"It looks like my brother's study," she mused with a smile as she sat down across from Philippe at the table by the window.

"What does your brother do?" he asked.

"He works for the Federal Bureau of Investigation," she said. "He's a senior agent. He used to be a Texas Ranger, though, and I think he misses it. His best friend, Judd Dunn, still works out of Austin. He keeps trying to get my brother to come back. But Marc's been with the FBI for two years now and although he likes the job, he says the constant traveling is wearing him out." She chuckled. "He used to hate living in our little town, but now he says he misses Texas."

His eyes narrowed. "Are you two close?"

"Yes," she said. "With our parents dead, all we

have left is each other. Do you have brothers and sisters?''

He looked out the window as he pulled an expensive cigar from his pocket, clipped the end, and lit it. "I had two brothers, both older than I. They were victims of a political assassination fifteen years ago."

"I'm sorry." She toyed with the ties that wrapped around her green silk dress. "Do you have to worry about enemies other than the man with the mercenaries?''

He leaned back in his chair, studying her. "Any head of state faces potential assassination, Gretchen," he said gently. "It goes with the responsibility."

"That's why you have Bojo and the other bodyguards, isn't it?"

He nodded. "I go nowhere in the world without them." He smiled faintly. "As my father's only living child, I have to bear a certain amount of overprotectiveness. When he can spare the attention from his precious orchids, of course," he added with a chuckle.

"Does he approve of you hiring an American woman to handle your social requirements?''

He pursed his lips and blew out a wisp of smoke. He considered his answer carefully before he decided he must tell the truth. "No. He has a fine distaste for Europeans because of the imperialism of years ago. And he thinks of Americans as decadent, so he may cause you some discomfort. You must not let him intimidate you," he told her firmly. "Most men will walk on a woman who permits it."

"Including you?" she asked demurely.

His black eyes narrowed and he didn't smile. "Especially me. You have no idea of the sort of life I've led. I was overly fond of giving orders even before I assumed power in Qawi, and I will warn you that I have been accustomed since childhood to total obedience."

"That doesn't surprise me," she confessed with a tiny smile. She found him even more fascinating now that she knew a little about his life. "Are all the women in your country veiled and kept separate from men?"

He began to smile. "Ah, the American press," he mused. His black eyes twinkled wickedly. "I understand. You Americans think that our women are oppressed, that they live in fear of mutilation and death from men."

She laughed softly. "Not since I've met you, I don't," she told him.

"I'm flattered." He took a small puff from the cigar. "And as it happens, you're right. I am working to change the status of women and my father rages at me unsuccessfully for the new laws I have had put in place. He says that I am as decadent as the Europeans and the Americans, wishing to give rights to women that should belong only to men!''

"Good for you," she said admiringly.

He laughed. "He is a Christian, too, you know," he remarked surprisingly. "He wrested power from his uncle and retained it for forty years. But his faith made his reign somewhat difficult until our religious population became so diverse. This is why he put it out that I was Muslim, and I permitted the assumption until I assumed office. I have the greatest respect for the Prophet and his writings, because a good deal of my family is Muslim," he added quietly. "We persecute no religion in Qawi."

"You said that your country was still rather...primitive."

His broad shoulders lifted and fell. "Compared to yours, certainly. But I have great plans for my people, for new educational facilities and modern hospitals and industry. Not polluting industry, however," he was quick to insert. "We have learned too much about acid rain and chemical spills to import them. No, our industry will be almost exclusively limited to electronics—computers and its accompanying hardware and software. We have already attracted an American franchise here, a corporation that now markets hardware and software together. You might know of its originator, in fact," he added. "Canton Rourke."

She drew in a sharp breath. "'Mr. Software!' But didn't he go bankrupt a few years ago?"

"He did, and regained his fortune. I know him through a mutual friend, an ex-mercenary who now lives in Cancún, Mexico, a gentleman by the name of Diego Laremos."

"You know real mercenaries?" she asked, fascinated.

He laughed with pure delight. He leaned toward her, glancing warily over her shoulder. "Who do you think Bojo is?"

Her green eyes widened. "Is he, really?"

"He belongs to a group of them, headed by a former physician named Micah Steele."

Gretchen made a sound in her throat. "Oh, if that isn't one big coincidence," she said at once. "For heaven's sake, I work…worked, that is…with Micah's stepsister, Callie Kirby, at the law office in Jacobsville, Texas!"

"Micah speaks of her. Well, then, you may also know Eb Scott and Cy Parks, former members of the group, and perhaps Cord Romero, who was…"

"Cord was blinded!" she exclaimed. "That's why my best friend Maggie went home, to take care of him. They were raised together as foster children. I only have this job because she had to forfeit it! We came to Morocco together.''

His hand reached out and smoothed over her graceful fingers. ''Fate,'' he murmured, meeting her sparkling eyes.

''Yes,'' she agreed breathlessly. ''Fate.''

His forefinger traced over the back of her soft hand and her lips parted as she struggled with her racing pulse. He saw it and thanked providence for sending him this woman, who made him come alive again, who made him feel like a man again. His body responded even to this light touch, and he caught his breath as he searched her pale eyes.

The plane began to move while they watched each other. Scant minutes later, it was airborne, high above the tarmac, reaching for the clouds.

Philippe's black eyes flashed as he studied her flushed, excited face. She looked as hungry as he felt. Abruptly he unfastened her seat belt and his and pulled her out of her chair. He shot a command to the other men as he passed them, tugging a curious Gretchen along with him to the back of the plane.

He opened a small door, put her inside, and closed it back. It was like a tiny apartment, complete with luxurious bed, writing desk, and two round windows. It was dark in the compartment, light coming in only from barely open shades over the two seating classes.

Gretchen started to speak, but he put a firm forefinger over her lips and bent to lift her clear of the floor in his arms.

He laid her on the bed and slid alongside her. She looked up at him with open puzzlement as he searched her eyes in the dim light.

"Consider this," he whispered amusedly at her lips, "a rabidly sexist interview for your new position...!"

And his hard, beautiful mouth reached down to brush over hers with a tender sensuality that pulled tight every muscle and nerve in her body.

Her faint gasp brought his head up. His tracing fingers were just above her collarbone, on the silky purple fabric of her long-sleeved embroidered blouse. Her eyes were wide-open, fascinated, as she watched his face tauten. The silence in the cabin was only broken by the high-pitched whine of the jet engines and the rough sigh of Philippe's breath as he searched her face.

He could hear her breathing jerk against his mouth, he could feel her galloping heartbeat. "It has been so long, Gretchen," he bit off. "I have been too intimidated by my condition to even approach a woman intimately for almost nine years." His hand was faintly unsteady as it drew tenderly against her body. Even through two layers of soft fabric, it burned like a brand. She felt her body go tight and sensitive in the oddest places and she moved involuntarily.

"Oh...glory!" she choked.

"You enjoy this? So do I." His fingers became bolder, tracing the soft curve of her breast. He looked down and, with pure male arrogance, watched her nipples peak. She caught her breath and reached up with nervous fingers to his broad chest in its shirt, gently pressing against it. He felt his body responding to that light, tentative pressure as if she were touching his own skin. He groaned softly.

Her fingers stilled. "Sorry," she began, and started to move her hands away.

He caught them at once and put them back. "I like it," he told her. "Don't stop." His eyes glittered. He guided one soft little hand to the buttons of his vest and nodded.

"This is uncharted territory for me," she said gently. "I don't know what to do."

"I'm going to show you," he said curtly. "There's nothing to be afraid of. I am, as you already know, not man enough to pose a risk to your chastity..."

Her hand had covered his mouth firmly. She looked at him with a fierce, unblinking scrutiny.

"You're a man who had a terrible accident," she said firmly. "It doesn't make you less a man. I'm the one who lacks all the usual skills," she added gently and smiled at him. "I don't even know what I'm supposed to feel, so it isn't as if I can be critical of anything you do."

His short breath was audible. "And I originally hired an experienced woman...!"

"We all make these little mistakes," she said wickedly. "You just didn't know what you'd be missing. That's okay. I won't hold it against you."

He was torn between amused laughter and a feverish hunger to crush her into the bed under him. These were new feelings. He felt himself begin to react to her silky warmth against him and he stiffened suddenly.

She felt the increased pressure against her hip and her eyebrows lifted. "I thought you said you couldn't do that," she whispered shyly.

"I haven't been able to make that happen," he agreed in a rough whisper. "Not for nine long damned years. And I have to feel it," he added hotly, "for the first time, with a woman who wouldn't know an orgasm from a potato!"

She burst out laughing at his sardonic expression. "Oh, you wicked man!" she whispered huskily.

Her amusement veiled a growing passion, and

he could see it in her eyes, in the faintly sensuous movement of her body against his hips.

"Wicked, am I?" he murmured, delighted by her eagerness for him, by her unexpected teasing, by her easy acceptance of his limitations and her pleasure in his touch. He began to smile. What had seemed like a potential ordeal all these years was suddenly fun. He reached under her and pinched her bottom, hard, laughing when she squealed and pushed at him, laughing back.

One of his long, powerful legs shot between both of hers and he came down on her with almost a decade of buried ardor making his blood hot.

"Torment," he breathed into her mouth. "You tease me with dreams of utter paradise...!" He broke her lips apart and began to brush them with his lips and his tongue. All the while, his hands were exploring the slender, warm shape of her body from her rib cage to her hips and back again.

"Philippe?" she whispered jerkily.

"What?" he murmured absently.

"I have breasts," she bit off as he nipped her full lower lip with his teeth.

He stilled. His head lifted and his surprised black eyes met hers. "I beg your pardon?"

"I just thought I'd mention it," she pointed out, breathless. "You seem to think my only assets are my rib cage and my hips."

"You're a virgin," he began.

"Yes, but I'm not dead from the neck down!" she whispered. Her fingers went to the buttons on his vest and then his shirt, and he hung poised just above her with his heartbeat shaking him as he tried to adjust to her mood.

"Aren't you uneasy?" he asked.

She was too busy with buttons to pay much attention. "Uneasy about what? Gosh, you're hairy here. That feels...wonderful!" She frowned. "Why should I be uneasy?"

"You little fool," he ground out. "This is dangerous. I wasn't making idle conversation when I told you I haven't had a woman in nine years!"

"Complaints, complaints," she muttered, shifting closer. "Oh! Oh, yes...!"

He felt the sinuous caress of her body against his and he grew even more aroused. He groaned harshly and his hands gripped the pillow under her head as if he wanted to kill it.

Her legs parted to invite him closer, and her hands smoothed roughly, trembling, up and down his hair-matted chest as she drank in the scents of soap and expensive cologne and cigar smoke that clung to him, filling her nostrils.

He was there...there! She arched up provocatively, involuntarily, and felt a shudder of such exquisite pleasure that she moaned.

His hand at her hip stilled her. He shivered. "Gretchen," he whispered.

She trembled under him as his hard mouth came back to hers and ground down into it with ardent fury. It felt as though he might devour her. Her head began to spin. Her arms slid under the shirt and around him. Her hand encountered a long, deep scar under his left arm and she stilled.

He seemed to have stopped breathing for that instant, when he felt her soft hand on the disfiguring scar that was only one of many. His head lifted. He watched her face, waiting for revulsion, distaste.

"There are others like this, aren't there?" she asked softly. Her fingers traced it to the belt line of his slacks. She looked into his eyes and began to pull the white shirt slowly out of the belt.

He hesitated, his hand going to slow the progress of hers as it reached bare skin.

She hesitated. "Is it...all right...if I touch you?"

His teeth were clenched. "Not below the belt," he gritted.

"Why not?"

His eyes closed. "Gretchen, the scars, some of them, go all the way to the bone. Those in my groin and my left thigh are...disfiguring."

"I'm not the swooning sort of woman," she

pointed out. "I love touching you," she whispered. "I love letting you touch me."

"I haven't. Yet."

Her hand stilled as she searched his face. Her heartbeat became even jerkier. "Would you…like to?"

His face hardened. "Of all the questions…!"

She drew back her hand and matter-of-factly began to unbutton her embroidered silk blouse. She watched his black eyes go involuntarily to the lacy little bra that she uncovered.

"I hope you didn't have too many expectations," she murmured, fascinated at her own boldness with him, "because this thing is padded. I…I'm not very big."

He frowned. "Padded?"

She grimaced as she tugged the edges of the blouse apart and unsnapped the clasp that held the cups together. "Padded," she said, embarrassed.

"You little fraud," he teased, but with tender mockery as she balked at pulling the cups aside. "But why should I be disappointed?"

"Most men like their women voluptuous, don't they?"

His lean forefinger traced a path down the valley between her breasts, making little ripples of sensation work their way down her. She lifted helplessly as he trespassed lazily on either side of the valley.

He laughed in a husky, predatory way. His eyes glittered with feeling. "Men vary in their idea of the perfect woman. Personally," he whispered as he began to move one of the cups slowly aside, "I like a breast that fits in my mouth."

Her expression was priceless. He actually laughed. "Don't you watch movies?"

"I watch movies and read books, too," she choked, lifting again as he traced the cup away to the hard nipple that ached for his touch. "But I never dreamed it would feel like this!"

"You make me ache to be whole again," he breathed, watching her eyes as he brushed the cup completely away from her breast and looked down with violent hunger at what he'd uncovered. His fingers traced her breast, lingering on the dark aerole that peaked even more when he took it between his fingers and tested its hardness.

She made a high-pitched little sound and he searched her face for a few heated seconds before his head bent to her body. "What a wise move I made, to have this cabin soundproofed...!"

She writhed as if she were being tortured as he took her whole breast into the warm, hot darkness of his mouth and suckled it hungrily. Her nails bit into his broad, warm chest. Her hips twisted into his, her breath seemed suspended in limbo while he made her a sensual prisoner in his arms.

He started to lift his dark head and she clung, her mouth at his ear.

"Please don't stop," she whispered frantically. "Oh, please!"

He renewed his efforts, moving from one breast to the other until she shivered, and then down her body to the fastening of her slacks.

He cursed the fabric as he fought with the closure, and then his mouth was on her flat belly, hard and feverish, and she began to whimper.

"That won't do," he murmured on his way back up to her mouth. "That won't do at all."

While she was trying to think, to make sense of what he was whispering, his lean hands smoothed her slacks and briefs out of his way and he touched her in a way she'd never dreamed a man would.

"Philippe!" she choked.

His mouth covered hers while he pleasured her in the tense silence of the cabin. He drew his lips back down to her firm little breast and he suckled her insistently while his hands explored her so intimately that she could have wept for the embarrassment. But even while she was trying to protest, he did something that lifted her completely off the bed. Her startled, horrified eyes met his glittering ones for just a space of seconds before she went over some hot, urgent precipice and began to shudder rhythmically with a pleasure she'd never experienced. Her eyes closed as she arched toward those skillful hands, inhibitions washed away by ecstasy as she felt the first climax of her life...

She wept then, clinging to him for comfort as he enfolded her against him and rocked her, pressing her naked breasts into the thick mat of hair that wedged down his broad chest. He'd satisfied her, and he was still aroused. It was more than he'd ever hoped for. If he could maintain it for even this long, there was every chance that eventually he could...have her!

He lifted his head and looked down at her faintly flushed face, her wide, secretive, shamed eyes. She was still trembling in the aftermath of what he'd given her.

He pushed back her disheveled blond hair, which was loose and flowing around her face. "When I told you that I could give you satisfaction," he murmured, "this is what I meant."

She swallowed, still embarrassed, but fascinated by the look in his eyes. "Is that how sex feels?" she whispered.

He smiled tenderly. "I think so. I'm not sure I remember," he teased.

Her nails curled into his chest. "Philippe?"

He bent and brushed his mouth over her eyes. "Yes."

"You...you're still aroused," she whispered.

"Very aroused," he admitted. "It comes as a surprise to me as well. I haven't been able to maintain it for this long before."

She touched his firm chin lightly and then his chiseled, beautiful mouth. "If you want to try..."

He watched her with dark, brooding eyes. "You would do that for me? Offer me your chastity without marriage?"

She bit her lower lip. "You're a head of state," she began. "When you marry, it will have to be someone equally important."

His hands smoothed into her disheveled hair and spread it on the pillow. "It will have to be a woman who can live with my limitations, whatever they turn out to be," he said quietly. "Just because I can maintain an arousal like this is no proof of my capability in bed. I have a genuine loss of sensation. It may never be possible for me to climax, Gretchen," he said bluntly. "No, don't turn your face away. We must speak of it. I can never give you a child, regardless of whether or not I can become your lover. The damage, as I let you discover in a small way, is terrible. Even more terrible than I can show you."

"Have you seen a doctor in the past nine years, since they made their original diagnosis?"

"I have no need to," he said heavily. He rolled away from her, onto his back, and stared up at the ceiling. "My mirror tells me everything there is to know, when I can bear to look at myself."

She crept up to his chest and slid an arm around him, pressing close to his side so that she could pillow her cheek on his bare shoulder. "You'd have to show me how," she said softly, "but I'm more than willing to try to do for you what you just did for me."

His heart stopped. His arm enveloped her and held her tight for a few seconds. "A generous offer, and one for which I am more grateful than you know. But I wouldn't subject any woman to the feel of me, much less a virgin who has no knowledge of men's bodies." He rolled over and put a finger over her protesting lips. "I am disfigured."

She caught his fingers in hers. "If you didn't trust me, you would never have allowed me to come in here with you in the first place."

"I was aroused," he corrected. "I wanted to see if I could function."

"But you had nothing," she said sadly. "It was all for me."

He drew her fingers to his lips as he rolled back over and lay looking at the ceiling. "Perhaps this is all there will ever be, for me," he said, his voice very quiet.

Her fingers tangled in the thick curling hair over his chest and her eyes closed. "Do you have any sensation there?"

"An odd sort," he replied after a minute. "I feel it most intensely when I touch you." He smoothed back her disheveled hair.

"Haven't you tried to make love to anyone since the accident?"

"The doctors told me it would be of no use, and I believe they were right." His hand tightened in her hair. "The reaction I have to you is a mystery."

"Perhaps you didn't feel anything because you wouldn't let yourself try."

"I did, once," he said bitterly. "With a woman in Europe."

"What happened?"

"Nothing, and she found the situation quite amusing." His voice became grim at even the memory of the woman's contemptuous laughter. "That was when I gave up. I decided that a charade was the only option left to me, the pretense of a serious relationship to put the old gossip to rest."

"I would never have laughed at you," Gretchen said with anger at the nameless woman.

He wrapped her up tightly in his arms and drew her over him, so that her hips lay angled across his. "I should send you back to Texas, right now."

"And I'd go back to my old, dismal job looking up legal precedents while somebody else gets to be the wild woman of the harem," she said with deliberate disgust. "How could you even think of doing that to me?"

He lifted an eyebrow and studied her, drawing his gaze lazily down to the soft breasts pressed into the thick hair of his chest. He was still aroused. She made him feel stronger than he ever had in his life. As he studied her, it occurred to him that what he was offering her really was a bad reputation. His Middle-Eastern roots shuddered at just the thought of such impropriety. She was innocent. It shamed him to have even considered dishonoring her in such a way.

He traced around her full lips. "So you would prefer to live with me and play doctor, hmmm?" he teased gently.

She gave him a mock glare. "Only if you play fair. I'm not going to be the only person taking her clothes off around here."

His black eyes danced. He felt joy as almost a tangible thing when she lay in his arms. "Pity," he mused, drawing her gently closer. "When you look so enticing without them."

"I suppose I'll have to learn to organize luncheons and meetings and social functions," she sighed.

He traced her soft blond hair. "I have an entire roomful of people who do nothing except that. Your only concern will be me."

Her eyebrows lifted. "I'll get fat."

He smiled. "You won't have the time. I expect to be at the palace for quite some time to come. I have plans which are about to come to fruition, especially in the field of education. You can help me convince the people in the outlying tribes to allow their children to be educated."

"I'd love to do that! But I don't speak your language," she said.

"You can learn it. It's a dialect of Arabic, and I'll have you tutored."

"Something else to look forward to," she mused, searching his eyes. "A mission of my very own."

"Something else, you said?"

"Mmm-hmm." She reached down and drew her lips tenderly over his, nibbling first the thin upper one and then the fuller lower one.

"Like this," he murmured, guiding her lips against his until she understood the pressure and contact he wanted. "Yes, that's it. What else?" he persisted.

She nipped his lower lip softly. "I want you to deflower me."

He was very still. He frowned. "The translation must be an idiom."

She chuckled and leaned down to his ear. "I want you to become my lover."

His lean hands spread on the soft, warm flesh of her bare back. "I want nothing more than that," he groaned, holding her even closer. "But you must realize that the odds are very much against it."

"The odds were very much against the condition you're in right now," she whispered. "Where there's smoke, there's fire, my grandfather used to say."

"More idioms, you little pest…!"

She'd put her open mouth on his chest, and he gasped.

She hesitated. Under her hand she felt the sudden violent shudder of his heart. He wasn't moving. He didn't even seem to be breathing.

She moved closer and did it again, deliberately moving her mouth against his tight nipple and suckling it, as he'd done to her, earlier.

His body came right off the bed. He shuddered. His hands caught the back of her head. He held her mouth to him. His fingers spread into her hair and coaxed her to suckle him again.

She barely lifted her lips as her hand slid to his navel. "Teach me how," she whispered as she put her mouth on his chest again.

He was muttering something, harsh and feverish, in a language she didn't understand. But he wasn't fighting her wandering fingers. He jerked the belt loose and worked the closure, bringing her hand onto silky fabric. But when she moved it under the waistband, he stopped her firmly.

"It won't matter," she whispered.

"It will," he ground out. "Don't stop."

He drew her hand onto him, feeling it jerk a little despite her resolve when she touched him. There was a velvety hardness under the silk, and he taught her how to brush it, how to explore it, in a silence that was loud with the sound of breathing.

He shivered, but despite the pleasure, there was no upsurge, no building heat. "Damnation!" he choked. "I...can't...!"

"What am I doing wrong?" she asked.

He stilled her hand against him and held it there as he exhaled roughly. His eyes closed. "The pleasure is there, but I can't reach it. The problem is in me, not in you. And this is not the time, nor the place."

He moved her hand and rolled away from her. He got to his feet efficiently and refastened his clothing. While he dressed, so did Gretchen, but she felt no embarrassment with him now. Her eyes told him so when he turned to look at her.

"I'm not sorry," she said before he could speak.

"Neither am I." His eyes met hers. "You belong to me now," he said, and he didn't smile. "We must marry."

"Why?" she asked huskily.

"Because if there's any possibility that I can have you, I'm going to," he said bluntly, holding her eyes. "In my world, no man has a virgin unless he is her husband."

"But I'm not your social equal," she protested.

"Gretchen, do you want me to turn the jet around and send you back to the States?"

"After that?" she exclaimed, her expression starting to fill with hurt.

He chuckled. He pulled her tight into his arms and rocked her, cradled her, cherished her against his heart. "It was the single most delightful pleasure of my life," he whispered. "If you're willing to take the chance, we can be married under my own customs, my own law." He hesitated. "Such a marriage would be binding only in Qawi," he added reluctantly, "so that if I am unable to consummate the relationship, you can go home still a virgin."

"And if you can consummate it?" she whispered back.

He lifted his head and met her eyes with his. "It will take an army to get you out of the country. Because if I can have you completely," he added huskily, "you will never escape me in this lifetime!"

Chapter Eight

Gretchen's warm eyes wandered over his face and she smiled tenderly. "I never dreamed anything like this would ever happen to me," she said softly. "I'd love to marry you. But you don't have to."

"Having you the object of lurid gossip in the palace would demean me and dishonor you. My father would cut off my hands," he pointed out. "He's a stickler for tradition. So am I." He pursed his lips and smiled at her. "So are you, in fact."

"I don't want to cause you any trouble."

"You make me a man again, and you think I see you as trouble?" he asked sardonically.

"You hadn't really tried to make love to anyone since the accident, had you?" she asked, seeing the truth in his face. "You might still be able to, with someone else. With that blond woman you said I remind you of," she added with a surge of jealousy that she fought to keep hidden.

"Brianne." He thought back to his relationship with Brianne, and his expression hardened. He had adored her, ached for her, and lost her to Pierce Hutton because he thought himself incapable with any woman ever again.

Gretchen saw the disappointment in his eyes and felt uncertain of herself. "Do you still care for her?" she persisted.

"I will always care for her," he said bluntly. "But she's happily married and she has a two-year-old son. Even if I were whole again, there's no hope. Not with her." He turned, his black eyes lancing into her green ones. "But my reaction to you is quite promising, and I have every intention of pursuing it. That should make my position crystal clear. If you want to run, do it now."

She pursed her lips and lifted her eyebrows. "Got a parachute?"

He chuckled. "No."

"Then I guess you're stuck with me. Monsieur Souverain," she murmured mockingly.

He caught her hand in his and opened the cabin door. "Out," he said on a laugh, nudging her into the aisle in front of him.

She laughed, too, and the bodyguards stared at both of them with varying degrees of puzzlement. Probably they'd heard all that gossip, too, Gretchen thought, but she was disheveled and her mouth was swollen and Philippe didn't look too neat himself. They looked shocked to see such radiance on their ruling sheikh's lean, hard face. Good. That ought to give them something to think about, she told herself smugly.

She sat beside Philippe until the plane landed in Qawi. It was no more what she'd expected than Morocco had been. There were date palms everywhere, sandy stretches that led to the Persian Gulf, and sparkling blue water. Inside the ancient wall of the old city, the buildings were a blinding white. There were beautiful mosques and a cathedral, and in the distance, she saw what looked like the beginnings of a new and modern city.

Philippe motioned to one of the stewards, and the neatly uniformed young woman in the head scarf smiled at Gretchen as she handed Philippe what looked like a bundle of black cloth.

"This is necessary," he told her solemnly. "It is the same as opening an umbrella during a rainstorm in your own country. I am sovereign of my country, and I must respect all its traditions as well as protect you from any extremists who live here."

"You don't have to explain it to me," she assured him. "I spoke to a Muslim woman in the hotel and she told me that to a lot of them who live strictly by the Qu'ran, the *aba* and *hijab* are visible signs of their pride and their purity."

He smiled radiantly. "Who taught you the words for cloak and head covering?"

"She did," she told him. "And it's a *thobe* that men wear with a *bisht* over the *thobe* and a *gutra* on the head held in place by that rope-thing called an *igal*."

He pursed his lips. "I'm impressed."

"*Shukran.*"

He chuckled. She'd thanked him in Arabic. "Now I'm really impressed," he added when she grinned. "Here." He stood and dropped the dark *hijab* over her head, covering her neat bun of blond hair. He added the huge black hooded cloak to it. "There are still those among my people who might do you harm if they see your shape blatantly displayed. I won't have you at risk, in any way."

She smiled up at him. "Thanks. But it's okay," she assured him. "If you came home with me, you'd have to put on a cowboy hat and somebody would probably try to trick you into getting on an unbroken horse."

He choked back a laugh at her assumption that he couldn't ride an unbroken horse. She had an interesting, if incorrect, opinion of him. She was going to be surprised when she saw him as he truly was, on his own home ground. He stood aside to let the bodyguards open the door of the huge black stretch limousine for them.

"You might have told me who you were from the beginning," she pointed out when they were flying down the paved road toward what must be the capital city.

"What, and take all the fun out of our relationship?" he replied with a grin. "Surely, men are more attractive to women when they remain mysterious?"

"You're a king." She was still getting used to that, and it helped if she reminded him occasionally, too.

"I'm a sheikh," he corrected. "The head of the tribe which traditionally held power in this part of the continent. The line has come down relatively unbroken through *imamates* for six generations, although my father is the first Christian leader."

"I see. You inherit the crown, so to speak, like kings do."

He lifted an eyebrow and for an instant, he seemed very foreign. "No one inherits a title among these desert people," he said softly. "It is won, and held, only by the man who can defend it."

That was confusing and she wanted to ask more

questions, but the phone rang and in seconds, the intercom came alive. Philippe listened and then picked up the receiver at his side, speaking abruptly and rapidly into it. He hesitated and then spoke again, grimacing as he put the phone down.

"More trouble," he said shortly. "A raid at the border. Several men were killed." He glanced at her. "It will mean a trip to the border on our northern desert. I must deal with this."

"Do you have an army?" she asked.

"Not in the sense you mean, not yet," he replied. "We are an old country, but without a modern base of power unless you include long-range tactical weapons and an elite but small military unit with a limited amount of equipment. No, the rebels will have to be met in the old way. And while we solve that problem, we can solve our own," he added with a lingering search of her eyes. "I will arrange the wedding at the same time."

"You're really serious?"

"I am."

"But you said your father didn't like Americans," she pointed out.

"Gretchen, you will enchant him," he said quietly. "All it needs is time."

"Will we leave right away?"

"Not for several days," he replied. "I have to

meet with my ministers and my father to discuss the treaties I have just signed, and the contracts I have negotiated. You will have enough to occupy you," he promised gently. "My minister of education will bring you up-to-date on my kindergarten project."

"I hope I can do what you want me to," she said worriedly.

"Of that, I am certain. And soon, so will you be," he said.

"You make me feel as if I can do anything," she confessed. "Until the past few days, I was sort of a bystander of life. You make me want to be a participant."

His eyes narrowed. "This man who wanted to marry you," he said, his eyes intent on her face, "what became of him?"

"Daryl?" She sighed. "He took up with a banker's daughter and left skid marks..." She saw the lack of comprehension in his face and laughed. "Sorry. I'm afraid that idioms are second nature to Americans. He started dating a banker's daughter. He couldn't get away from me fast enough. He thought my mother would leave a great deal of insurance money. But there was none."

"An opportunist," he commented.

"Yes, and I hadn't the experience to recognize that when I saw him," she said self-consciously.

"Mother was very possessive of me, especially when I got old enough to date. I think she knew she was dying and she was afraid of being left alone. As if I would ever even have thought of leaving her by herself!"

"No," he mused, studying her. "You are not the sort of person to abandon a loved one in need."

"At least he was around when she died, so I wasn't totally alone. Marc was in Florida working undercover. He didn't get home until after the funeral."

He muttered something, his eyes flashing. "You had no one to help with the arrangements?"

"I sort of had Daryl, at least until he felt safe mentioning the will." She shook her head. "But I guess there aren't a lot of men who'd want to settle for life on a run-down cattle ranch in a small Texas town."

"You sell yourself short," he said curtly.

Her eyes widened. "Speaking of selling women," she said, leaning toward him, "did white slavery *really* go on over in this part of the world?"

He burst out laughing. "Why do you want to know?" he teased. "Do you think I might be tempted to sell you?"

"I guess not," she said with a smile. "You wouldn't need the money."

"No, I wouldn't," he agreed. His eyes slid over her warmly. "White gold," he murmured. "That's what they would have called a woman like you. You would have fetched a handsome price."

"There, you see, it did cross your mind!" she chided.

He chuckled softly. "Even if I were a brigand, would I sell the greatest treasure in my storehouse?" he murmured.

She smiled back at him. It was like a new beginning, this foreign place with a man who was already fascinating to her in every way. Her small hand reached for his under the cover of the *aba*. Without turning his head toward her, his long fingers curled into hers and pressed them tightly before letting them go. She remembered then that public shows of affection were unacceptable in this part of the world and she moved her hand back from his unobtrusively. He noticed, and his eyes twinkled approvingly.

Gretchen's first sight of the palace was a revelation to Philippe, who watched her reaction with pleasure.

"The *Palais Tatluk*," he murmured as it came into view, a towering, sprawling white stone structure with arched doorways and arched windows with black grillwork on both stories. There were no balconies, but then she remembered that in Arab households, the balconies always faced inward, not outward, so that the women were hidden to the eyes of the world. "The seat of power of my family."

"It's magnificent," she said, lost for words.

"It was the only structure Brauer's men didn't destroy two years ago," he said through his teeth, and for an instant, he looked so menacing and fierce that he seemed like a stranger. "Brauer intended using it as his headquarters when he and his mercenaries took over my country."

"How did you escape?" she asked. "I mean, if you don't mind telling me?"

"I slipped through the perimeter and joined a small caravan bound for Oman," he murmured. "Then I managed passage with my pocket money to Martinique, where I…borrowed funds to launch a successful counterinvasion."

"Against mercenaries?"

His head turned toward her, and the expression in his eyes was odd. "You know nothing of us. You may find that all your assumptions are far short of the mark. In all the Middle East, there are no mercenaries, no soldiers, equal to my *sha-KOOSH*."

"Your what?"

He smiled. "My personal bodyguard. They are

my *sha-KOOSH*—my hammer, you would say in English. They have no equal in combat, except perhaps the British SAS. The Special Air Services,'' he enlightened her. "A unit of exceptionally gifted soldiers whose training methods are, shall we say, also exceptional.''

"Oh, I see. Like our Green Berets and Navy SEALs,'' she agreed. "You send them in against terrorists.''

"Send them in…'' He seemed puzzled.

"I can't get away from idioms,'' she groaned.

He lifted an eyebrow and smiled at her. "I understand. The general sits at his desk and sends his men into battle, yes?''

"Well, not all of them,'' she amended. "But no one expects the head of state to lead a charge.''

He averted his eyes before she could see the merriment in them. "Of course not.''

"You said your family had been in power here for generations.''

"So they have,'' he replied. "Originally, it was part of the Turkish Ottoman Empire. Then when the French and British fought over us in the nineteenth century, foreign missionaries came in and began to convert us. We won our independence in 1930, when my grandfather defeated a detachment of the French Foreign Legion and drew together the remaining nomadic Bedouin tribes under one sheikh. My father succeeded him, but not until after he was won over to Christianity, which caused no small disturbance. He was forced to go to war to defend his position. My two half brothers were Muslim, and I was raised to honor both traditions. But some years ago, I, too, converted. This caused some dissention and my father thought it wise not to make an issue of religion. As you might understand already, there are many Muslim sects, some of which are more reactionary and militant than others. We coexist with them, and the Jews, with laws in place that protect no right more than that of freedom of worship."

Her eyes admired him. "I think you must be a very good leader."

He smiled at her. "I have a long way to go before I become such a man. But having a fierce little desert hen to protect might hasten my journey."

She dropped her gaze shyly. "I'm not fierce."

"You will be," he replied quietly. "You have the heart of a falcon. It is only that you lack the self-confidence to realize your potential. I will make you believe in yourself. I will make you strong, as you will make me stronger."

She glanced at him curiously. "I don't understand."

His eyes narrowed. "The experiences of your

life have combined to strengthen you, but you've never really tested yourself, have you? Gretchen, most of the women of my experience—with one exception—would have run screaming for cover when the bullets started flying in Asilah. You stayed right by my side.''

"Did you think I could run away and leave you to face the danger alone?" she asked, aghast.

His chest swelled. His body tautened. His eyes began to smolder in his lean, taut face as he looked at her. "Did you know," he said huskily, "that the falcon mates for life?"

Her lips parted as the heat built in her body from the unblinking scrutiny of those black eyes. She felt her breasts swelling, peaking, and she caught her breath at the intensity of desire that consumed her.

His gaze fell to the shapeless *aba,* where the small peaks were just barely discernable under the thick fabric. His face hardened even more as pleasure shot through him. He hated his impotence. He groaned and dragged his eyes away to the passing landscape outside the speeding car.

"One day," she said very softly, so that she couldn't be overheard by the bodyguards in another compartment of the car, "you're going to be very glad that Maggie couldn't come to work for you. I promise you, I'm going to do everything in my power to make you happy."

He seemed almost to flinch. "How, by marrying half a man?" he choked.

"You're more man than anyone I've ever known, Philippe Sabon," she said huskily. "I'd rather have only kisses with you than a full relationship with any other man in the world."

He turned back to her slowly, frowning, his eyes wary and strange. He looked at her with pure longing. "I feel that way, with you," he whispered.

Her eyes lit up. What he could see of her face was suddenly radiant.

"I could love you," he said harshly.

"I know. I could love you, too," she whispered back.

His whole body tensed, as if he were about to throw convention and formality to the four winds. But just as he moved all but imperceptibly toward her, the car swerved and when he looked out the window, they were going around the long paved driveway that led through legions of straight palm trees to the front entrance of the palace.

As if his sudden weakness irritated him, Philippe left the car as soon as the chauffeur opened the door, leaving Gretchen to follow, with the huge ponytailed guard still at her side. He looked totally

Arab, but there was something in his face that reminded her whimsically of the late singer, Elvis
Presley. She wondered what Philippe would say if
she called his burly bodyguard a nickname. In the
days to come, perhaps she'd find out!

The interior of the palace was as captivating and
beautiful as the exterior. The floor tiles were done
in a dozen shades of blue. There were graceful
arches everywhere and expensive carpets on the
floors. There was a staircase that Gretchen fell in
love with the instant she saw it beyond the enormous crystal chandelier sparkling in the foyer. She
turned around slowly, mesmerized by her surroundings, so intent on looking that she backed
right into something warm and solid and suddenly
turned to find herself at the mercy of black eyes
that made her feel hunted.

A spate of rapid Arabic came from Philippe to
the slight, formally dressed man in the dark suit
who was glaring at Gretchen.

"This is Ahmed," Philippe introduced him.
"He is my uncle, the brother of my father. Ahmed,
this is my fiancée," he said. "Gretchen Brannon
from Jacobsville, Texas."

For an instant, pure hatred flashed in the older
man's eyes. "Fiancée? An infidel? An...Amer-
ican?" he made the word sound obscene.

Gretchen drew herself up and started to speak, but Philippe moved in front of her before she could. There was another rapid-fire burst of Arabic and the older man's eyelids flinched. He bowed quickly, murmuring something, and moved away. The bodyguards followed, except for Gretchen's "Elvis."

"I told you it would be difficult," Philippe told Gretchen gently. "But you must not involve yourself in verbal altercations with him. He is Muslim. It would cause grave offense. You understand?"

She drew in her breath quickly. "I understand. Really."

His eyes softened. "I would not mind for my own sake. It is for your safety that I worry. He is powerful and he has allies at court. Save for myself, and my father, he is the only other claimant to the robes of state. He would like to be sheikh."

"Oh, I see. Well, I won't give him any reason to use me against you."

His eyes twinkled. "As if he could." He moved forward, his expression lightening. "I can't talk to you like this." He reached down and whipped off the *aba*, mussing her hair in the process. He tossed the garment to "Elvis" and indicated that Gretchen should join him as he walked down the long hall. "Now for the next hurdle," he mused to himself.

He led the way through another archway, down another hall, and suddenly they were in what looked like a tropical paradise. The tiled room was huge. Fountains sang from every corner. There were palm trees and tropical vegetation and, everywhere, orchids. Hundreds of orchids.

"Oh, glory," Gretchen exclaimed. "Oh, how beautiful. How beautiful!" She went close to a yellowish-green bloom with speckles on it and leaned forward to breathe in its exquisite fragrance. Her fingertips caressed it lightly.

"Do not touch them!" came a harsh, furious voice from behind them.

She stumbled in her haste to move away from the orchid and barely saved herself from a hard fall. The old man staring at them was wearing a white *thobe* and a matching skullcap, called a *taiga*. He looked formidable for a gardener, and he was heavyset and big. He wore a beard and mustache, both white like his thick hair.

"They're exquisite," Gretchen said, pushing back her disheveled hair. "I'm sorry, but I love flowers. I can't bear not to touch them. I have an orchid of my own—just a phalanopsis, a little inexpensive one—and I pamper it, too."

"Only one?" the old man mused.

She flushed. "Yes, well, I don't have a proper place to keep them. And I couldn't afford many of them even if I did," she added with complete honesty.

His eyes narrowed. "You are unveiled in front of men who are not your husband," he replied. "And you wear garments that offend my eyes and those of my brother and my male household."

Philippe moved forward. He spoke to the old man sharply, although with great respect.

The old man gaped at him. "You would marry *that?*" he exclaimed, indicating Gretchen. "An American? An infidel from the very pit of hell?!"

Gretchen gasped. He had a lot of gall for a servant.

"A skinny infidel, at that," he added, with a disapproving stare.

"How dare you!" she exclaimed before Philippe could intervene, and her green eyes flashed furiously. "I go to church, I'll have you know, and I'd lay a man out with a horsewhip before I'd let him touch me without a wedding ring on my finger!"

The old man's eyebrows lifted. He pursed his lips and cocked his head to stare at her outraged, flushed face. *"FIL-fil,"* he murmured dryly, and suddenly burst out laughing.

Philippe chuckled and exchanged a brief couple of sentences with the old man.

The older man grimaced, but he was silent. Philippe bowed and his older counterpart waved his hand dismissively and, with a last glare in Gretchen's direction, turned away and went back to his orchids with a magnificent air of indifference to them both.

Philippe motioned for Gretchen to go with him.

"My goodness, what a bigot," Gretchen said angrily. "And he called me a name, too. What did he call me?"

"Never mind," he murmured with a chuckle. "I told you he would try to intimidate you. Had you let him get away with it, you would be halfway back to Texas by now, forcibly escorted to the airport by his entire personal bodyguard."

"Your gardener has that sort of power?" she exclaimed.

"Not my gardener, Gretchen. My father."

Her lips pursed. "Ooops!" she murmured self-consciously.

"Don't worry, he'll adjust to you," he said. He turned to the ponytailed bodyguard who'd been waiting in the corridor with them, and shot a command at him. The bodyguard bowed and walked away.

"Where's he going?" Gretchen asked.

"So you miss him already, hmm?" Philippe asked with a grin. "I have assigned him to protect you with his life. He will never leave you, except while you sleep. Even then, he will sleep at your door.''

"You're taking my safety very seriously," she said, impressed and a little curious.

He stopped and turned to her. "I think that Brauer has a spy among my household," he said bluntly. "I also think he had a part in the border attack today. I can't afford to relax my guard, especially now. You must never leave your quarters without Hassan."

"You mean 'Elvis.'''

His eyebrows lifted. "A nickname, yes? Have you spoken to him?" he asked suddenly.

The question puzzled her. "I don't speak Arabic yet."

"Ah. I see. A lucky guess, perhaps."

"Now you're being enigmatic," she accused.

"A private joke, nothing more. Call him what you like, then. In my country when people marry, the bride is given a dowry by her husband."

"I don't want money from you," she said firmly.

His eyes twinkled. "Very well then. I will give you Hassan. He is yours."

"He doesn't look like white gold to me, but maybe he has hidden talents," she murmured dryly. Her eyes sparkled. "Since he belongs to me, if you divorce me, can I carry him home and keep him?"

He laughed out loud. "That need will not arise. Divorce will be out of the question, you understand?"

"Yes." She searched his eyes. "But we're not being married in a church, are we?"

His smile faded. "Not yet, no. The ceremony will be a very simple one, a tribal one, with a minimum of witnesses and no formal festivities. Marriage in a grand cathedral—and we have such a place here—would be binding for life." His eyes were sad and bitter. "If there were a possibility of children, it would require a state wedding. But that is impossible."

"Who will inherit this when you die?" she asked with equal sadness.

"Did I not tell you? Brianne's little boy will become sheikh at my death," he said simply. "A beautiful child, with the dark eyes and hair of his father," added with cold distaste. "And, of course, his father will oppose this, as he opposes anything that might necessitate meetings between his wife and myself. He is a violently jealous and possessive man."

And this Brianne meant something important to Philippe still, if he was willing to give his kingdom to her child. She wondered how his uncle would react to this news, not to mention his father.

He sighed irritably at the thought of Pierce Hutton. "God knows what she sees in such a man," he muttered.

"What's her husband like?" she asked curiously.

"Rich."

She laughed. "Besides that?"

"He owns an international construction corporation. He builds oil platforms, among other things." He glanced at her. "A brave man, although I find him distasteful. He and Brianne and I barely escaped Qawi with our lives during Brauer's attack. It was Hutton who loaned me the money for the counterrevolution here." His eyes glittered. "A fact of which he never tires reminding me."

It sounded as though there was still a rivalry between the two men. Gretchen was curious about the unknown Brianne. She must be a raving beauty to have two such men vying for her. It was natural that her husband should love her, but Gretchen was intensely jealous of Philippe's pointed references to her.

"Will I see you again today?" she asked abruptly.

"Perhaps," he said, gesturing to the pretty

young woman in an embroidered beige *gellabia* that fell gracefully to her ankles and a neat beige patterned *hijab* who came back with "Elvis."

"Here is Leila to take you to your quarters. I have had my paternal grandmother's rooms made ready for you. I think you will like them. She was Turkish. Her late husband was French."

"Is she still alive?"

He shook his head. "She died twenty years ago. I remember her love for orchids. She passed it on to my father."

"At least he likes something," she said wistfully.

"Yes. His beloved orchids," Philippe said with a mocking smile. "And very little else, except his country. Never mind. You will have little enough to do with him. Go with…Hassan," he said, grinning, and she knew he'd been about to use her nickname for the man. He said something to "Elvis" that made him smile and then followed the remark with an obvious command in Arabic. The bodyguard nodded curtly and bowed.

He turned and spoke to the pretty dark-eyed young woman, who smiled and caught Gretchen firmly by the hand.

"You will come with me, please, Lady FIL-fil," she said respectfully.

Philippe gave a loud laugh. "Now you, too,

have a nickname, *mademoiselle,*'' he teased. ''You can thank my father for it.''

''What does it mean?'' she asked apprehensively.

His black eyes twinkled. ''It means pepper. And I assure you, it was not of a mild species my father was thinking when he used the term!''

Chapter Nine

Leila took Gretchen into the luxurious confines of the white and gold quarters in the women's section of the palace. The Texas woman stood and stared at it with disbelief. It was like something out of a luxury magazine, she thought, with lavish tile on the floors and even the walls, with a bathroom the size of her house back in Jacobsville, complete with huge bathing pool and skylight. The pool was surrounded by the same tile that graced the floors, and potted palms and flowering plants all but concealed it.

"You like?" Leila asked with twinkling eyes.

"It's so beautiful," Gretchen remarked dreamily.

Leila leaned toward her. "It was the old

harem," she said confidentially. "The *sidi's* great-grandfather had twenty concubines, and this is where they stayed, surrounded by eunuchs."

"*Sidi?* What does it mean?" she asked curiously.

"It means lord."

"Lord of the desert," she mused, picturing a sheikh in flowing white robes on a huge stallion riding like the wind in front of his warriors. She smiled at her folly. Philippe probably couldn't even ride a horse. What a fanciful woman she was getting to be. The mystique of the place was affecting her.

"He is a strong man, the *sidi*," Leila continued to speak, moving to unpack the suitcases the body-guard had brought to the women's quarters. She shook her head disparagingly over Gretchen's few clothes. There were two skirts, a blouse, and a pair of slacks, besides the white Mexican dress and accompanying shawl. "No, no, this will not do at all! I must make the *sidi* aware of your wardrobe, Lady FIL-fil," she continued. "He will expect you to dress as befits a woman of your station here."

"My station?" Gretchen asked, diverted.

"You will be my Lady, of course," the Arab woman said simply. "You will be the bride of our sheikh." She smiled at Gretchen's expression. "We know of the *sidi's* desire to marry you, my

Lady," she added. "We had feared that he would never take a bride. In fact, there were whispers that he had no use for a woman…"

Gretchen's face flamed and she knew she looked guilty as sin.

But Leila saw the expression in an entirely different light, and began to laugh secretively. "Ah. So it was not the lack of need for a woman, it was the lack of someone for whom he could care, eh?" She chuckled. "I see."

"He is…very attractive," Gretchen said demurely.

"He is very much a man, my Lady," Leila replied. "A tiger of a man. They still tell stories of him around the Bedouin campfires, of the fierce battle he waged to regain Qawi from the mercenaries."

"Yes, he told me about his personal bodyguard," Gretchen recalled.

Leila gave her an odd look. "The battle was joined by all the tribes, my Lady," she said softly. "By every tribe in our country. You cannot possibly imagine the divisions, the clan feuds, the vendettas that had to be overcome to unite them."

"I know so little about Qawi," came the quiet reply. "I have a lot to learn."

"You will enjoy the learning," Leila assured her

with a smile. "And now, my Lady, would you like to soak in the whirlpool bath?"

"A whirlpool bath?" she exclaimed with delight.

"One of many modern amenities we have here now," the young woman giggled. "And large enough for a woman and her husband to share," she added with a blush.

"Leila!" Gretchen exclaimed, flushing.

The other woman's smile was deeply approving. "I can see that you are like us in your beliefs, my Lady, and it pleases me very much. The tribespeople value morality."

"I come from a very small town," Gretchen told her. "I'm very old-fashioned, too."

Leila's eyes twinkled with affection. "Then you must learn a little about our traditions. It will be my pleasure to instruct you, with my *sidi's* permission."

"Do you have to have permission from men to do things here?" she asked without sarcasm. "I mean, do all women?"

"In much of the Middle East, we live by the Qu'ran," Leila said solemnly, "which means that we permit no sexual exploration outside marriage and no access to immoral things or pursuits. This is the law for men as well as women. We are a clean and moral people." She paused and glanced at Gretchen to see how the liberated American woman would react to the statement.

"Those who believe in the old values are pretty much thought of as prehistoric these days in my country," Gretchen told her quietly.

Leila raised her eyebrows. "Then welcome to the caves, mademoiselle," she said impishly.

Gretchen laughed with pure delight. She was going to enjoy this new friend's company. "From one cavewoman to another, thanks!"

"And now, shall I draw your bath?"

Despite Philippe's assertion that he wouldn't see her again that day because of the pressures of his office, she was sipping coffee and eating almond pastries after her evening meal when he came through the door into her apartment. Surprisingly, Leila was with him, although he motioned her curtly into an antechamber and had her close the door behind her.

"A chaperone?" she teased as he came to sit down in the chair across from hers at the small glass table. "How exciting!"

He chuckled. He was wearing a *thobe* now, like the ones called *djellabahs* in Morocco, but his was elegant, deep blue and embroidered in gold thread. On his feet were the heel-less shoes called *babouches* in Morocco. He cocked his head and stared at her, approving the way she looked in a gold-embroidered white silk *gellabia,* which was thin enough to show the long embroidered thick cotton gown she wore under it.

"You dress conservatively," he said approvingly. "But not well enough, I'm afraid. I've arranged for a woman to come tomorrow and measure you for a new wardrobe. I particularly like you in white, but I think a deep, rich green would suit you equally well."

"You shouldn't spend a lot of money on me," she protested. "I'm really not that clothes-conscious, and when I go out, I'll wear an *aba,* even if I go out with you."

"You must dress the part I brought you here to play," he said gently, and with a smile. "Besides," he added, leaning back to study her with faint arrogance, "it will please me to buy you pretty things. Indulge me."

She grinned. "Okay, then, but will you get me at least one pair of jeans so that I can go riding with you?"

His heart leaped. "I would love to take you riding," he told her. "But you must have jodphurs and a helmet, Gretchen. Riding clothes."

She grimaced. "I like blue jeans."

"When in Rome...?" he teased.

"All right." She studied his hard face, seeing

faint new lines in it. "You're tired," she mused. "And you look as if someone's tried to take several bites out of you and been poisoned in the process."

He chuckled. "An apt description." He stood up and stretched lazily. Hard muscle rippled in his powerful body with the action. "Have they fed you?"

"Very nicely," she said. "I had pigeon pastries. They were delicious. So are these," she added, lifting a small crescent-shaped almond pastry. "Want one?" she asked, offering it.

He bent over her and opened his mouth, holding her gaze as she fed him. He chewed it deliberately and swallowed it before he bent and opened his mouth against her soft lips, brushing it lazily with a featherlight pressure.

Her breath caught and she reached up, but he stood up and pursed his lips, studying her with deliberate intensity.

His gaze went to the huge, four-poster bed with its gauzy curtains and then back to her, sliding down her body in the silky garment. His black eyes began to glitter faintly as they met hers.

"Hours seem like days to a thirsty man," he murmured softly. "Come here, little one."

He bent and lifted her out of the chair and up into his hard, strong arms. He bent, brushing his lips over her eyes as he carried her to the bed and placed her gently onto the heavily embroidered coverlet. She lay still, looking up at him with wide, hungry eyes.

He slid onto the bed beside her, his hands on either side of her head as he poised there, with a look of eminent conquest on his lean face. Resting his weight on one forearm, his fingers went to the pins that contained her hair and loosened its soft weight so that it fell around her head like a golden halo.

His eyes dropped to the tiny buttons of the *gellabia* and his lean fingers followed them. He began to unbutton them while he held her eyes.

Her heartbeat went wild. She knew that he could see it, because the garment she was wearing jerked with every hard, quick pulse. Her body moved almost imperceptibly, aroused by the brief touch of his knuckles against the soft skin barely concealed by the thin embroidery of the gown.

His hand went under the concealing overgarment and to the buttons under it. He flicked them open with a lazy, teasing pressure and then slid his hand under the fabric and onto the silky soft skin barely contained by the tiny little lacy brassiere she was wearing. "Ah," he whispered as he found the hard peak and felt her body jump with pleasure. "No pads this time?"

She shook her head slowly. "Not with you. Not ever. You make me proud of my body."

"As you should be," he said tenderly. "How soft you are here, Gretchen," he murmured, brushing his lips over her closed eyelids as he traced her firm little breast. His lips moved to her mouth and he nipped her lower lip gently with his teeth as his fingers became bolder. "Listen to me," he said urgently. "I want to put my mouth on you and make you cry out. I want Leila to hear you. But if this would be too embarrassing..."

While he was talking, her hands were getting fabric out of the way. She eased out of the top of the overgarment and the gown under it, and lay back down, inviting his eyes to her soft nudity. Her arms reached up to him, without coyness or pretense or embarrassment.

Her soft green eyes made him feel like a true king as she watched his head bend to her body. Her back arched, just a breath, just enough to invite his mouth over that hard, dark pink little nipple...

The quick, jerky cry that pulsed out of her made him violently hungry. His mouth became demanding, insistent, as he suckled her in the fierce tension of desire. His body moved over hers. He'd forgotten Leila, his resolutions, his reticence, all his misgivings about her reputation. He was on fire. His body was throbbing, pulsating. He was so fiercely aroused that he barely felt her sharp nails biting into his back below the waist. He moved on her, edging between her long, trembling legs, his mind focused on nothing more immediate than satisfaction. Perhaps he could, perhaps he could, perhaps…!

"*Sidi!*"

He shuddered. His eyes were terrible as he forcibly dragged his eyes from Gretchen's misty, hungry eyes and her soft body and looked toward the doorway into the room that contained the whirlpool path.

Leila stood there with her arms folded, her face set disapprovingly, glaring at him.

He said something in a furious tone in Arabic to her and she replied very calmly, and firmly, in the same language.

Philippe cursed in French and English and Arabic as he looked down at his handiwork and was barely able to stop shivering with unsatisfied desire. This time was worse than it had ever been. He'd felt more aroused than ever before. He still was. He wanted to rip away the fabric between himself and this woman and drive himself into her soft body. He wanted…

He groaned harshly and rolled away from her to sit on the side of the bed with his face in his hands.

Gretchen could hardly breathe. She dragged her

gown up over her taut breasts and stared at Leila with a mixture of confusion and embarrassment.

"You come with me, my Lady," Leila said firmly, moving forward to tug Gretchen out of the bed. "Not before the wedding, *sidi*," she told Philippe in firm English. "Shame on you!"

Philippe burst out laughing even through his agony. "Pest," he groaned. "I should have given you to Mustapha al Bakir when he begged for you!"

"He aspires far higher than his worth. I had sooner marry an ox," she returned haughtily. "Now, I will take my Lady into the other chamber until you leave, *sidi*," she continued, drawing Gretchen along with her. "You must not dishonor her."

Philippe managed to get to his feet. He didn't face them as he stared over his shoulder toward the women, one commanding, the other trying to keep her breasts covered with a garment that was still unbuttoned and steadily slipping. He pursed his lips with a wicked grin.

"Then keep her locked carefully away until we leave for the desert," he advised Leila. "The temptation she presents is difficult to resist."

"So Hassan told me," she returned, nodding when his eyebrows rose. "Yes, I heard all about what happened on the airplane! My Lady is not safely left alone with you, *sidi,* and it will be my chore to keep her chastity intact until the ceremony takes place. Whether you like it or not!''

''I won't like it,'' Philippe assured her, but his eyes were twinkling as they met Gretchen's. ''Third time lucky, *mademoiselle,*'' he added to Gretchen in a low undertone, and chuckled when she blushed.

He left the apartment, and Leila helped Gretchen back into her gown and *djellabah,* frowning. ''What means this third time?''

''An idiom,'' she told the Arab woman. ''And never mind what it means,'' she added primly but with a smile.

''That man is a menace,'' Leila said, shaking her head. ''And to think I trusted him alone with you!''

Gretchen didn't say a word, but she could only imagine how it flattered Philippe to be thought of as a potential seducer. Leila's fierce protection had amused and delighted him, for reasons the Arab servant could never imagine.

Remembering the fierce arousal of his lean body and the increased urgency of his embrace, Gretchen had very little doubt that one day soon she was going to learn all the secrets of the bed-chamber. She could hardly wait for the wedding ceremony that would make Philippe her own. If she could seduce him, the mysterious Brianne would never be able to hold his affections. And she was going to seduce him. By any means, by all means, possible!

A week went by very quickly while Gretchen learned her way around the enormous palace and got to know the people who served in it. She felt sorry for the poor servants who had to wash down the walls. They used bleach, and it made their hands raw. She complained about this to Philippe, who provided them with rubber gloves. She found one of the women in the kitchen barely able to stand, sick with some female problem, and this problem, too, she insisted on addressing. A doctor was sent for and the woman was treated and given sick leave.

There were other problems she noticed, to the amusement of her future husband. She found the working hours too stringent and the lack of day care facilities and kindergarten worrying. She met with the servants at the end of a particularly long day with a translator Philippe provided, and she listened to their shy requests with patience. Each one was given a chance to speak, even the long-suffering cook who had no modern tools or appliances to produce the delicious French dishes Philippe preferred. The household manager was at first resentful and appalled at the interference of a foreign woman in such business. But as Gretchen accomplished remarkable changes in working conditions, he soon looked upon her as an ally and even conspired with her to have china replaced and new linen ordered for the tables.

Nor did she stop at the household. She found children playing in the dirt with sticks. There were no toys, and there was no place to play. With the translator, she went to the small, meticulously clean houses that filled the kasbah and gathered the mothers together. Most of them worked at making textiles for the palace and its occupants, but there was no one to look after the children. They played outside in the dirt, because there was no other facility. She went back and told Philippe, and asked for a proper fenced playground and a supervisor to watch them while their mothers worked. A kindergarten, she added, was going to be a necessity, and it must have a capable educator to run it.

Philippe agreed, all but shell-shocked at the change in her since her arrival. She seemed to be everywhere, watching, listening, learning. She saw things that needed changing and went right to work changing them. She became mature under his very eyes. She was charming his household. She was charming him, as well. He wanted her more each day, but Leila managed to keep him from Gretchen except for rare occasions in the evenings. And now, she refused to leave the room when he entered Gretchen's apartment.

Philippe glared at the woman with her embroidery in her lap, and said something to her in their language.

Unperturbed, Leila grinned at him and went right on with her embroidery.

"We leave for Wadi Agadir in two days," he told Gretchen. "By then, the first of your new things should be delivered to the palace. Leila will come with you on the journey."

"A caravan?" Gretchen asked enthusiastically. "Camels and horses...?"

He chuckled. "A Land Rover," he corrected. His eyes twinkled at her disappointment. "I am a city man," he said lazily, darting a warning glance at Leila, whose mouth was open. "Why should I suffer the discomfort of riding on a camel when I can travel in comfort?"

"I read too many novels, and watch too many Valentino movies," Gretchen confessed sheepishly. "I'm sure that traveling in a Land Rover will be an experience, too."

"This entire trip will be an experience. One which I expect neither of us will ever forget," he added softly. He lifted her hand to his mouth. "I must retire. Sleep well."

"You, too. Thank you for not minding."

"Minding what?" he asked, curious.

"I've been making waves around the palace," she confessed. "I'm sorry I've caused you so much trouble. Perhaps I should have stayed in my quarters..."

Leila was laughing uproarously. So was Philippe.

"The cook makes those little almond pastries you enjoy so much with his own hands—a man whom his underlings call 'Napoleon.' The washwomen use the most expensive perfumes on your clothing. The children swarm around you whenever they see you. My own valet carried a pot of orchids stolen right out of my father's conservatory—an offense for which he could have been beheaded once—and put them in your sitting room. Trouble? I live in constant apprehension, wondering if a servant who brings your tea late may slit his own throat for fear of offending you!"

"It is so, my Lady," Leila agreed, chuckling at Gretchen's stunned expression. "The household loves you."

"They've all been so kind," she replied. "I felt I must do something for them."

Leila got to her feet, still smiling. "It is not hard to be kind to such a woman." She gave the sheikh a wry glance. "I shall have to change my thread.

But I will only be gone for a very short time, *sidi,*" she warned firmly.

He gave an exaggerated sigh. "Then I shall be thankful for even a short time."

Leila bowed and smiled wickedly at Gretchen as she went from the room.

Philippe held out his arms and Gretchen went into them, pressing close, her ear at his chest, listening to the heavy, hard beat of his heart.

"I have been thinking about this desert trip," he said at her temple. "Perhaps I should leave you here."

"But why?" She drew back and looked up at him. "Have you changed your mind, about wanting to get married?"

He touched her soft mouth with his forefinger, watching it intently. "Never that," he said quietly. "But I have second thoughts, serious ones, about taking you into a situation that may prove more dangerous than I anticipated."

"I'm not afraid," she told him.

"Neither am I, for myself. But you would be at risk."

"Are just the two of us going, then?" she teased.

"Impossible woman!" he said with a mock growl, and bent to kiss her hungrily. "No, my bodyguard will go as well, and there will be many representatives of the tribes in residence. We make a formidable force when we unite.''

She was worried. ''You sound as if you're getting ready for war.''

''I may be,'' he said, surprising her. His face was unusually somber. ''I have spent this week collecting intelligence from my spies. Brauer is in Salid, the country on my northern border. I have proof of it. He has collected a small band of cutthroats who will do murder for a price, and he contemplates his next action camped at my border. I cannot allow him to stay.''

''How will you make him leave?'' she asked, worried. ''He has automatic weapons and things, doesn't he?''

He nodded. ''Plastic explosive, rocket launchers, land mines and grenades. He has friends who owe him favors, and his credit is good with most of the major arms dealers. If he can start a war, he can recoup his losses in commissions for arms sales. With the current political situation, he might just manage it unless I can stop him in time.''

''What can I do to help?'' she asked simply.

He brought her forehead to his lips. ''If you plan to heft a rocket launcher and march along with me, forget it.''

She chuckled. ''I couldn't shoot one, but I can

use a rope and shoot. Marc taught me how. And I can ride anything with four legs."

"Skills that may prove useful," he agreed. He drew away and searched her soft green eyes. "If only Leila could lose her way here…" He bent to catch Gretchen's warm mouth with his own. He enfolded her in his hard arms and strained her to him, feeling the quicksilver response of his body to her silky warmth. She was already like a part of him.

"And here I have returned," came a familiar, cheerful voice from the doorway, followed in by its owner.

Philippe glared at her. "After the ceremony," he informed her, "if you come within a hundred meters of us, I will have you substitute for the target on my firing range."

"And then who will draw my Lady's bath?" came the amused reply. "And who will arrange her things and care for her wardrobe and make her beautiful for you?"

Philippe touched Gretchen's soft cheek. "She doesn't need to be made beautiful. She already is."

"She will need her sleep to remain so. Good night, *sidi*," she said pointedly.

"You forget that I am lord here," he agreed, staring at her. "My word is law."

"Indeed it is, *sidi*, in any other part of the palace. But in here, you are a trespasser and the final word is mine, not yours. Good night, my lord!''

Philippe threw up his hands. He glanced at Gretchen with wry resignation and turned, muttering in Arabic all the way out the door.

Leila giggled. "I have been here for many years," she told Gretchen. "But never have I heard the *sidi* laugh. All the servants speak of this change in him since your arrival, my Lady. You have enchanted him."

"I'm the one who's been enchanted, I think," came the absent reply. She was still looking toward the door he'd left through. "It's like a fairy tale come true. I never dreamed that a man like that would ever look twice at someone as plain as me."

"Plain. Ha! You have the inner beauty as few others I have ever known," Leila said softly. "And it is this to which my lord responds. You will be a fine wife for him, my Lady. You will give him many strong sons!"

"That would be lovely," Gretchen said, turning. She would carry on that part of the charade, willingly, but she knew there would be no children. It was sad to think of it. Of course, there were plenty of children at court, and she was going to be very much involved in their care and education. Perhaps it would make up for the lack of them in her own life. The alternative was to leave Philippe and find a man who could give her children, but the thought was unbearable. Whatever happened now, her life was inextricably merged with his. It was truly fate, and she bowed to it eagerly.

Chapter Ten

Three days later, the big white Land Rover was sitting at the side steps to the palace, being loaded by servants with supplies. Behind it were several camels bearing carpets and household goods. Gretchen was almost jumping with excitement, because among those goods was her wedding costume, handmade by the palace seamstresses. She was going into the desert to marry the man she'd never expected to meet, much less to love. Even if the ceremony had no relevance anywhere else in the world, in Qawi she would be Philippe's wife. At least, until he decided to send her away. She wanted so desperately to belong to him, in such a way that he wouldn't be able to let her go, ever.

Philippe, like herself, was wearing khakis. She'd

expected him to don traditional robes for the journey, but his eyes had twinkled and he'd informed her that he was much too Westernized to like traditional clothing. One of his bodyguards had almost tripped over his own feet while listening to this remark, but Gretchen's eyes had been on the camels, so she hadn't noticed.

There had also been a heated argument between Philippe and his father. Gretchen had assumed that it was about the marriage. But while the supplies were being loaded, Leila came to tell her that the old sheikh, Philippe's father, wanted to see her. She was faintly apprehensive about it, because she knew he didn't like her. She'd been careful to stay out of his way, although she couldn't resist an occasional trip to see his beautiful orchids—when nobody was looking, of course. She wondered if he knew that she'd been invading his conservatory and was angry.

Leila led her to the huge greenhouse that adjoined the palace. The old sheikh turned at her entrance, his eyes disapproving of her figure-enhancing long tan safari skirt and matching blouse and hat that she wore with knee-high boots. The traveling outfit had been part of the new wardrobe Philippe had ordered for her, and the single ensemble that pleased her most.

"No *aba*," he said curtly, indicating her lack of the traditional overgarment.

She sighed and smiled. "No. I'm sorry, I forgot. I grew up on a ranch in Texas, you see, so I usually wear jeans and T-shirts. Even this is dressy, for me…"

He said something she was glad she couldn't translate. "You mock me," he accused.

"No," she said gently. "Not at all. You don't know me. I'm not sarcastic and I don't try to hurt other people. I was telling you the truth. I'm an absolute dunce when it comes to dress and social behavior. You mustn't worry," she added solemnly. "Philippe is only marrying me in a tribal ceremony. It won't even be binding, except in your country. He won't be stuck with me."

"Stuck?"

She shook her head. Nobody in this country understood English idioms. She was going to have to relearn how to speak her own language properly. "He won't have to stay married to me," she corrected. "I know that he needs to marry a woman of his own background and status when he does it for real." She colored a little. "He has…other reasons for going through this ceremony with me," she added, embarrassed.

His eyes narrowed. He still hadn't smiled. "It is not right," he said shortly.

She shrugged. "You stop him, then," she said. "I've told him that he doesn't have to marry me."

"He doesn't listen to me, either," he muttered. He turned back to his orchids with an odd movement of his shoulders. "Go with him, then." His eyes caught hers. "But make sure the bodyguards are close by, always." He motioned her closer, watching warily for any sign of other people before he leaned toward her and spoke earnestly. "One of the servants ran away this morning, one of the household staff assigned to my brother," he said very quietly. "I think that this is no coincidence. Someone is watching Philippe's movements."

"Do you think the servant might be connected to the man Philippe helped put in prison?" she asked. "The man Philippe told me about?"

"Kurt Brauer," the old man agreed coldly. "Very possibly. He lost money and prestige and he seeks to regain both at my son's expense. I have tried to convince Philippe that the army and our long-range weapons are best suited to deal with this border dispute, but he will not hear me. He said that Brauer could use it against him if he sent the army and remained behind. The rural clan chiefs might see it as a sign of weakness and join the invaders." He raised a hand when she opened her mouth. "And he is right. I withdrew my objections, but not my concern. He is lax about his personal security. You tell Bojo that I want my son watched night and day, regardless of what he says!''

"I will," she promised, and her eyes narrowed. "Can someone loan me a pistol?"

His eyebrows arched. "Mademoiselle?"

"I'm a dead shot," she explained, recalling that she'd lied about that once to Philippe. "My brother is in law enforcement. He taught me to shoot. If all else fails, and Philippe won't let Bojo keep close, I'll sit up every night at the end of Philippe's bed and guard him myself."

He didn't speak for so long that she wondered if he might not have heard her. He was studying her intently, his heavy white brows drawn together in a puzzled frown. Suddenly the frown vanished, and his whole expression softened. "You love my son," he said slowly.

Her faint color was betrayal enough without the immediate averting of her eyes. "I'm fond of him," she corrected gruffly.

"You love him." He drew in a slow breath. "I have misunderstood everything," he said after a minute. "It all begins to make sense to me, now. I had wondered, you see," he added when she glanced at him quizzically, "why a young American woman would be so eager to go along with a rather shameful charade that would put her moral character at risk. But if you love him," he continued softly, "and he is willing to risk a war to keep you with him…"

"Risk a war?" she interrupted.

"My brother has threatened him with civil war if he goes through with this wedding ceremony, but Philippe will not hear of canceling it, even of postponing it." He began to smile as her eyes widened with surprise. "And he wants you. Perhaps there are forces at work here that medical science cannot explain, hmm?"

She went scarlet, and the old man began to chuckle. "Go to the desert and get married," he murmured. "All the doctors in Europe could not cure him, but I think that you will." He shook his head. "And I thought he was out of his mind."

"He still is," she said. "Listen, you can't let him do this if it will cause a war. I won't be responsible for people getting killed!"

"It was a bad joke. Nobody will get killed," he told her. "My brother makes a great deal of noise, but he is frightened of my son. As most of the tribal leaders are," he added. "Few have dared to provoke his anger in recent years."

"Philippe?" She frowned. "But he's such a gentle man…why are you laughing?"

"He may be gentle with you, my girl," he said

gleefully. "Ask him sometime how he came to happen upon that land mine in Palestine."

She blinked. "I did. He told me it was an accident. He just stepped on it while he was there on a business trip."

He gave her a wise, steady look. "And you think a man on a business trip to the city would walk over a land mine on the sidewalks, I suppose?"

That had never occurred to her. Many cities suffered war damage, but it would be difficult to lay land mines on sidewalks. Why hadn't she questioned that when Philippe first told her about it?

A horn sounded impatiently. "Your intended grows impatient," the old sheikh said with a smile. "One moment." He raised his voice and called to a servant, spoke to him rapidly, and sent him running. That servant spoke to another, and he went toward the entrance. Seconds later, the first servant came running back with a bundle of cloth.

The old sheikh took it, unrolled it, and produced a Colt .45 single action revolver, fully loaded, and a box of cartridges. He wrapped it back up and handed it to Gretchen. "A present from one of your heads of state, who never imagined that it would ever be put to such a use," he chuckled. "Go with God, child."

"I will. And I'll take care of your son."

He pursed his lips. "You think he requires a nursemaid, hmm?"

She shrugged and smiled a little sheepishly. "Well, he's not really the rugged sort. He's a sophisticated city man. And I shoot straight."

The old man's dark eyes were dancing with glee. He looked as if he could barely contain it. "Go," he said, waving her away. "When you return, we will speak of orchids, at great length. I think by then you will have a good knowledge of how deceptive appearances can be."

She wanted to ask what he meant, but the horn sounded again. She made him a neat bow, turned, and ran toward the side entrance with her bundle held tight under one arm.

"Where have you been?" Philippe demanded hotly. "We must make the oasis before the sun is high."

"Sorry," she said, indicating the bundle. "Forgot my undies."

His expression was priceless. She tucked the bundle in her bag and got into the Land Rover beside him in the back. Bojo gave them both a grin as he got in under the wheel, with "Elvis" at his side. They were all wearing khakis and black boots. Philippe's hat matched hers. Bojo and "Elvis" were wearing skullcaps. Everyone had sunglasses, even Gretchen. Philippe had ordered designer ones from America, and she wore them with a flair. She wondered what her brother Marc would think if he knew she was riding shotgun for a sheikh with a borrowed Colt .45 in a Land Rover. She had to fight laughing out loud at the absurdity of it. She must be careful not to let Philippe think she was protecting him, of course. She didn't want to embarrass him.

"Where were you?" Philippe asked when they were underway.

"Your father wanted to tell me something," she said. "One of the household servants, one of your uncle's, ran away this morning. He thought it suspicious."

He lifted an eyebrow and exchanged a complicated look with Bojo in the front seat. "My uncle is fond of creating complications. This one could be the undoing of him," he added in a softly menacing tone. He snapped something at Bojo in Arabic and gestured with one lean hand.

Bojo produced a cell phone and tossed it to him. It didn't look like the phones Gretchen had seen at home. It had all sorts of buttons and two screens. He pushed a button, noticing her puzzled look.

"GPS," he said. When she frowned, he added, "It contains a global positioning function. With this, I can find my exact location wherever I am, even in the high desert. It enables me to send targeting coordinates to a remote outpost, in case Brauer has more sophisticated equipment than I give him credit for.''

"Targeting coordinates." She nodded, but she wasn't getting it at all.

"Gretchen," he said patiently, "I can call an air strike if I have to. We do have an air force here, and long range missiles, even if our military lacks the sophistication of the United States."

"Oh!" She laughed with pure embarrassment. "Sorry. I don't know what I was thinking."

He shook his head and punched buttons on the unit. "Now, I can triangulate on the oasis...here...and get an estimate of travel time. Yes, we should make it there on schedule." He shot another question at Bojo, who replied in Arabic. Philippe nodded and tossed the cell phone back to him. Bojo caught it neatly without even looking at it.

Something was definitely going on. She wondered if Philippe was already in contact with his military forces and planned to let them attack Brauer, while making it appear that he was going there to do it himself. If so, there must be someone watching them even now. She felt cold chills run down her spine. She glanced toward Philippe. Well, one thing was for sure. She wasn't going to let anything happen to him, if it meant sitting up for a week with that Colt in her hands!

"There has been another development, one I haven't shared with you," Philippe said a few miles down the road. "Brauer sent an assassin to Paris and an attempt was made on the life of Brianne Hutton."

She drew in a sharp breath. "The woman you told me about, the one with the little boy?"

"Yes," he said through his teeth. "I only learned of it this morning. I have sent a small unit to accompany her and the child here while Hutton and his security chief round up the would-be assassin."

"Wouldn't the police be the people to do that?" she asked.

"I trust no one with her life. Not even her husband," he said shortly. "He was reluctant to let her come, but he knows she and the child will be safer with me than with him at the moment. The palace is all but impregnable. I can protect her."

"Should we be going into the desert now?" she asked, her heart sinking at the thought of Brianne in residence in Qawi. Knowing how Philippe felt about the woman, she knew that her own place in his life would be insignificant after this trip. Ceremony or not, she would be no match for the beautiful, elegant Mrs. Hutton.

"She arrives in five days," he said. "It will take that long to make the proper arrangements. Hutton is taking no chance with transport. He's having one of his own jets, and his bodyguard, bring her here. But first he wants to eliminate any chance of sabotage, so there will be elaborate details." He looked worried. "I sent members of my own bodyguard to assist them. Hutton has a new security chief and I don't know him. I'm sorry Tate Winthrop left, but his wife was uneasy having him in the middle of firefights, especially since the birth of their son."

"I can understand that," she said quietly, thinking how glad she was that Philippe was a diplomat and not a mercenary. "What about the ceremony?" she added reluctantly. "Shouldn't you postpone it?"

His dark eyes narrowed. "No," he said at once. "That I will have, Brauer or no Brauer." His gaze went down her body in the well-fitting safari outfit and his face tautened. "You should have worn an *aba*," he said suddenly. "We'll appropriate one when we reach the oasis."

Her eyebrows lifted. "Not you, too," she groaned.

"Me, too?" He scowled. Then he laughed. "I see. My father." He shook his head. "His upbringing was extremely strict." He pursed his lips. "So was mine, in many ways, when he brought me back here. I was a child of the streets, unused to restrictions or discipline. I learned both at his hands.''

Poor little boy, she was thinking. She almost said it aloud, but a cloud of dust up ahead stopped the words on her lips. The wide, sandy road was coming to the desert now, and she expected another party of vehicles to meet them. But as the swirling dust gave way to glimpses of white, she sat up straight and her lips parted on a startled breath. It wasn't a caravan of vehicles. It was a mounted regiment of white-robed men with rifles, on some of the most magnificent horses she'd ever seen in her life. Arabian horses.

The guns fired wildly, accompanied by hearty yells as the riders surrounded the Land Rover. Bojo stopped, chuckling, and Philippe got out as the leader of the approaching tribesmen jumped down from his horse. The two men exchanged greetings and embraced like brothers and spoke in an enthusiastic jumble of foreign words.

''Achmed,'' Bojo said when he noticed Gretchen's curious stare. ''He leads one of many tribes which owe allegiance to the Tatluk family. He is a blood relative of the *sidi*, sworn to fight to the death in his service.''

The man was almost Philippe's height. He was

wearing robes that covered him entirely from head to toe, and he was indicating Philippe's manner of dress and speaking about it very loudly.

Philippe chuckled and said something back with a wave of his hand. The other man nodded, glanced toward the car, and grinned.

"What's that all about?" Gretchen asked Bojo.

He cleared his throat. "Just, uh, discussing the vehicle, *mademoiselle.*"

She wondered why he looked so amused. But Philippe came back and got in beside them as the tribal leader swung gracefully into the saddle and led his men back in the direction from which they'd come.

"Oh, look at them ride!" she exclaimed, breathless. "What magnificent horses!"

"Arabians," he told her, amused at her rapt expression. "The finest blood stock in the world."

She was spellbound, barely hearing him. "I've never seen anything like that!"

"Wait," he murmured dryly. "I think you have many surprises in store."

"What?" She wasn't really listening, she was still watching the riders in the distance. "Are they going where we are?"

"Yes. You can see the horses close up," he added, amused at her eagerness.

"That would be wonderful," she said dreamily.

He cocked an eyebrow and grinned at Bojo, who had to hide his face before Gretchen saw it.

The desert camp wasn't too unexpected. Gretchen had seen documentaries about the desert and its nomadic tribes. But she wasn't prepared for the luxury of the tents. She was taken to a separate one while some of the tribesmen set about erecting Philippe's. It was a sprawling, impressive affair, and expensive carpets were carried in one after another, along with ornate hanging lamps. She smiled as she thought of elegant Philippe "roughing it." He looked as out of place here as a mink coat.

When the tent was finished, Leila took Gretchen inside and unpacked for her. She sprawled on the puffy cushions and looked around here, thinking how foreign a place it was to feel so much like home. She closed her eyes with a long sigh and only opened them when she felt Leila tug on her boots.

"The boots are better off, yes?" the Qawi woman said with a grin. "Are you tired, Lady?"

"Bone-tired," came the weary reply. "I thought we were never going to get here, and I'm sure they never turned on the air conditioner once. Come to think of it, I haven't seen car windows closed anywhere in the Middle East." She grimaced as the other boot came off. "I suppose I eat alone?"

"Yes, Lady," Leila told her. "For tonight, at least. Tomorrow is the ceremony. Tomorrow night, you will not spend alone," she added with a giggle.

Tomorrow. Gretchen felt as if she were in some sort of dream world, where nothing was as it seemed. She worried briefly about the wedding, about the uncertainty of the future. Even if Philippe could never be a husband to her physically, she loved him enough to accept him on those terms. But he would never agree. If he couldn't consummate the marriage, she had no doubt whatsoever that he would send her home to America without a second thought. If only there were something she could do, some way to help him...

Right, she thought whimsically. As if she knew anything about seducing men.

"You rest now," Leila said gently, removing the boots to a far wall of the tent. "I will be back soon with food and water. Or would my Lady prefer coffee?"

"Oh, coffee, please," Gretchen said.

"Very well."

Gretchen stretched out and closed her eyes. When she opened them again, Philippe was sitting beside her, his brooding eyes on her face.

She smiled up at him. "Hello."

"You slept through the evening meal," he mused. "Were you that tired?"

"I'm afraid so. I haven't really slept well in a long time. Not since Mama died," she added, before he could think it was her new surroundings that kept her awake.

He searched her drowsy eyes. "Tomorrow we marry."

She smiled. "Yes. Are you sure?"

He drew her hand to his lips and kissed it very softly. "I'm sure."

"How late is it?"

"Bedtime," he murmured dryly and chuckled at her blush. "No, my girl, not tonight. But hold that thought," he added with a grin.

She smiled back, so comfortable with him even through the excitement. "My brother will never believe this."

He lifted an eyebrow. "If there was time, I would have him flown here for the ceremony. But it will have to wait. Brauer is not far away and I have much planning to do." He kissed her hand again. "Sleep well."

"You, too." She waited until he got up before she asked, "Where do you sleep?"

He chuckled. "Through there," he indicated a compartment behind hers in the huge tent. "Leila will sleep at your door, as Hassan will sleep at mine," he added. "So don't get any ideas about seducing me in my sleep."

She laughed heartily. "I wouldn't dream of it!"

She watched him go before she got up and unwrapped her neat little bundle. She put the pistol under her pillow, along with the cartridges. She would pretend to sleep, but nobody was going through here to get to Philippe. She would protect him from any intruder.

She stayed awake most of the night, which gave her a drugged appearance the next morning and dulled her wits. She had time to hide the gun before Leila brought breakfast, and all too soon, she was being prepared for the wedding. Several tribeswomen bathed and dressed her, hennaed her hands and feet, and veiled her face. When they finished, with her blond hair carefully concealed under the headdress and veil, she looked very mysterious, and very nearly pretty.

She was watching for Philippe as they walked through the alley between the tents toward the place where the ceremony would be performed. She didn't see him, not until she was brought to a stop before a little old man in white robes. And then, glancing up, she recognized the laughing black eyes of her husband under flowing white robes with a white head cloth secured by the *igal,* the doubled black cord that signified his rank. He was wearing a curved ceremonial dagger with a silver jewel-encrusted handle in a case carved of ivory. It was stuck in a sash around his lean waist, and he looked very dangerous for a city man.

While she was trying to reconcile this new look, the old man began to speak in an Arab dialect. Philippe gently led Gretchen through the ceremony, teaching her the proper words and when to speak them as the ritual continued. When it was over, their hands were briefly bound and then Philippe pulled out a scimitar and with a very professional sort of motion, he sliced a loaf of bread, handing part of it to Gretchen before he resheathed the sword.

"Another tradition," he said gently. "Eat the bread."

She obeyed, taking a small bite and praying that it wouldn't choke her. She washed it down with a sip of water.

"And we are," he told her softly, "married."

"Already?" she asked, glancing around at the beaming faces. "But you didn't lift the veil or kiss me."

"That is done in private, Lady FIL-fil," he chuckled. "Your face is now for my eyes only."

She smiled wickedly. "We could make that binding both ways. You could wear a veil, too."

He chuckled. "Only when I ride in sand-storms."

Her eyes went over his tall form with pride. "You look very nice in those robes. Did you borrow them for the ceremony?"

He cocked an eyebrow. "We have a few minor misconceptions to clear up," he began, and started to speak when a rider came barreling into the camp. He rode right up to the gathering and literally jumped out of the saddle. He knelt in front of Philippe and a frenzy of Arabic followed. Philippe questioned him curtly and listened to his answers before he threw up his hand and men started moving toward horses.

"Go into the tent, and stay there," Philippe told Gretchen firmly, nudging her toward the tent. "Don't stick your head outside for any reason. Hassan!" he added, tossing orders to the bodyguard.

Hassan bowed, took Gretchen's arm, and led her to the tent and put her inside.

Leila shook her head at Gretchen's fury as she struggled to free herself from the bodyguard's grip. "They go to fight," she told the American woman. "You must not be in the way of danger."

"Danger!" she scoffed. "Philippe's the one in danger, and I promised his father I'd take care of him. I am not letting him ride into a war without backup! You tell "Elvis" to get out of my tent or he's going to be beheaded for watching me change clothes!"

Shocked, Leila obeyed, and as soon as Hassan left, before Leila could say another word, Gretchen was scrambling into her safari outfit with the pistol tucked in her belt and the cartridges in her pocket. Mindful of Philippe's status and her obligations, she threw an *aba* over the whole outfit, leaving her hat behind because it wouldn't fit under the hood. She ran out the back of the tent, the place where Hassan wasn't. There were many horses still in the camp. Far in the distance already, the tribesmen were throwing up clouds of dust as they rode furiously toward the horizon.

Grimacing, she looked around until she noticed one horse standing quietly near a tent, saddled. She hoped they didn't hang horse thieves in Qawi, but she really had no choice. She couldn't let Philippe go into a firefight alone. She'd pretend to be one of his men and keep an eye on him. The tribal leaders could do that, of course, but he was the sheikh and they might be too much in awe of him to keep close enough to protect him. Without counting the cost, she flung herself into the saddle of the horse, and took off after the cloud of dust that was Philippe and his men. In the doorway of the tent, Leila was yelling at Hassan, who went in search of a horse.

Even under the circumstances, riding an Arabian was the experience of Gretchen's life. She thrilled to its perfect motion under her body, to its speed and grace and stamina. She rode like the wind, her hair coming loose from its pins and wisps of it flying into her mouth. In the distance, she could see the column and she dug her heels into the horse's flanks, urging it on.

She had almost caught up to the end of the column when her mount stopped suddenly and reared up, unseating her. She landed in an undignified heap in the middle of a sand dune. She got to her feet a little gingerly. The hood had fallen back from her blond hair, and it shone like gold in the sunlight. While she struggled to regain her breath and catch the horse at the same time, a party of riders came over the dune from another direction. She stood very still, because it was immediately noticeable that these men weren't locals. They were wearing khakis and armed to the teeth. One of them, a redhead, laughed out loud and called something in a foreign language to another man, who rode her down as easily as if she'd been a stray calf.

He looped a hard arm around her waist and

pulled her roughly up into the saddle in front of him. She fought, kicking and biting, but a sudden hard tap on the head with something hard put an end to her struggles. She went limp. The horseman turned and rejoined his party.

"You have found her! My stepdaughter!" a man with a thick German accent said mockingly. "Let me see her face!"

The man holding Gretchen moved her head so that he had a good look at her. Kurt Brauer cursed hotly. "This is not Brianne!" he said furiously. "They said Brianne was on her way here!"

"It is the American woman who stays with Sabon," came the reply. "It is said that he means to marry her."

Brauer's eyes were thorough. "Look at her hands. They have been hennaed. And she came from the direction of the camp. Why, gentlemen," he added with a cold smile, "I believe we have Mrs. Sabon herself!"

Chapter Eleven

Gretchen came to her senses in a smaller tent than the one she'd left, with a horrible headache and some nausea. She held her aching head and sat up, glancing around at the makeshift quarters. A man was sitting at a writing table. He turned his eyes toward her when she stirred.

"Who are you?" he asked.

"Gretchen Brannon," she replied huskily, disoriented enough to forget that she was married for a few seconds. Her head hurt terribly. "Who are you?"

"Kurt Brauer. You might have heard Philippe speak of me," he added darkly.

Her eyes widened. "You!"

He smiled mockingly. "Yes. Me. And now I

have Philippe just where I want him," he added. "I think that he will be very willing to talk terms with me once he knows I have you. My spies have been very helpful in providing me with information about you."

"You really think he'll care that you have his social secretary?" she asked, trying to sound nonchalant.

"Ah, you are more than that," he mused wryly. "My informants tell me that you were married to Monsieur Sabon not more than a few hours ago."

"A marriage of convenience," she said haughtily. "So that I can work for him in the palace without gossip."

He raised an eyebrow. "Philippe has made it widely known that he will never marry at all, and I know why," he added sarcastically. "He is no longer a man." She forced herself not to react to the flat statement. He watched her closely and then laughed coldly. "You see, you do not deny it. This is a fact which I intend to share with all his countrymen, so that they will know what their ruler is. In this world, a man is judged by his ability with women, his ability to father children. I think that his throne will be a little less secure once the truth comes out. And his uncle will pay handsomely. He inherits, with Philippe out of the way."

Her eyes narrowed. "Why are you telling me

this? Don't you know that the first thing I do will be to tell Philippe?''

"You will never tell him anything again, *madame*," he said in a deadly tone. "I intend to leave you in the desert for the buzzards. I shall tell your husband in a few days where to find you. How I wish I could see his face then. They tell me that he is fond of you.''

Her heart jumped. She must not panic, she told herself. She must not panic. If she lost her nerve, she lost her life.

"I notice," he observed again, intently, "that you do not deny your husband's condition.''

"Why bother to deny a lie?" she asked, completely calm—at least on the outside. "My personal maidservant would laugh herself sick if she heard your suspicions." She smiled slowly. "She knows better, you see.''

For the first time, Brauer looked uncertain. He hesitated.

"You should never trust gossip, Mr. Brauer," Gretchen said quietly. "It can be deadly.''

He watched her for a few seconds and then he began to smile. "Then I assume that you would not object to a physical examination? If your husband has actually consummated your relationship, a physician would know.''

Easy, girl, easy, she told herself, and forced a

smile to her lips. "Of course he would. Bring him on."

Now uncertainty turned to anger. He glared at her. "No matter. Your captivity is a fact. I have lost everything I own. I have spent two miserable years in a Russian prison. Now I have a chance to pay Philippe Sabon back for my torment, and that is what I mean to do, even if it costs me my life. He will pay!"

"Pay for what? For letting you and your hired gorillas kill his people and destroy half the city?" she asked hotly. "What sort of man mows down innocent people?"

He walked over to her, drew his hand back, and slapped her so sharply that she fell. But she got right up again and swung on him with her fist, hitting him hard enough to break his balance. But he hit her back, and with his fist this time. She went down with a cry, rubbing her sore knuckles and her jaw.

Furiously angry, her hand went to the slit in the side of the *aba* and she felt in her waistband for the Colt .45—only to find that it was missing.

"Is this what you search for?" he asked, picking up the pistol from his writing table. The box of cartridges was there beside it. He aimed the gun and her and cocked it. "Perhaps I should spare you the desert and just put a bullet in you."

It was the closest to death she'd ever come. But she wasn't afraid. She lifted her chin and stared at him, her jaw throbbing. "Go ahead," she invited with icy green eyes. "It takes a big brave man to knock a woman around, doesn't it? I guess it takes an even braver man to shoot one!"

He cursed furiously. He put the pistol down and yelled for someone to come inside the tent. He and the man, the redhead who'd hoisted Gretchen into the saddle, spoke quickly in what seemed to be German, and he gave the man a note. The redhead nodded, gave Gretchen a strange look, and went back outside. Seconds later, there was the sound of an engine revving up.

"My helicopter," Brauer told her. "I am sending my man to the *Palais Tatluk* with a ransom note."

"Philippe's father will barbecue him over an open fire," she said with pure menace.

"Unlikely. The old sheikh has no stomach for a fight. He will tell Philippe what I wish him to be told—that I have you and am willing to bargain for you. Then Philippe will walk into my trap and be dealt with."

"You seem very sure of yourself," Gretchen said harshly.

"I am. Philippe is a sophisticate, not a fighter. It will hardly be worth my time to subdue him at

all, but I want him to suffer before he finds you."
His eyes narrowed with perverted pleasure. "Perhaps I will turn Eric loose on you with the bowie
knife and let him find you skinned alive."

She didn't even flinch. She just stared at him.
"And when my brother finds out," she said softly,
"there won't be one place on earth you and your
cutthroats can hide where he won't find you."

"Your brother," he scoffed. "And what is this
brother?"

"A former Texas Ranger," she said, watching
his expression flicker. "Someone might have mentioned that once a ranger starts tracking you, he'll
follow you to hell to get you. That's my brother."

"You will be dead by then," he assured her.

"And you will follow me in short order," she
assured him.

"You are a woman of rare courage," he said.
"I had heard that my stepdaughter was being
brought here. It was she I hoped to kidnap. Philippe's feelings for you are unknown to me, but I
know he would die for Brianne. She is the only
woman he ever loved."

Brianne again! She lifted her chin. "Mrs. Hutton
isn't even in the country. Looks like your intelligence network needs updating. Or wasn't working
for the skeikh's uncle close enough for your spy?"

His eyes widened. "What do you know of that?"

"I know a lot about your intelligence network," she replied cautiously. "I have friends who are professional mercenaries. I knew you had spies in the palace."

He chuckled. "I doubt you knew about the head of security," he mused. "Or the cook's assistant. But that knowledge will do you no good now. You have hours to live."

"Enjoy your own last few hours," she tossed back.

He glared at her. "Do not leave the tent or I will have you tied and gagged. In this heat, in that—" he indicated the thick *aba* "—you would probably smother to death."

"Don't you wish!" she shot back, infuriated at her helplessness.

He shrugged, opened the flap of the tent, and went out. Gretchen dragged to her feet and looked around for anything she could use as a weapon. There wasn't a gun or a knife nearby. She heard Brauer speaking to someone outside the tent. On the writing table was an instrument like the one Philippe had used, a GPS cell phone. She grabbed it up, fumbled Philippe's number, which he'd had her memorize days ago, into it, and waited for someone to answer. Someone did, but in Arabic.

"It's Gretchen. I've been kidnapped by Brauer!"

She quickly closed the phone, cleared the number, and put the device back in exactly the spot and position it had been in, moving to lie down on the pallet as if she was hurting too badly to get up.

She closed her eyes and prayed that Philippe or his men had heard her. Brauer came back in seconds later, glanced at her, retrieved the cell phone and went back out.

"Where did the call come from?" Philippe was raging at the tribesman who'd picked up the phone when it started to ring. "Never mind!" He pressed buttons on the sophisticated instrument, got the number, then was able to fix on the location where the call had originated. He motioned to his men and gave a spate of orders.

He'd just had a phone call from the palace, from his chief of security, informing him that Brauer had Gretchen and wanted to make a trade. Philippe told him to do nothing, that he would make decisions and then notify the man. He wasn't certain that it was worth paying ransom for a social secretary, he told the security chief in a deliberately careless tone, even if she was his wife. It had been a business arrangement only, he added craftily, not a love match, so Gretchen was more or less expendable. The other man sounded surprised and asked if the American government might step in, since she was a U.S. citizen. There was, after all, a border dispute.

Philippe nodded to himself. So it was like that. Brauer would enjoy starting a war. It would set him up in the arms business with a client like the neighboring country, not to mention embroil Philippe in a vicious war just as his country was becoming prosperous from oil. It was the same plot that had put Brauer away in the first place. But now he had nothing to lose, apparently, and he was determined to carry it through to the end, whatever the cost in lives. He was not, Philippe thought, a man with many original ideas, and that would be his downfall.

Philippe told the security chief that he'd have to have time to discuss this with his cabinet ministers. He was on his way back to the palace, he added, and they could discuss it then. He hung up and tossed the cell phone to two of his men, indicating that they were to take it and travel back to the palace. If anyone traced it, they'd notice that it was en route to the city, not the border. He grabbed another cell phone from the pocket of the Land Rover before it left and pondered his next move.

The security chief had been hired by Philippe's uncle and desultorily approved by the old sheikh.

Philippe didn't trust the new security chief, and had been having him watched for several weeks. It had proved useful, because the servant who'd run away had had many secretive conversations with the security chief. The man was probably a direct conduit to Brauer, so anything he told the man would get back to Brauer. Good. Brauer would think he was on his way back to the palace to undertake a diplomatic solution to the kidnapping. Brauer had never seen Philippe on his home ground. Not yet. He was in for a surprise.

Meanwhile, Gretchen had taken a huge risk to get those coordinates to him. He mustn't waste time. Kurt was crazy for revenge and with the grapevine on the desert, he would know by now that Gretchen was Philippe's wife. He'd kill her. He'd kill her in the most horrible way he could think of, and then he'd phone Philippe and tell him where to find her. It was the sort of thing Brauer did. Philippe groaned aloud, just thinking of that sweet, gentle woman in the grip of such monsters. He couldn't lose her now. He couldn't!

He motioned a shame-faced Hassan to him and told the man in biting tones just what he thought of his efficiency as a bodyguard. The man apologized profusely and offered to do anything to make reparation.

"Pray that she lives," Philippe told him, his

black eyes glittering with fury. "If she doesn't, pray for yourself!"

He whirled furiously, still in his flowing robes, and went out to his men. He ordered the tribal chiefs to go to their villagers and bring back every able-bodied fighting man available. He phoned the chief of staff of his small air force and gave him the target coordinates, cautioning them not to begin shelling until he gave the order. It would take time to organize an attack, and every second would count. He was furious that Gretchen had permitted herself to be captured. Hassan had sworn that he hadn't seen her leave the tent. But Leila had. She threw herself at Philippe's feet, wailing, as she imparted what had happened. She'd tried to stop the young, headstrong woman, but it had been impossible.

"She had a pistol, you say?" Philippe asked, aghast.

"Yes, *sidi*," she replied. "And cartridges. She stayed up all night, watching to make sure no one harmed you. I think it was the old sheikh who gave her the pistol," she added. "She had it concealed in a small bundle of cloth."

He knew immediately what she meant, having seen the bundle when Gretchen came out of the palace. His teeth ground together. "Then why did she follow me?"

"She said that she must protect you," she said simply.

He laughed curtly. "Protect me!" He threw up his hands and turned away. "Against a force of professional mercenaries led by a vengeful madman with state-of-the-art weapons? And she meant to protect me with a Colt .45?" He was still muttering when he swung into the saddle of his big, swift Arabian and motioned his men to follow. Leila watched, her eyes troubled, her heart heavy. If the lady was not found alive, she feared for everyone who would be blamed for it—including herself.

Gretchen was waiting, biding her time for one chance to save herself. Her brother, Marc, had always told her not to ever try to struggle with an armed man. But she knew self-defense. If she could get close enough to Brauer, she might have a chance of escape. She wasn't up to his weight, but she might not have another opportunity. Once his men returned, it would be impossible to get away.

It was early afternoon before Kurt came back inside the tent, accompanied by three other men, armed to the teeth.

"Your husband is nothing if not persistent," he told Gretchen. "But it will do him no good. I can't imagine how he thinks he can attack me with a handful of tribesmen on horseback. Perhaps he thinks we are still living in the last century." He said something to two of the men. They left and an engine revved up. The other man, the redhead, stood rigidly next to Brauer's writing table.

"Where are you going?" Gretchen asked as Brauer searched through the contents of the writing table.

His eyebrows arched. "You think I would tell you? You are an optimist, madame."

"If I'm going to die anyway, who can I tell?"

"Eric is going to escort you out to the desert while my men and I prepare a nice surprise for your husband," he told her coldly. He spoke to the other man in German. "It has been an interesting experience to meet you, *madame*," he mused. "A pity that we have so little time to become better acquainted."

"Doesn't bother me," she muttered.

He only laughed. He gathered up some papers from his desk and stuck them into the pocket of his safari vest. He said something to Eric, who looked at Gretchen in a way that made her skin crawl.

Brauer went out, and Gretchen eyed her new companion. He was thin and scarred, with receding red hair and freckles and intensely blue eyes. He had a knife in one hand.

Gretchen forced herself to breathe normally, and wait and hope for an opportunity to get away. The man was obviously her superior in strength, and he was armed. She tried to remember everything Marc had taught her about self-defense. *Let the enemy come to you*, she thought, *it gives you the advantage. Use his own strength against him. Never try to fight if you can get away.*

Outside there was the sound of a vehicle leaving.

Eric twisted the knife in his hand. His eyes narrowed and he smiled coldly. "Kurt said to leave you in a condition that your husband won't forget. But he didn't say I couldn't enjoy you first," he added in a tone that made nausea rise in her throat.

She sat very still on the cushions, hands folded in her lap. Her mouth was as dry as cotton. Her palms were sweaty. Her heartbeat was shaking her. Think, she told herself, think what Philippe would do, what Marc would do.

The man, put off guard by her docility and lack of movement, shrugged and tossed the knife onto the writing table. He approached her with a slow, methodical gait, his hot eyes already anticipating pleasure.

She waited, trembling, until he bent over to catch her arms. Instantly, her booted foot came up and she threw him right into the wall of the tent. Without hesitation, she grabbed up the bowie knife and ran out of the tent toward the mountains.

She could hear him behind her, cursing and raging for her to stop. The heavy black *aba* was slowing her down, but it would take precious seconds she didn't have to rip it off. She kept running, her heart bursting. If she could get into the mountains, perhaps...

But distance was deceptive on the desert. The mountains seemed farther away as she ran. The heat was stifling her lungs. She could hardly breathe. There was a wind and it was forcing sand into her eyes, her nostrils, her mouth. She felt covered by it, whipped by it. Eric came closer. She could hear his harsh breathing. Any minute now, she was going to give out, and he'd have her. *Oh, Philippe,* she called silently, in anguish, *if only I'd done what I was told and stayed in camp!*

She stumbled and turned her ankle. Tears of frustration and anger burst from her eyes. She went down, holding the bowie knife close in front of her, waiting. He might get her, but she was going to get him first!

He was laughing. He slowed his pace and came toward her with a mocking, victorious smile. She was done for. He could do what he liked, now, and he was anticipating all sorts of perverse pleasures when he felt something thump him in the chest...

The expression on his face puzzled Gretchen. He stopped and his eyes seemed shocked. In the same instant, she heard a loud crack, like a firecracker. Blood issued from the soldier's lips and he suddenly pitched headfirst to the desert floor.

Gretchen saw a cloud of dust, and riding out of it was a tall man on a creamy Arabian stallion, yelling orders. He was holding a rifle and even as he yelled, he sighted it and shot an armed man running toward them. The camp was instantly in an uproar. Mercenaries poured out of tents, firing as they came. The party of Arabs rode like gods on their exquisite horses, standing in the stirrups to fire on the run. Gretchen had never seen anything like it. The mercenaries, though better armed, were routed almost at once and running for their vehicles.

She managed to get to her feet, thrilling at the way those men rode, at the very primitive rampage of native tribesmen against modern guerillas. That tall Arab on the stallion fascinated her. One of the mercenaries charged him. He leaped from his horse to meet the man, taking him in and throwing him with exquisite grace. The man came up with a knife, which was immediately kicked from his hand, and a hard blow from a big fist put him down for good. The Arab picked up the man's automatic weapon and swung back into the saddle as gracefully as any Texas cowboy. Gretchen couldn't take her eyes off him. He took her very breath away.

He wheeled the horse, still holding the weapon in the other. He rode toward her, not even breaking speed when she stood up. He leaned down and a long arm caught her around the waist, pulling her up in front of him. He never even slowed down, wheeling the horse back toward his men. His face was covered with a white fold of cloth, his head was in the traditional headdress with black ropes securing it. He looked like every dream of heroism Gretchen had ever had. A sheikh on a stallion, saving the heroine from great danger in the desert...

He looked down at her, and the black eyes that met her own were glittering with rage.

"You little maniac!" came a familiar deep voice from the fold of the flowing white cloak. "I should have given you to that German dog and let him show you the consequences for disobeying orders!"

She thought she might faint. "Philippe?" she asked, aghast.

He tugged down the fabric to reveal his angry face. "Reckless fool of a woman!" he shot at her. "As if I need protection in the first place... Achmed!" he yelled, and added a stiff command in Arabic. He waved his hand, motioning his men out of the camp and back the way they'd come.

"Why are we in such a big hurry here?" she asked, gingerly handing Philippe the bowie knife, which he stuck in his belt next to his ceremonial dagger.

"I called an air strike on these coordinates," he told her through his teeth. "Where was Brauer?"

"He rode out of camp before you rode in," she said, still fascinated by this rugged warrior who'd been hidden in a camouflage of expensive suits and city sophistication. "I've never seen anybody ride like you."

"I learned to fight and ride before I learned English." He glared down at her. "Leila told me you came to protect me. How kind of you," he added icily. "Your concept of me is less than flattering."

"I didn't know!" she said, flushing. "You always wore suits and I thought you were a city man without any survival skills. Your father said you needed protection, what was I supposed to think? I wasn't sure you'd let your bodyguards close enough to do the job, and I knew I could. I'm a dead shot."

"I had half a regiment of seasoned veteran warriors with me, didn't you notice?" he demanded furiously. "In fact, I trained them myself! I was one of the few heads of state ever to go through the SAS training course in one attempt! I united the warring tribes in Qawi when they fled under Brauer's attack and organized a counterrevolution here. And you think I need protection?''

"All right, I did a stupid thing! You don't have to go on and on about it!''

He drew in an angry breath as he urged his horse to go even faster as he raged on, "If I'd been five seconds later getting here, that redheaded lump of horse excrement would have raped you!''

"I almost got away," she said with hurt pride, trying to hold on and keep her seat at the breakneck pace of the powerful animal under them. "And I did throw him into the tent wall! That's how I got outside.''

He wasn't budging. His face was harder than rock. He was almost shivering with rage and fear and, unexpectedly, fierce desire. His body rippled with pleasure from the close contact with her. He felt more potent than he'd been in years. Perhaps it was the combination of danger and relief. Whatever it was, he ached for her.

His arm contracted around her. "How did they get you?''

"I was trying to catch up to you and the horse reared up and unseated me, God knows why," she muttered. "They were on me before I knew it.

Brauer planned to have his friend with the knife peel my skin off. They were going to leave me in the desert for a few days and then tell you where to find me. They thought,'' she added bluntly, "that I was Brianne Hutton."

His breath left him in a rush as he contemplated what might have happened to her. It was the sickest terror he'd ever felt. Then he realized what she'd said. His arm contracted involuntarily. "So he knows that Brianne's coming here."

"Yes, he does, and a lot more besides. Your chief of security is one of his spies, and so is an assistant cook." She grimaced at his shocked expression. "He thought I was going to die before I could tell anyone. Your uncle is helping him, too."

"My uncle will regret it," he said, and his face looked dangerous. He glanced down at her hotly. "And you are going to regret, deeply, having put me through this torment today. I thought he was going to kill you before I could get to his camp!"

"He did think about it," she murmured, and gingerly touched her jaw.

"He hit you?" His voice was almost strangled with fury when he saw the discoloration. "He hit you!"

"Yes, well, I hit him back," she said curtly. "Marc taught me how to throw a punch. I promise you, he looks worse than I do. And if I ever see him again, I'll pump him full of lead!''

"Gretchen." He drew her up close to him, burying his face in her throat where wisps of disheveled, damp blond hair had come loose from her bun. "You crazy, outrageous, brave little fool," he groaned.

She linked her arms around his neck and held on hard. She could feel the effect she was having on him and she laughed, low in her throat, at his ear. "Mr. Brauer thought you can't have a woman," she whispered. "But he doesn't, anymore."

She felt his heartbeat stop and start again. "What did you tell him?"

"That my maid would laugh at his assumptions. She would, too. Leila thinks we're already...well, doing it."

"Doing it?" he asked curiously.

She smiled, and shivered a little with reaction. "You know."

He glared down into her eyes. "This would be a very bad time to...do it," he said through his teeth.

"Why?"

"Because I'm furious with you!" he said bluntly. His eyes went over her in a sensual appraisal that made her heart catch in her throat. "I couldn't be gentle, even if I could manage it at all.''

Her lips parted. "I wouldn't mind," she whispered. "I wouldn't mind any way you made love to me.''

His powerful body shivered. He bent, uncaring if the whole planet watched, and caught her mouth hungrily with his own. She held on for dear life, opening her lips, welcoming him, wanting him. Her heartbeat shook her with its mad pounding. His ardor became faintly violent, his arms bruising, his mouth hurting. She almost protested, but she held back. If he couldn't have her in cold blood, perhaps the very fury that rode him would work the miracle.

Chapter Twelve

Philippe lifted his head, finally, and his black eyes smoldered as they met hers. He drew her flushed face up into his throat and held her there while he urged his horse across the desert ahead of his men. His heartbeat was shaking him. He'd never felt such blatant desire in his life.

The minute they arrived at the camp, he eased her to the ground and jumped down beside her. He shot orders at his men and then at Leila, who went dashing out of the tent and into another one.

Without breaking stride, he lifted Gretchen into his hard arms and walked straight into his own apartment, lowering the flap before he ripped away the cover and put her down on white cotton sheets. He tore off his headdress and his cloak and his boots and did the same with hers before he bore her back into the cushioned surface of the make-shift bed. He'd never felt such hope for himself as he did now, anger and all. He must try, he must!

She was almost beside herself with excitement. She reached up to him as he turned to her, wanting to speak, but afraid to break the spell. So much depended on what happened next.

He started kissing her before she could say a word. His ardor was insistent, feverishly intense, almost brutal. He wasn't thinking about his capa-bility or the lack of it. She was warm and sinuous under the crush of his powerful body. He could feel her heat, breathe in the faint smell of lavender soap that clung to her skin. He felt her hands on his back, her eager submission. She wasn't in the least afraid, if her kisses were any indication of what she was feeling.

His hands jerked her blouse the rest of the way out of her skirt and moved up over the lacy little cups that enfolded her firm breasts. He tore it out of the way and caressed her, moving his hand again to scatter the few pearl buttons that secured her khaki shirt. Her body arched as he brought his mouth down squarely over one taut little breast and began to suckle it. All the while, his hands were busy with the skirt and everything under it. In seconds, he'd stripped her, and he was enjoying her as if she were his first woman.

He was burning up with desire. He eased up the *thobe* and unfastened the silk trousers, the *chalwar,* that he wore under it and moved away the silk boxer shorts while his mouth fed on her breast. He touched her, and was surprised to find her ready for him. She was saying something, but he couldn't hear her. His mouth shifted over hers, teasing her lips apart so that his tongue could penetrate the warm, soft darkness inside it. She moaned huskily. Her nails were at his nape, digging in, her body was writhing seductively under him.

One lean hand caught her upper thigh and moved her legs apart. He didn't stop to worry about his capabilities. He wouldn't let himself think of anything except the softness of her yielded body and the eagerness of her mouth under his lips. He pinned her under him and penetrated her in one smooth, hard motion of his hips. Her tiny, helpless cry of pain was stifled by the hard, hungry pressure of his insistent mouth.

This ability was unsurprising. He was aroused, as he had been many times before with her. It was his own inability to reach a peak that disturbed him. But he could give her pleasure, even if his body denied it to him.

While he was thinking it, her hands were

smoothing steadily down his spine to his upper thighs, caressing him tenderly. Her mouth opened even more, and she moaned again, twisting her hips up toward his to invite him to move even more deeply inside that secret place.

"Tell me what to do," she whispered frantically. "I'll do anything, anything to give you pleasure!"

His breath caught. He lifted his head and looked into her eyes. He moved deliberately and her arms tightened around her.

"Teach me," she moaned, lifting to put her mouth on his. "I don't want pleasure unless I can give it to you as well!"

A shudder went through him at the pure unselfishness of the soft, husky plea. Her young body was unused to the demands he was placing on it, and he was sorry that he'd hurt her. He wanted to cherish her. His lips touched all over her face, down to her lips, brushing, teasing them apart. His body teased as well, fencing with hers, deliberately prolonging the contact and then denying it.

She caught her breath. Her eyes were looking straight into his and she gasped faintly with every slow movement of his powerful body.

He bent and whispered something very softly into her ear. She made an embarrassed little sound, but she obeyed him, contracting the lower part of her belly in a slow, sensuous motion. He groaned sharply.

"Is that...what you want?" she whispered shyly, and did it again.

"Yes," he managed hoarsely. "Yes, darling, yes...!"

He twisted his own hips against hers, intensifying the soft moans. Her soft body clenched again, and as he felt her contract around him, something happened. A fierce surge of pleasure took him unawares. He felt heat, like a living, breathing thing, traveling along nerves that had been dead for years. There was a sensation of terrible tension, and then a storm crest of white-hot pleasure that lifted him above her in a taut arch and then brought his hips crushing down over hers forcefully. He felt her body resist him once more, just briefly, heard again her soft, sharp little cry.

His head lifted and he looked straight into her eyes as his lean hips fell in one smooth, hard movement. Her lips fell open. She couldn't seem to focus on his face. It came closer and then faded away, and her whole body seemed to be fading in and out with it. She dug her fingers into Philippe's back, holding tight while he intensified the deep, powerful movements of his hips.

"Is this hurting?" he asked in a hoarse whisper.

"Not...anymore. Oh, no, no, it isn't...hurting!"

She shivered as the pleasure grew by the second. Her eyes held his. She touched his face, his cheek, his mouth tenderly. "Oh, I want you," she whispered brokenly. "I want all of you. I want you to be whole again. I'll do anything for you, anything, Philippe…!" She cried out, shivering wildly as pleasure shot through her.

Something arrogant and possessive came into the taut face above hers. He watched her intently, and the movements of his body became more demanding. He pinned her wrists to the bed above her head as his body moved furiously against hers. She began to lift toward him with her last ounce of strength, moaning as each thrust brought a new, higher level of pleasure.

Her reaction made him violent. He hadn't felt excitement like this in so long…so long! He could feel the spiral, the old familiar spiral of ecstasy, beginning! He could actually feel it…The wave was coming. It was almost on him. He couldn't bear it…!

He arched himself above her, groaning harshly as he intensified his possession. Her long legs wrapped sinuously around the backs of his and her face began to clench as the change of position made the pleasure rip through her like a knife blade. She cried out.

"Yes," he breathed hotly. He let go of her

wrists and caught her head in his hands. "Look at me," he ground out. "Let me watch...let me see it!"

It was unbelievable. She was dying. No human being could survive such waves of searing pleasure, so deep that they were like pain. She began to sob, her cries loud in the silence of the tent. The sound seemed to galvanize him. His mouth found hers and he turned her into his body, rolled over with her, so that she was beneath him and then above him. And all the while, his body teased hers, promising delights beyond imagination.

She begged him to end it, sobbing, moaning harshly as he built the tension to flash point.

"Yes, now," he bit off. "Now, Gretchen. Now, now...!"

She went off the edge of the world. Her voice broke on a shrill, husky little cry that arched her body, her eyes wide-open, like her mouth, as she gave in to the ardent demands of his body.

Watching her, feeling the helpless convulsions of her body, sent fire through his body. He could feel it in his spine, feel it climbing, ripping, tearing, possessing. He felt it take him, unexpectedly, with a suddenness that left him hanging in midair. He felt the heat explode up from his loins in a violent, shocking, intense flood of exquisite physical sensation. He groaned and began to shiver. Ecstasy. It was ecstasy. He'd never thought to feel it again in his lifetime. Nine years, he was thinking while he still could, nine years, nine years…!

He gave in to the hot, sweet tidal wave. He groaned harshly and his body corded, convulsed above hers, rippling over and over and over again with exquisite sensations of pleasure. He groaned again. He cried aloud harshly, his voice rasping as the intensity of delight all but cost him consciousness. Never in his life…!

There were running feet and a loud, quick spate of Arabic outside the chamber. Philippe, his hair damp with sweat, his face still taut in the aftermath of passion, his body shuddering with ripples of ongoing pleasure, yelled something at them harshly. The footsteps went away quickly.

Philippe took a slow, steadying breath, and looked down into drowned green eyes in a face flushed with shock and uncertainty. His own eyes were fierce, dark, shocked. He shivered again and again in the slowly diminishing waves of pleasure, looking straight into her soft, curious eyes, letting her share his ecstasy until, finally, the spasms began to ease and his body relaxed all at once, with all its formidable weight pressing her into the thin mattress under them.

Barely able to breathe, he lifted away from her, quickly concealing himself before she could see him, and his eyes went to her thighs. He touched them gently, bringing away a faint smear of blood. He looked down at her yielded, trembling body, his eyes dark with possession as he registered her silky smooth pink skin.

"You bled," he said quietly. His voice was faintly unsteady, because his heartbeat was shaking him. His hair was damp, as if he'd been running.

Gretchen swallowed down a wave of shyness. She had nothing on, and he was making a meal of her with his eyes. She was still shivering, too, in the aftermath of something unequaled in her life. "Yes. It's natural."

"Was it bad?" he persisted.

She shook her head. She smiled shyly, her eyes twinkling as she looked up at him. "You felt it, didn't you?" she whispered. "You felt it all over, at the end, just like me."

"Yes," he whispered. "I felt it. I felt it!" He bent and brushed his lips softly over hers, and then over her eyes, tasting the tears that came readily to them. "Don't cry," he whispered, smoothing his eyes over her face. "It was beautiful. It was so beautiful, Gretchen. I never dared hope that I would ever know fulfillment again in my life."

Her arms clutched at him, dragging him back down over her shivering body.

He laughed softly. "No. Not just yet." He drew

away from her with an expression that was puzzling. He touched her face with soft, tender fingertips. His eyes were possessive, jubilant. He chuckled, deep in his throat, and slowly got to his feet, refastening his clothing with hands that still held a fine tremor in the aftermath of joy. He looked at her hungrily for a few seconds, sprawled on the sheets with her hair all around her head. He smiled tenderly as he pulled the sheet slowly over her. "First things first, my lady," he said huskily, and turned away.

He called Leila and went out before she could say a word.

An embarrassed Gretchen found herself pounced on by Leila as well as four other women, who went about sorting clothes, filling a bathtub and stripping the bed.

Leila helped her into the small tub. "It will be all right," she said gently, as if she knew what had just happened. It would have been hard not to know, Gretchen supposed, embarrassed as she remembered Philippe's shout of pleasure and the concern of the guards outside the chamber.

"Leila," she began.

"The *sidi* said to bathe and pamper you, and he will be back to have supper with you. It is your wedding night, Lady," she added with a grin. "I think that it will be a very long one!"

Gretchen closed her eyes on a moan. Well, there was no longer any doubt in her mind, or probably in Philippe's, about his condition. That had been real lovemaking, not foreplay. And it was a certainty that these women who'd stripped the bed would have seen evidence of the consummation of the marriage. That would solve Philippe's dilemma. Never again would he have to fear gossip. But it also meant that he could marry now. He would be able to find a wife befitting his station in life, and it wouldn't be a nobody of a little country girl from Texas. She felt miserable at the thought of losing him when she'd only just begun to love him.

She felt a soreness that the water seemed to ease, and when she was finished, Leila brought her a small jar of salve to use where the tissues were torn. These women were obviously all married themselves, and they knew about first times. They were kindness itself.

Later, they dressed her in a filmy lavender silk *gellabia* with exquisite embroidery in many colors and left her, her long hair brushed and clean, in the bedroom chamber.

She waited on pins and needles for Philippe to come back. Today had been a revelation. She'd discovered a side of him that she hadn't known existed. Her husband, and he was no sophisticate.

Well, he was, but he was a tiger as well. She remembered him riding right into the camp to rescue her—unafraid, relentless. It would be a story to tell her grandchildren, if she ever had any.

It seemed like an eternity until she heard Philippe's voice outside the chamber. She sat up, feeling half dressed and unbearably shy when he pulled the curtain aside and joined her.

He, too, had bathed. He was wearing a white silk *thobe* with gold embroidery and a slit down the front to his collarbone, showing a thick patch of black curling hair. He wore those same odd pants under it. His hair was still damp. He looked handsome and very dangerous, and altogether different from the man she'd met and thought she knew in Morocco.

There was a difference in the way he looked at her now. There was a faint smile on his lips, and his black eyes glittered with possession. He stood aside to let Leila in with a tray of food and hot tea. She gave Gretchen a speaking look and grinned at Philippe as she darted out again. He closed the flap behind her and threw himself down on the cushions beside Gretchen.

"Here," he said, popping a small flaky pastry into her mouth.

"Mmm," she murmured as she chewed and swallowed. "It's delicious." She poured tea into two cups, loving the smell of mint that rose from it. She handed his to him and gave him a shy glance. "Are you still angry with me?"

The corner of his mouth went down. "I should be," he replied. "You could have been killed. From now on, madame, when I give an order, obey it!"

"So speaks the master," she said with a wicked grin.

He caught her arm and pulled her down onto him, rolling her under him with a graceful movement. He smiled at her consternation. "I am the master here," he said in a deep, soft tone. "In every way, now."

She searched his dark eyes. "The women bathed me."

He nodded. He touched her hair lightly. "It is a tradition among my tribe. That, and the saving of the bridal sheet." His eyes glittered. "It is proof that you came to the marriage bed a virgin and that any child that comes of it is mine."

Her eyes were sad. "I wish there could be a child, Philippe," she said genuinely. "I would have loved having a son with you."

His face went hard as he looked at her. "One miracle in a lifetime is enough, don't you think?" he asked quietly. "So you felt what happened to me?"

She flushed. "Oh, yes."

He brushed his fingers over her mouth. "It was...unexpected. I knew that I could remain aroused long enough to pleasure you. But I didn't realize that I could take pleasure from your body as well as give it." He bent and kissed her tenderly. "You made me a man again," he whispered. "It is a gift I will cherish all my life."

She smiled under his hard mouth, her hands tangling in his damp, thick black hair. "Can you, again, do you think?"

He looked vaguely worried. "I don't know," he said honestly. He smiled a little stiffly. "The combination of danger, relief, desire, the aftermath of violence...it would be difficult to recreate such circumstances."

She traced the scar down his lean cheek and to the corner of his mouth. "I suppose so. But you didn't think you could at all, before."

"That is true." He bent and kissed her again, softly. "Nine years of celibacy, Gretchen," he said roughly. "And in a space of weeks, you gave me life all over again."

Her arms linked around his neck. "Only because you let yourself go with me," she pointed out. "Perhaps that was what was missing all along. You thought you couldn't, so you didn't even try."

"You realize that our marriage is binding only

in Qawi?'' he asked, just to make sure she understood.

Something went out in her soft eyes. She pulled her arms from around his neck. "Yes, I remember what you told me," she said, moving away. She forced a smile to her lips. "I'm starved. This looks good."

She began to eat, subdued now. He watched her absently while he, too, ate, his eyes bold on the soft contours of her body that were visible in the light from the ornate hanging lantern above them. She was beautiful in her way. And her body aroused him as no other body ever had. He felt himself tense with the same inexplicable stabs of pleasure that had sent him running to her bed earlier.

She wasn't noticing his preoccupation with her figure. She was thinking that he was anxious to send her packing, now that he was whole again. He probably had some other woman in mind to share his throne. Perhaps this Brianne Hutton wasn't as happily married as he made out, and he had ambitions in that direction. She had a picture of a beautiful blond woman with Philippe straining her to his powerful body. She swallowed and put down the last bit of a flaky roll that she couldn't manage.

She sipped what Leila called "fizzy water" absently until she noticed that Philippe had called the servant to take the tray away, adding another curt command that she couldn't hear. But she noticed that the big tent flap was quietly secured in place behind the servant.

Philippe's black eyes cut into hers in the sudden silence of the chamber. He got up without another word and lowered the chain that secured the hanging lantern so that he could extinguish the flame.

He hung it once more, secured the chain, and then bent to draw Gretchen to her feet and tug her along with him to his bedchamber.

With her heart shivering in her chest, she felt him search for the hem of the *gellabia* and strip her out of it. She was bare underneath, as his lean hands quickly discovered. They slid easily over her soft curves with the delicate scent of the powder Leila and the other women had dabbed on after her bath.

"You feel like warm silk," he murmured, drawing her to him. He bent his head and began to kiss her slowly, softly, tenderly. "I ache for you. Is it too soon? Do you need time to recover from the first time?"

"No." She linked her arms around his neck, eager for whatever he wanted of her. She was still a little sore, but not enough to discourage her from the pursuit of more delicious intimacies.

"Wait," he said gently. He moved away from her and there was another sound of fabric sliding away from skin.

When he came back to her, she felt his nudity in close, thrilling contact with her own and she gasped with pure delight, reaching up to draw herself even closer to that power and heat.

His hands slid down her long back to her hips and drew her hungrily to him. As he felt her against him, his body began to tauten and swell, and he laughed with delight, with pure joy in his returned manhood.

Her arms went around him and she returned his soft kisses with equal pleasure, lingering on the soft contacts as he taught her to prolong the slow giving and taking of caresses that kindled raging fires.

His hands caressed her soft, firm breasts lazily until he bent and his warm mouth replaced the silken caresses of his lean fingers. She lifted, catching her breath, to coax his lips even closer, to increase the soft suction that made her shiver with delight.

He parted her lips with his and his hands contracted on her upper thighs, lifting her, pressing her down on him, so that they were suddenly in intimate contact. She gasped as she felt the hard probing of her softness, and the immediate invasion of herself in one long thrust that her body protested.

She clung to his neck, shivering, lifting herself away because she was sensitive to this sort of invasion, and he seemed even more potent than he had the first time.

"You flinched," he whispered. "Are you sore?"

"Not...inside," she replied, glad that he couldn't see her flush. "But you seem...more potent," she added shyly.

He inhaled sharply. "I am," he murmured against her mouth. He eased her down onto the thick pallet and stretched out on her taut body, nudging her thigh aside to admit the slow descent of his masculinity. "Try to relax," he whispered as his body fenced lazily with hers and began to probe it. "Your body clenches so tightly that it resists me."

"I'm sorry. It isn't that I don't want to, you know," she whispered. "I love being with you like this."

He lifted his head and kissed her eyelids, his body resting intimately against hers. "I had forgotten the difficulties," he murmured enigmatically, and a deep chuckle sounded at her forehead. "Especially with an inexperienced lover."

Her breath caught. "Difficulties?"

"Never mind." He nudged her long legs into parting even more and he moved sensuously between them, teasing her body in a new and very arousing way, so that she began to lift toward him. "I must be more patient, that is all. Here…"

He moved her lazily from side to side while his mouth fed on hers. She moaned as the motions took her from one surge of hunger to the next, higher, one.

She felt him move, lowered himself slowly onto her yielded body, coaxing her long legs to bend and lie close to his, so that they were cocooned together in the most poignant intimacy they had yet shared.

Her breath was audible when he began to rock her under him, his tongue probing her mouth as his body tenderly probed hers.

His hands were under her, between their locked bodies, touching her in ways he hadn't before, making her shiver with little surges of quick pleasure.

She wanted to touch him, too, but she was wary of it since their earlier conversations, so she contented herself with tracing lazy patterns on his shoulders while his body brushed hers in an increasingly arousing way.

"Here," he whispered, repositioning her. "There?" he asked tenderly when she stiffened and moaned. "Yes. Don't be frightened," he whispered, and then he began to move again with skillful, quick motions that had her nails biting into his shoulders and her breath suspended in her throat as a new and alarming sensation began to build in her body. He moved closer and she felt her body accept the invasion of his with delight, felt herself lift to entice him even closer. The pleasure became violent, like jolts of high voltage, and the contact, even so intimate, was suddenly not intimate enough. She arched up to him with a harsh little moan.

"Philippe!" she cried quickly, almost panicked by the surge of explosive pleasure, far greater than anything they'd shared before. "It's not... close...enough!" she sobbed, clinging to him urgently.

His hand shot out and grabbed a cushion. He lifted her abruptly and placed it under her hips and when he moved again, she cried aloud and shuddered.

"Even this," he whispered deeply into her ear, "is hardly close enough, is it?" He moved sharply and groaned as she shivered again. "I've never possessed a woman this completely," he bit off. "I've never wanted to go so deep...!!"

His hands hurt her hips as he tilted them and pushed down fiercely. His body arched with a pleasure that was almost painful. He shuddered and groaned into her open mouth. He felt her sharp little teeth biting into his shoulder and he laughed, deep in his throat as he moved more violently. "Yes, bite me," he ground out. "Bite me, claw me...!"

She lifted up to him with her last sane impulse, straining for the elusive pleasure that suddenly shot through her like silver fire as her sharp nails bit into his hips. She sobbed, her voice breaking as she stiffened and then convulsed under his powerful body, feeling him cover her mouth to silence her as he brought her to ecstasy.

His own body rippled with the sensation of unbearably sweet tension. It climbed into a fierce spiral and suddenly snapped in explosions of pure delight. He felt the rigor lift him, arch him down into her own straining body. He whispered her name harshly, like a prayer, over and over again until finally he groaned it and his body shuddered rhythmically with the most exquisite fulfillment he'd ever had from a woman.

He lay on her with his full weight, feeling himself pulse helplessly, feeling her around him, under him, part of him. His hands tangled in her cool, disheveled blond hair and his mouth searched hungrily for her own. He tasted it in an exhaustion that left him vibrating with the strain.

Her mouth was against the hard arm she'd bitten. She was soothing it with her lips and her tongue in a silence that throbbed with spent pleasure.

"I felt your teeth," he whispered, lazily brushing his mouth over her parted lips. "Did you feel mine?"

"Yes. Is it normal?" she asked hesitantly.

His mouth smoothed over her eyelids, closing them. "If we have pleasure from it, yes."

She moved and shivered with the tiny little spasms that seemed never to end. She moaned. "It goes on and on," she whispered.

"Rarely," he replied. His hips moved deeply and he laughed as she shuddered under him. "Yes. We could satisfy each other continually now with no more than these tiny movements." He drew in a shaky breath. "And I am selfish enough to want that. But your body is raw and exhausted. It will make you very sore if we continue much longer." He kissed her once more and slowly pulled away from her, noticing her tiny flinch when he rolled over onto his back and stretched lazily.

She couldn't see him in the darkness, but she heard him slip back into the *thobe* just the same. It had been heady and sweet to hold him in her arms like that, with nothing between them. But he was far too self-conscious about his scars to do it in the light, and she would have to accept that.

He handed her the purple *gellabia* and drew her to her feet before he slid it over her head.

"Come," he said gently, and lifted her, carrying her back through the tent to her own chamber. He placed her tenderly on her own pallet and knelt beside her, watching her face in the dim light from the torch outside the tent.

"Why can't I sleep with you all night?" she asked.

He touched her bright hair. "I have nightmares," he said simply. "You would not sleep."

"You're my husband," she began.

"In Qawi," he said curtly. "And only in Qawi." He got to his feet abruptly. "There has been a change in plans. We start home in the morning. Brianne will be at the palace by the time we arrive, and I must make sure adequate safeguards are in place. She arrives much sooner than I had expected."

"What about Brauer?" she asked worriedly.

"We shelled his headquarters. Many of his men are missing, most of his equipment is destroyed. Even if he wishes to provoke another border skirmish, it will not be right away. He must raise more money for arms and men. In the meanwhile, all of us will be relatively safe. Especially with my uncle under guard, and his accomplices in prison.''

"You had them arrested?" she asked.

"Yes. They will be tried. As will he, if he is not careful.''

"And I thought you needed protecting," she mused, moving a little gingerly on the pallet.

"Perhaps I do," he mused. "You have an unexpected effect on me," he added quietly. "I'm not sure I like it.''

"What effect?''

"These unexpected lapses of physical ravishment," he said bluntly. "It was not what I intended when I brought you here.''

"You wouldn't have known you were still capable if you hadn't.''

His face would have shocked her, had she been able to see it. Capable. He was so obsessed by what had happened that he felt vulnerable. He'd never really known vulnerability in his rough, difficult past, but this woman could reduce him to his knees. She had power over him, and it was disturbing. He knew the treachery of women who used men for their own purposes. He didn't think Gretchen would ever behave in such a manner, but how could he be certain? Rushing headlong into physical ravishment had not been wise, even if circumstances had sent him racing to her bed. Now he had to manage the aftermath, and he was too confused at the moment to make sense of it all. Brauer was still loose, and Brianne was on her way. He looked at Gretchen and his whole body clenched. He needed time...

"You aren't sorry about what happened, are you?" Gretchen asked, quickly reading his dark mood.

He wouldn't look at her directly. "I don't know," he said tautly. "It may prove as much curse as blessing," he said curtly. "Sleep well."

He turned and left her without a backward glance. She huddled under a thin sheet and wondered what she'd said or done to make him suddenly so remote. The most wonderful experience of her life had turned him into a stranger. Something had changed drastically between them, and not just intimacy. He'd taken several mental steps away from her. She wondered if he hadn't meant to seduce her at all now that Brianne Hutton was coming to stay, and if he felt guilty that he'd given in to desire now that his old love was making a reappearance in his life. Only time would tell, but she felt more dejected and uncertain than she ever remembered feeling in her life.

Chapter Thirteen

The next morning, Philippe was back in his flowing white robes, looking as much a part of the desert as his hard-bitten fighting men. He was still acting remote with Gretchen, although unfailingly polite and courteous. But she had her own horse going back, and he didn't offer to share his. The Land Rover had been sent ahead, on its way to the airport to pick up Mrs. Brianne Hutton and her little boy, who were arriving ahead of schedule.

By the time they arrived at the palace, the newcomers were already in residence. Brianne came out to meet Philippe, who took the palace steps two at a time to grasp her hands and kiss their palms warmly. He bent and picked up the little boy who was with the pretty blond woman, who looked no older than Gretchen herself. As Mrs. Hutton turned, Gretchen almost gasped. The woman could have been her sister, they resembled each other so much. While she stared, transfixed, without a backward glance or even an introduction, Philippe took Mrs. Hutton and her son into the palace and he never looked back once.

Hassan, Gretchen's bodyguard, escorted her inside and let Leila take charge of her. But he stayed close behind as they went toward her quarters.

"There is still danger," Leila explained when they were sequestered in Gretchen's suite. "The *sidi* has told Hassan to stay always near you, while Monsieur Brauer is free."

"They said he won't pose much of a threat for a while, since Philippe blew up his base," Gretchen said.

"That is so. But it is never wise to take too much for granted." Leila gave Gretchen a wise, quiet look. "You need to rest, Lady," she said. "It has been an unsettling time for you."

Gretchen flushed, and averted her eyes.

"There, there," Leila said gently, and smiled. "It is something which all women share, this learning of men and their needs. It is not altogether a fearful thing, is it?"

Gretchen smiled shyly. "No," she admitted.

"And the *sidi* is a man of great experience,"

Leila chattered as she began to unpack Gretchen's things and put them away in drawers. "When he was younger, there were always beautiful women stalking him. In recent years, he has been quite circumspect, especially since he assumed power in Qawi. But he will want an heir. And an American wife," she added with a grin, "is quite a coup for him. It will be of great help when he asks for technical assistance from your government to help with his modernization programs."

Gretchen sat down in a low chair and smoothed her hands over the carved wood arms. "Mrs. Hutton is American," she mentioned.

"She is married, Lady," came the surprised reply. "A guest, certainly, but hardly in the same class with the wife of the sheikh!"

"Do you think so?" she asked absently, and sighed. She leaned her head back and closed her eyes, seeing again the painful sight of her husband walking away with Brianne and her son. Remembered bits and pieces of conversation filtered through her misery, and she recalled what Philippe had said about Pierce Hutton's young wife. Now that Gretchen could see the resemblance, she was frightened that what Philippe felt for herself was the desire he couldn't express for Brianne. It didn't help to wonder if he'd been pretending even in their most intimate moments that she was no more than a poor shadow of the woman he really wanted. She remembered his remoteness after they'd made love, and his sudden and total lack of awareness of her presence the minute he saw Brianne. She had a feeling that it wasn't going to be an isolated incident.

It wasn't. That first day set the pattern for the next few weeks. Philippe found time to take Brianne around his kingdom and show her all the sights Gretchen had longed to see for herself. The child was always with them, and Philippe paid so much attention to him that Gretchen felt her heart breaking in her chest. They would never have a child. But it seemed that he thought of Brianne's as his own.

To Gretchen, he was polite and courteous, like a host with a guest. He no longer came to her chamber, even in the daytime. She felt as if she had no status at all, that she remained in the palace on sufferance. She had been an experiment, to see if he could be a man again. And now that he knew he could, he was in hot pursuit of Mrs. Hutton— whom, gossip said, was temporarily estranged from her husband. They had argued, apparently, over her presence here with Philippe.

Gretchen found an unexpected ally in her former adversary, Philippe's father. He invited her one day into his conservatory and began to instruct her about orchids. She was an apt pupil, listening with rapt attention as he explained the different species, their growing conditions and the quality of their exquisite blooms. They grew in a bark mixture instead of in soil, which fascinated Gretchen.

She touched a fragile phalanopsis blossom with delicate fingers. "They're so individual," she remarked. "Just like people."

"I like to think that they have personalities as well," the old sheikh told her with a warm smile. "Some are shy and show their blossoms only under persuasive care. Others are flamboyant and showy. Still others are recluses, hiding their blooms under their leaves. I find them fascinating."

"Yes, so do I," she agreed, her eyes embracing them. "Do they all have names?"

"Every one," he replied. "And many are old enough to be my children, much less my grandchildren," he added on a chuckle.

They walked quietly down the long rows of plants, surrounded on all sides by various tropical and subtropical trees and shrubs. It was a wonderland of a conservatory, one which any gardener would envy.

He glanced down at her in the all-enveloping white and rose *gellabia* with its hood drawn up around her coiled blond hair. She fit in so well, he thought. She never pushed or tried to command; she persuaded and coaxed people to do what she wanted them to do. She was gentle even with servants. The cook sneaked her little treats through Leila. The seamstresses went to extra pains on her robes and dresses. The candy merchant sent her samples of his best chocolates, and the pastry chef sent her a selection of his best sweet rolls in a ribbon-festooned box every morning. Not since the old sheikh's grandmother had there been a woman so beloved by the staff.

But she wasn't happy, either. He had heard through the servants about her wedding night with his son, and there was more than ample evidence that the marriage had been consummated. Even if Philippe couldn't give her children, he was apparently able to give her a full and complete marriage. This was delightful news to a man who grieved for his only surviving son's impotence. But something had gone wrong, very wrong. Philippe was spending every available moment with the visiting Mrs. Hutton and her son, and Gretchen was left to entertain herself.

"Why does he desert you for the woman from Paris?" he asked suddenly.

She stopped and turned to face him. "He loves her," she replied honestly.

"Have you no idea of competing with her?" he prodded gently.

"How?" she asked with a sad little smile. "I'm not in her class socially, and I haven't her looks or her history with Philippe. The minute he saw her, he went to her and never looked back at me. It's been that way for weeks." She stared down at the marble floor and thought irrelevantly how nice it would feel on bare feet. She wished she dared to go barefoot. "You must have noticed that I favor her," she added, rubbing salt in the wound.

"He wants you," he said bluntly, ignoring the comment. "There is a weapon you could use."

"It wouldn't be enough," she said softly. "Not if he loves her." She glanced out at a nearby palm tree in its nice ceramic pot. "I've been thinking about going home."

"What?"

"You must see that it isn't going to work," she said with a gesture of her hands. "He wouldn't have chosen me for his wife in a hundred years if I hadn't appealed to his senses and his conscience. He knows that he can be a complete man now, and I think he's already considering the qualities he wants in his consort. Believe me, I'm not even in the running."

"Mrs. Hutton is married and has a son," he said firmly.

"She and her husband had a terrible fight before she came here," she said, relating the gossip that Leila had whispered to her. "Philippe loves her and she has some sort of feeling for him." She shrugged. "How do I fight that?"

"You must try, if you love him," he said.

"And if I fail?"

"If you fail…then I will help you to leave. On the condition that Hassan goes with you," he added sternly. "Brauer has a long reach, all the way to the United States. Whatever my son's failings, he will not want you in danger."

"Hassan would hate being away from here," she tried to argue.

"That is my condition."

She sighed. "Oh, very well."

"But not until you make one last effort to mend your marriage, young woman," he told her. "I do not like the thought of sending away the one person in this palace who wants to learn about orchids!"

She chuckled. "Fair enough. And thank you."

He shrugged and picked up a pair of clippers. "Now. Let me instruct you about the art of propagation!"

That night, Gretchen bathed and pampered herself, adding perfume to her water and her hair. She dressed in her most beautiful blue velvet caftan with gold braid, and left her hair flowing and long. With every hope and prayer she walked on soft slippered feet to her husband's suite with her heart beating like mad as she proposed seducing him. It was the last-ditch stand, she thought. She was like the last of the Texas Rangers holding off an outlaw gang. She was walking in where angels feared to tread. At least he did want her, and she was the one woman he'd been physically successful with. It was the one point in her favor, even if he didn't love her.

With her breath in her throat, she rounded the corner to the double door that led to his suite of rooms—and was stopped by two armed guards.

She actually gasped. One of the men stared at her with narrowed eyes. "What do you want?" he asked. "No one may enter here without invitation. Especially not a woman who is improperly clothed and flaunting her body!"

He spoke as if she were some mindless concubine. He didn't know her. She didn't know him, either. But his condescending attitude made her furious. Why did Philippe have guards who didn't recognize his own wife? "I want to see my husband," she said, gathering courage.

"And why should you expect to find him here? Who is he?" he demanded curtly.

Her green eyes flashed. "He is Philippe Sabon," she said icily.

The guard's eyes narrowed. "I do not believe this. The *sidi* is not married."

Gretchen's eyes burned like fire. "Yes, he is. And you get him. Right now!"

"Oh, very well. Wait here," he said irritably. He glanced at her, frowning, and went into the chamber, leaving the other guard standing rigidly at attention.

There was muffled conversation, and the guard came back with Philippe at his heels. Her husband was still wearing his robes. He looked very foreign, and very attractive. He lifted his chin, staring at Gretchen as if he didn't recognize her. A minute later, she heard movement and saw Brianne Hutton move into view. The woman was dressed in a nice green silk pantsuit, and she didn't look ruffled, but the fact that she was with Philippe in his quarters at this hour of the night spoke volumes.

"What do you want, Gretchen?" he asked formally. "It's a little late for dictation, isn't it?"

She saw in his lean, hard face that whatever rapport they'd shared in the past was gone. The comment surprised her. "Dictation?" she stammered.

"You are my social secretary, Miss Brannon," he reminded her shortly. He looked very uneasy, and he wouldn't quite meet her eyes.

So that was his game. He was going to pretend that they weren't married at all, that he was still single. No wonder he'd placed guards unfamiliar with Gretchen at his door, to protect him from her unwanted intrusion. It occurred to her unexpectedly that she didn't even have a wedding band or a written marriage certificate. Only the people at the wedding, and Philippe and Gretchen and Leila, knew they were married. Leila, of course, would say whatever he told her to say.

She lifted her chin proudly. Her heart was breaking, but she wasn't going to beg. If Brianne was what he wanted, she couldn't very well force him back into her arms.

"Yes, Monsieur Sabon, I am, indeed. That, and nothing more," Gretchen said calmly, barely catching the flicker of his eyelids. "You must excuse the intrusion. I only came to tell you that I am returning home tomorrow and you will have to replace me. Good evening!"

Having delivered that bombshell, she turned to the young guard who had been insolent to her and was now looking perplexed. She shot a furious oath at him in the Arabic dialect she'd been painstakingly learning since her arrival, in a secretive effort to please her husband. It must have been a good oath, because he blanched. She'd learned it from the old shiekh, who was eloquent when a servant broke one of his orchid pots, and the orchid inside it. He'd repeated the phrase enough that it had stuck in her mind. He did love those orchids.

"Mademoiselle!" the guard choked. No woman had ever spoken to him in such a way in his life. He was dumbfounded.

"Madame, to you, you sidewinder!" Gretchen raged, infuriated by her whole situation, not the least in having her identity denied by her own husband. And lifting one slippered foot, she kicked the guard in the shin as hard as she could and stormed back down the corridor.

Philippe's eyebrows arched almost to his hairline as he stood, shocked, watching Gretchen's fiery retreat. His now-lame guard was hopping on one foot and trying to look dignified in the process. Philippe shot a curt order at him and let him go back to his quarters. He glared hotly at the other guard, who was trying very hard not to grin. The guard stood at attention and faced forward, quickly.

Philippe went back into the chamber and closed the door, ill at ease with Brianne. He was behaving badly. His uninhibited ardor with Gretchen had shocked and frankly embarrassed him. Even in his younger days, his prowess in bed had been largely silent, controlled. With Gretchen, he had said and done things that would never have occurred to him

to do with any woman. His weakness and vulnerability had made him uneasy around her. He didn't
completely trust her not to take advantage of his
vulnerability, as well. Women did so enjoy having
a man at their mercy. His past was full of women
who would have used that vulnerability to get what
they wanted from him. But in the weeks since their
return from the desert, his wife had not come near
him, not to flirt, not to demand. Her avoidance of
him had shamed him, and now he was fighting
guilt as well. His treatment of her tonight would
haunt him. What did he think he could have with
Brianne Hutton now, except friendship? She loved
her husband. She grieved like a widow since her
arrival, after their estrangement.

Besides that, the sudden arrival of Brianne and
her ordeal in Paris had been much on his mind. He
had loved her once. He had avoided Gretchen, living in a land of dreams where Brianne and her
child were his family. But the dream had not been
realized. And tonight he had come to his senses
abruptly and with shock. Gretchen was going to
leave him. He would be left with nothing, because
that was all he could expect with Brianne Hutton.

He still adored Brianne, but she was married and
so was he. If there had ever been a chance for
them, it was far too late now. All she talked about
was Pierce and how miserable she was since they'd

parted in anger. There was another problem, one that had shaken him to his very soul—he was un- aroused by her. His body, so receptive and im- mediately responsive to Gretchen's, was as dead as sand when he was near Brianne. Amazing, he thought, that it had taken him weeks to realize how indecent his behavior would seem to the people around him. And tonight he'd committed the worst error of them all, by denying his marriage and let- ting Gretchen walk away.

"Why did you have an American secretary?" Brianne was asking curiously.

He ran a hand through his thick, black hair and sighed heavily as he looked down at her with trou- bled eyes. He grimaced. "I have made many mis- takes in my life. Tonight is the crowning glory of them all." He smiled faintly. "Gretchen isn't my secretary, Brianne. She's my wife."

Brianne's face was a study in fascination, sur- prise, and then, amusement. "Your wife?" she asked, almost with glee.

He shrugged, looking embarrassed. "She's from Texas," he said, smiling. "She rides like the wind and shoots a Colt .45 like a movie cowgirl." He chuckled. "She rode right into an ambush and was kidnapped trying to save me from harm."

"What an interesting woman," Brianne said warmly. "Trying to save you…?"

"She'd only ever seen me in business suits," he explained ruefully. "She thought I was a, what is the word, a wimp."

She chuckled. "Oh, my."

"My father adores her," he added. "He permits her to touch the orchids, a privilege even I do not enjoy." The smile faded. "It is dangerous for her to leave now. Your stepfather is still nearby, probably plotting more mischief."

"Then shouldn't you go and tell her to stay?" Brianne challenged with an impish grin.

"It will take a brave man to walk in there unarmed," he pointed out. "I fear my guard will limp for a week as it is. And he may never recover from the shock of her insults." He burst out laughing. "I had no idea she knew such curses, and in a very archaic dialect of my people. I suspect my father has been giving her lessons, without proper definitions. I really must speak to him."

Her eyes softened as she looked up at him. "I've hoped for a long time that you might find someone who could, well, who could accept you as you are and make you happy. You're my friend. I care about you."

He took her hand to his lips. "As I care about you," he said gently. "As I always will. But Gretchen..." He hesitated, self-conscious. "I am...whole...with her."

Brianne caught her breath. "Philippe!"

He smiled. "I never believed in miracles until she wove herself into the fabric of my life. I have been unkind to her. Now I must try to redress the balance. You will excuse me?"

"Absolutely." She chuckled. "I think I really must call Pierce and see if he's as miserable as I am. If he grovels nicely, I'll even go home."

"With a contingent of my men," Philippe said firmly, "not alone. I refuse to let you put yourself at risk."

"I'll tell Pierce." She went on tiptoe and kissed his lean cheek. "Thanks, Philippe. You've been wonderful to Edward and to me."

"I adore your son. I wish..." He shrugged again. "But, then, one miracle is all many of us can expect. I must not be greedy."

"I've discovered in my life that miracles happen most often when you least expect them to," she said. "Even doctors can be wrong." She laughed wickedly. "As you've already found out, I gather?"

He laughed, too. He left her and went down the long corridor toward Gretchen's chambers. On the way he met Leila, who looked harassed and overwrought.

"*Sidi,*" she exclaimed, running to him. "The Lady is packing. She will not listen when I try to reason with her, and she is speaking the most horrible sort of words…!''

"You're lucky you weren't holding a rifle," he murmured dryly. "She kicked one of my guards."

"She is out of her head!" Leila said.

"I'll deal with her. Go to bed," he said.

"But, *sidi*…"

"Go."

She bowed and went along without argument.

When Philippe reached Gretchen's room, he met his own father coming out of it. He glared at Philippe from the doorway.

"Go and look at your handiwork!" he raged in Arabic. "She is leaving, and this is your doing!"

"How self-righteous you sound, when her language sent one of my guards into spasms of horror!"

The old man cleared his throat. "She heard that from me when one of the guards tipped over one of my grandchildren and broke his stem. I did not translate the words."

"You should have. I expect to be chastised by the entire household. And she kicked one of my bodyguard so hard that he cannot walk."

His father pursed his lips. "Did she? Why?"

Philippe cleared his own throat. "He, uh, stopped her at my doorway and refused to believe that I was her husband."

"One could be forgiven that, since you spend so much time with the woman from Paris and so little with the woman you married." He gestured toward the door. "I cannot stop her. But I have insisted that she take Hassan with her when she goes."

"She is going nowhere," Philippe said haughtily.

The old man looked down at Philippe's legs in the gold and white *aba* he was wearing over his *thobe* and *chalwar.* "I suggest more padding before you confront her," he murmured dryly, and walked away.

Philippe took a deep breath and walked into Gretchen's room.

Her big canopied bed was covered with her few articles of Western clothing. The *gellabias* and robes and silk and velvet *abas* he'd given her were piled in two chairs by the window. Her long blond hair was loose and falling into her face as she muttered, trailing the sash of a bathrobe as she deposited it with the rest of her unwanted clothing.

She spared him a glare as he entered the room. "Come to say goodbye, have you?" she asked coldly. "Fine. You've said it. Goodbye."

He hesitated, uncertain of his next move. "Brauer is still in the vicinity. This is a bad time to travel."

"I'm taking 'Elvis' home with me," she said. "He'll protect me."

He folded his arms over his chest, glaring at her. "I will not give you permission to leave the country. I will have you stopped at the airport."

"Your father has already given me the necessary papers so that I can travel, in his personal jet, without your damned consent," she shot back.

His eyes began to glitter. "You are my wife!"

"Like hell I am!" she replied, eyes blazing as she walked right up to him. "I'm only your secretary. You just said so!"

He winced. "I want to explain," he began.

"There isn't anything to explain. Now get out of my room!"

His chin lifted slowly. The menace in his face grew with every deep, measured breath. "You do not command me in my own palace, *madame!*"

"This is my room, and I want you out of it!"

"I will leave when it pleases me," he growled. "Not before!"

"If you don't get out of here, I'll—Philippe!" she cried sharply.

He had her up in his arms and his face was furious. He turned, walked to the door, slammed it shut and locked it.

"You put me down!" she raged, fighting him. "I'm going home! I'm going to marry my ranch foreman and live happily ever after, do you hear me?''

Ignoring her struggles, he carried her to the bed and tossed her down onto it. With a savage smile, he bent and ripped the caftan she was wearing from neckline to hem, whipping it away from her body, nude except for tiny white briefs. He jerked those off as well and stood over her, vibrating with anger and jealousy of the faceless man back in Texas that she'd once confessed to being in love with.

"You monster!" she choked, grabbing the sheet up against her nudity as she glared up at him. "How dare you!"

"You are my wife," he said harshly, so eaten up with desire that he was shivering from the force of it.

She was angry, too, her lips tremulous as he stood over her. "That isn't what you said a few minutes ago! And just what are you planning to do?" she demanded.

He laughed coldly. "Since I have nothing left to lose, I am going to show you what you married," he said harshly. "If you think I am a monster, let me prove that you are right before you leave me."

He caught the hem of his *aba* and *thobe* and threw them off, pausing long enough to step out of his slippers and unfasten the silk pants he wore under the robes. When he turned, the scars that covered the left side of his body were blatant white streaks against the natural olive tan of his skin. But it wasn't the scars that drew Gretchen's shocked, fascinated eyes. She'd seen photographs of nude men, but Philippe was in a class of his own. She wasn't looking for flaws. In fact, she wasn't certain she'd have recognized them if she'd seen them. She sat up in bed, suddenly uninhibited, and stared at him with parted lips.

"Well?" he asked furiously, his fists clenched at his sides. "Don't you have anything to say?"

She swallowed and lifted her eyes back to his. "No wonder it hurt, the first time," she said in a husky, fascinated tone.

Chapter Fourteen

Philippe's rigid stance relaxed. His fists un-
clenched. "What?" He scowled.

She swallowed again. "You heard me." Her
eyes fell back to his hips and she colored furiously.

Something changed in his lean face. He moved
toward her, sitting down on the edge of the bed
facing her. "I wanted you to see the scars," he
began hesitantly.

"Oh." Her eyes met his, curious and soft.
"Why?"

He laughed in spite of himself. "I thought it
might be a suitable revenge for your defection."

"Revenge? I don't understand."

Quite obviously she didn't. His eyes fell to her
mouth. He bent and kissed it slowly, teasing her

lips apart. He felt her shy hands go to his hair-roughened chest and bury themselves in it. His body rippled with sensation. He eased her down on the mattress and moved over her. He felt her arms slide around him, felt her long legs soften and slide against his in a slow, lazy caress.

His hands framed her face as he kissed her. His tongue went slowly past her lips and into the soft darkness of her mouth. His body became one long caress, teasing hers, whispering against it in a silence that grew explosively by the second. He felt as he had in his teens, when he was inexhaustible and eager for experimentation. He treated her as he would have treated a virgin, slowly arousing her, denying her the pleasure she begged for. Minutes grew long with the exquisite pace of their loving. By the time he curled her into him and began to possess her, she was shivering helplessly with the fierce urgency of her need.

She cried out softly at his ear, gripping his powerful upper arms with her nails as he moved into total intimacy with her. He felt her hips straining upward in a rigid arch and he lifted his head to look at her.

He read the thought in her eyes. Without moving, he reached for one of the small cushions and placed it gently under her hips. "Yes," he whispered as he moved down again, this time in a stark penetration that made her gasp. "For me, too, it must be...very deep..."

She whimpered as his mouth moved to cover hers. He whispered to her, savage, shocking things that made her writhe under him. She felt the pleasure climb like a spiral of pure fire as she clung to his strength and felt the potency of him increase with every brush of his body. It had never been like this. She was barely certain, in the last few lucid seconds, that she could even accommodate him...!

He felt her body convulse under his, again and again. He gloried in her pleasure until his own need demanded fulfillment. He gave himself to it, his body fierce on hers, hoping that he wasn't going to hurt her in the frenzy of passion. He soared, burned, consumed in flames that pulsed and pulsed and pulsed endlessly.

He heard his own ragged breath jerking out at her ear as he lay heavily upon her damp body, shaking in the aftermath of their explosive lovemaking. Finally, he forced his head to lift and he looked into a face that was white with misery and tears.

"Gretchen!" he whispered, startled. "Did I hurt you?"

Her lips trembled. She felt sick all over. She'd welcomed him, shamed herself with him, when all the time she knew it was because he wanted Brianne and couldn't have her. He'd used her, and she'd let him, out of a helpless, shameful love that she couldn't help. But it was wrong. Wrong!

She pushed at him and he withdrew from her, rolling onto his back and then his side. She curled into a ball and refused to look at him.

"Did I hurt you?" he demanded.

She shook her head.

"Then what is wrong?"

She swallowed, hating him for the very pleasure he'd given her. "She's married," she whispered harshly. "But a blind man could see that she looks just like me. I guess I'm her stand-in tonight, is that right? You couldn't have her, so you had me. I hope you enjoyed it."

His heart seemed to stop. "I beg your pardon?"

"I'm so ashamed," she sobbed. "I've never been so ashamed in my life. I didn't even have enough willpower to deny you. I let you...use me!"

He couldn't remember ever feeling so outraged. He slammed out of the bed and back into his clothing, so furious at her intolerable insult that he forgot to be embarrassed about his scars. She wasn't looking, anyway. Her back was to him.

He took the coverlet and threw it over her, his face like stone. He raged at her in three languages, the content of which was muddled and barely comprehensible.

She rolled over under the cover and sat up, glaring at him from a ravaged face. "You just can't stand the truth, can you?" she demanded on a sob. "You want her, but you're too noble to do it with her. You wouldn't even introduce me as your wife, but when you want sex, here I am!"

"You aren't my wife any longer," he raged back in heavily accented English. "I divorce you!" He snapped his fingers. "You can go back to Texas and marry your foreman, with my blessing!"

"And you can get Brianne Hutton a divorce and marry her, can't you?!" she cried.

"Believe what you like, *madame!*" He spun on his heel and stormed out of the room, scattering servants as he continued to curse, eloquently and audibly, the entire length of the corridor.

Leila came running, having feared that her Lady would have need of her. When she saw the sobbing woman in the bed, she knew she was right.

"Lady, what can I do for you?" she asked gently.

Gretchen's lower lip trembled, but she raised her face proudly. "You can help me finish packing and call Hassan! I'm leaving here right now!"

"But, Lady," Leila began.

"You heard him," she pointed out. "The whole palace heard him. He just divorced me. I don't live here anymore!" She got out of bed, totally uninhibited, and put on her *gellabia*. "I want a bath and then I want you to call the driver to take Hassan and me to the airport."

"I will go with you," Leila offered.

"I'll miss you. But you can't go with me." She turned away. "You'll have a new Lady to take care of very soon, anyway."

"She is married, Lady!"

"She can be divorced as easily as he divorced me. Come on. I want to get this over with."

A week later, she was not only back home in Jacobsville, but she was back at work as well. The girl who'd taken her place at the law firm of Barnes and Kemp had gotten pregnant and gave up her job while morning sickness kept her bedridden. The job was temporarily open, and Gretchen had to support herself until she could look for something permanent.

The surprise was to find that Callie Kirby wasn't there, either. Something very hush-hush was going on, and nobody was talking about what it was. Gossip was that a drug lord was involved, and that Micah Steele, Callie's stepbrother, was also missing. Beyond that, nothing was really known publicly.

Gretchen could have found out from her brother, Marc, but he hadn't been at home when she arrived, either. Conner Mack, the elderly ranch foreman, and his wife, Katie, welcomed her with open arms. Marc's old friend and fellow Texas Ranger Judd Dunn was home on vacation. He stopped by to see Gretchen and was surprised to find her with a six-foot-four-inch Arab bodyguard who went everywhere with her.

"Where did you get him?" he asked.

"Hassan? Oh, he's my dowry," she told him with a grin. "I suppose he's my marriage settlement, too. I must say, I've never felt safer in my life. He takes very good care of me."

Judd's black eyes flashed with humor. "Do you get to go to the ladies room alone?" he asked wickedly.

"He stands right outside the door," she said with a chuckle. "He's intimidating, isn't he?"

"Does he speak English at all?"

She shook her head, smiling at Hassan, who nodded and smiled back. "But he's a darling. I feel ever so safe with him."

Judd noticed a flicker in Hassan's eyes, but he didn't mention it. "What are you going to do about your marriage?"

Her face hardened. "There's nothing to do. He divorced me before I left the country. I'm free."

"Doesn't sound quite legal," he remarked.

"The marriage was only legal in Qawi," she pointed out. She folded her arms over her chest, fighting a bout of nausea. Ever since she'd come home, she'd been having these irritating queasy spells. She must have picked up a bug in Qawi, while they were in the desert. "How's the job?" she asked.

"It's hard," he said flatly. "They've got me working with a new partner, and we don't get along. I miss Marc." He shoved his hands into his jean pockets. "He's never going to be happy living from pillar to post. Why doesn't he come home?"

"He's wondering that himself. He isn't happy with the Bureau. He doesn't like all the traveling he has to do."

"Good. I hope it gets so bad he can't sleep at night."

She grinned. "Give it time. He's weakening."

He glanced at her as they turned and started back toward the house. "I wondered why he went off in the first place. He loved the Rangers."

She wasn't about to give Marc away, especially not to Judd. His reason for leaving was still painful. "He thought he wanted a change of scenery."

"Uh-huh." He pursed his lips. "And to get away from somebody in the process, maybe."

"I haven't said a single word. And I won't."

He chuckled. "Never mind. I know when to quit, too."

He came over twice more before his vacation was up and he headed back to headquarters in Austin for his next assignment. She liked Judd, but she was still a little intimidated by him.

She wasn't at all intimidated by the ranch foreman and his wife, who did the cooking and housecleaning. Connor was in his fifties and so was Katie. She wondered what Philippe would think if he knew that she'd had her "crush" on Connor when she was six years old. He was much more like her father than an employee and she loved him and Katie dearly. She'd given Philippe a wrong impression, but it didn't really bother her. She was still seething about Brianne and being treated like a slave girl in her own bed while she stood in for the other woman. Her pride was crushed, but nothing helped her loneliness. She missed Philippe more every single day.

She brooded over her own problems, but worry wasn't going to solve them. She'd hoped that Philippe might call or write, or even show up one day at the front door. But a month passed with no word from him at all, and Gretchen gave up. She was lackluster and miserable, sick half the time and tired the rest, but she put on a good face for her co-workers. The only bad thing was the continuing ill health that finally drove her to Dr. Lou Coltrain after she passed out in the office where she worked.

When she came to, Hassan had her in the ranch truck and had driven her to the doctor's office. Heaven knew how he found it, but he was resourceful. He helped her out of the truck and frog-marched her, in the gentlest possible way, right up to the receptionist's desk and patted her shoulder with a hand the size of a ham.

"Hassan thinks I should see Dr. Lou," Gretchen said irritably. "I fainted," she added.

"Is Mr. Hassan your husband?" the receptionist asked, staring at the big man wide-eyed.

"What he is would make a book," Gretchen said with a sigh. "Can you work me in, since he won't let me go home?"

"Of course! She's only got one more patient. She was leaving early, but she won't mind seeing you. Have a seat."

She did. Hassan sat and waited with her, ignoring the fascinated glances of the other people in the waiting room. Ten minutes later, the nurse called her name and led her back to a small cubicle. Hassan followed, standing at attention outside the door.

Lou Coltrain came in seconds later, giving the huge man a speaking glance before she closed the sliding cubicle door and looked at Gretchen.

"You have a shadow," Lou remarked with a grin. She had long blond hair, too, and was married to "Copper" Coltrain, the other doctor in the small practice.

"Hassan," Gretchen said complacently. "Although I call him 'Elvis.' He's my dowry."

Lou blinked. "Excuse me?"

"My husband gave him to me as a dowry. I get to keep him, even though my husband divorced me. He's my bodyguard."

Lou grinned. "Do you need one?"

"I am...I was," she corrected, "married to the head of state of a small Middle-Eastern country. He divorced me and sent me home, but one of his enemies is trying to blow him out of his palace. He thinks I may be a target, so Hassan has to live with me until one of us dies or Kurt Brauer is arrested again."

Lou cocked her head. "Nice story. Thinking of getting it published, are you?"

Gretchen glared at her. "It's the truth."

Lou nodded. "Of course it is," she said, humoring her patient. "Now let's hear your symptoms."

Gretchen elaborated on them. Lou asked a question and Gretchen gasped out loud as she realized that she hadn't had a monthly in two months. Lou frowned and called the nurse in to draw blood.

"What do you think it is?" Gretchen asked, worried.

"I think you're pregnant," she said flatly. "We can tell with one of these tests. Considering that it's eight weeks since your last period," she added, "I don't think there's going to be much guesswork."

Gretchen grabbed up an old magazine and began fanning herself furiously. "I can't be pregnant," she said breathlessly. "It's impossible."

"You said you were married..." Lou offered.

"No, it's not that." She looked up. "He was injured in a land mine explosion years ago," she said. "The specialists told him he could never have sex again or father a child. They were wrong about the sex part, but he'll never believe they were wrong about fathering a child. He won't think it's his." She buried her face in her hands. "I can't even tell him. I can't bear it...!"

Lou took both her hands in hers and held them tightly. "It's very early days," she began. "If you want to consider other options..."

Gretchen shook her head. "Oh, no. No." She took a slow breath and let go of Lou's cool, strong fingers. "I want my baby. I'll just have to make sure he doesn't find out."

"Your bodyguard is right outside the cubicle," Lou pointed out. "And the door is paper thin."

"Hassan can't speak English." She smiled. "He's very handsome, isn't he?"

"Very. And big as a house." Lou paused while the nurse came back with the results, grinning from ear to ear.

"Yep," Lou said, reading the results. "You're pregnant."

Gretchen felt as if a magic wand had been waved. Her eyes softened. Her face became radiant. She looked at Lou with an expression that was a little confused, a little enchanted.

"First order of business is going to be an obstetrician," Lou told her. "The best one I know is in Houston, but we do have a specialist who comes here every Friday and is on staff at Jacobsville General."

"I'd rather have a doctor who could treat me here," she replied.

"Good enough. I'll send you to Dr. Genoa. You'll like her."

"A woman doctor."

Lou nodded. "And a very good obstetrician. I'll have Tilly set you up an appointment for next month. Meanwhile, get lots of rest. In addition to prenatal vitamins, I can give you something for the morning sickness, something safe.'' She wrote out a prescription. She handed it to Gretchen and smiled. ''It's none of my business,'' she said gently. ''But your husband has a right to know, even if he did divorce you.''

Gretchen nodded. ''I'll tell him. Eventually.''

''Go home.''

''Yes, ma'am.''

Hassan escorted her back down the hall and into the ranch pickup. He drove her home instead of back to work, and he was smiling secretively. She was so tired and worn and worried that she didn't notice that smile.

But two days later, as she was typing up a brief for Mr. Kemp in his law office and fielding half a dozen interruptions, a black stretch limousine with diplomatic flags flying, followed closely by another dark limousine, pulled up in front of the office.

''Gadzooks,'' one of the other secretaries exclaimed, peering out the venetian blinds. Her eyes almost popped as she caught a glimpse of the dignified man being let out of the limo by a uniformed driver.

''What is it?'' Gretchen murmured, her mind still on her typing.

''Somebody important! Two stretch limos!''

"My, my, maybe Mr. Kemp is representing the mob," Gretchen chuckled.

"Not unless it's an Arabian branch," came the amused reply.

Gretchen's fingers froze on the keyboard. She looked up as the door opened and went white in the face as Philippe Sabon walked into the room, flanked by two bodyguards wearing head cloths and *igal* and three men, obviously American, in suits wearing earphones.

He glared at his companions. "Couldn't you go stand on the sidewalk and intimidate pedestrians?" he asked with some disgust.

"We have very strict orders, Your Highness," one of the earphoned men said politely. "Sorry."

He shot something in Arabic to his own bodyguards, who obediently opened the door and went out. Philippe turned to pierce Gretchen with furious black eyes. She glared right back at him, remembering their last confrontation when he'd torn her clothes off and ravished her, and she flushed despite all her intentions.

He moved his neck as if his collar were choking him. He was dressed very expensively in a silk suit and tie, and an impeccable white shirt. His hair was immaculate, like his nails. He always looked as if he'd just come from the shower.

"Yes?" she asked coldly. "Can I help you?"

"I wish to speak to you. Alone," he muttered, glaring at the other secretary, the openmouthed receptionist, and the suited men behind him.

"I don't wish to speak to you, alone or any other way," she replied with hauteur. "Go back and romance your houseguest. Remember me? We're divorced!" she added hotly.

"We are not divorced!" he flashed, his accent growing stronger by the minute.

"You said we were!"

"I lied!" He threw up his hands and exploded in a spate of Arabic curses that, apparently, Gretchen was the only one who understood.

She flushed and got to her feet. "Don't you use language like that in front of me! I shall have to speak to your father about your language!"

"I've already spoken to him about yours!"

She straightened. "What do you want? I'm not going back with you, no matter what," she added firmly. "I'm very happy where I am."

"Yes, I remember what you told me about your beloved foreman," he said through his teeth. "I hope you remember that you are still a married woman!"

"For the last time, I am not married!"

He glared at her and she glared back for long minutes. Mr. Kemp, blissfully unaware of anything unusual, came barreling out of his office reading a brief and collided with one of Philippe's companions.

"What the hell...?" he exploded.

Philippe glowered at him. "Who are you?"

The other man's eyes narrowed and he scowled. "I'm Kemp. This is my office." He glared. "Who are you?"

Philippe lifted his chin pugnaciously. "I am Philippe Sabon, Sheikh of Qawi, protector of the innocent, defender of the faithful, the lord of the desert...etc., etc."

Kemp was impressed. He pursed his lips and glanced at Gretchen, who was trying to shrink. "So this is your ex-husband," he mused, having been told the bare bones of the relationship when she returned to work for him.

"We are not divorced," Philippe said furiously.

"You said we were!" she reminded him.

"I know of no country in the world where a legal document is not required to terminate a marriage," Philippe retorted. "Ask your employer."

Kemp grinned. "He's right, you know."

"You said...!" she exclaimed.

"I spouted a great deal of nonsense," Philippe said, calming a little as he studied her. "I want to talk to you." He glanced over his shoulder and grimaced. "We shall have to take the Secret Service, my bodyguard, and Hassan along, but perhaps we can gag and blindfold them and stand them together in a corner while we discuss our differences.''

"That's against regulations, Your Highness,'' one of the Secret Service men drawled in a thick Georgia accent.

Philippe glared at him. "If I used my influence, Russell, I could have you assigned to guard the single U.N. delegate from Salid. I understand he keeps cobras and belongs to an obscure ancient cult that bathes yearly...?''

"I love corners, sir,'' the man returned at once.

Kemp was fighting a grin. "Go home,'' he told Gretchen. "Melly can finish the brief for you,'' he added.

"Sure I can,'' Melly said.

Gretchen had already gathered up her purse. She took her work over to Melly's desk and showed her what was left to do. "And don't forget the breakfast meeting in the morning about the new water project,'' she reminded Mr. Kemp.

"I won't forget. Take care, Gretchen.''

She smiled. "Thanks.''

Philippe and the Secret Service stood aside to let her out the door. Hassan, grinning from ear to ear, was waiting on the sidewalk.

"You turncoat,'' she told him. "I don't know how you understood what Dr. Lou Coltrain said to me, but I know Philippe's here because of you! You overprotective big lug!''

Hassan grinned again. ''Thank you very much,'' he said, in a perfect imitation of Elvis's voice.

She gasped.

''Didn't I tell you?'' Philippe murmured as he joined her and motioned the limo driver to open the back door for her. ''Hassan was born in Tupelo, Mississippi. He has an atrocious accent, but he speaks English quite fluently!''

Chapter Fifteen

Gretchen was too inhibited by Hassan's presence to speak to Philippe in the car. She folded her hands in her lap and chafed at the level, steady appraisal her husband gave her. She was aware of the other car following them, and realized that the U.S. government must also consider Kurt Brauer a threat, to go to so much trouble to protect Philippe. It made her uneasy.

They arrived at the ranch ten minutes later, and Philippe left his bodyguards on the porch with Hassan and the Secret Service as he and Gretchen went inside.

Katie came out wiping her hands on her apron and stopped dead at the sight of Philippe.

"Katie, this is my...husband," Gretchen said

hesitantly. "Philippe, this is Katie. She and her husband, Conner, run the ranch when Marc and I are away."

Philippe's eyebrows went up as he acknowledged the woman and her obvious age, and Gretchen knew he was remembering her "crush" on the foreman. She'd never mentioned Connor's age or the fact that he was married. But even as he stared at Katie, he said nothing, and his face was as unreadable as a rock.

"Katie, would you make some iced tea and take it out to the porch? I think we've got six people—three bodyguards, including Hassan, and three Secret Service agents.

"Secret Service agents!" The older woman looked as if she might faint.

"It's all right, Katie," Gretchen interrupted quickly. "They're just along to protect Philippe while he's in the country."

Katie frowned worriedly as she looked at Gretchen. "Does he know?" Katie asked uncomfortably. About the baby, she meant, and before Gretchen could answer, Philippe did.

"Yes, he knows," Philippe said curtly and stared at her until she cleared her throat and went back into the kitchen.

"We can talk in here," Gretchen said, walking into the small study and closing the door. There was a desk and chair, where Marc liked to do the book work, and a bookcase, along with comfortable leather chairs that faced a picture window overlooking the pasture. Longhorn steers grazed out there just inside a well-kept barbed-wire fence.

Philippe looked around the room, noting the gun cabinet and the shooting trophies, as well as the electronic gadgets that Marc used in his work from time to time. "Impressive," he commented.

"Yes." She sat down in one of the chairs and waited for the explosion.

He moved to the desk and perched on the edge of it with his arms folded, his angry eyes searching Gretchen's. "When Hassan phoned me, I could barely believe what he told me," he said curtly. "You have seen a doctor, of course."

She averted her face.

He waited, but she didn't say a word. He frowned. "Surely it is too soon for pregnancy tests to be accurate."

"It's been over eight weeks," she said gruffly.

There was a shocked silence, followed by an audible intake of breath and a furious curse as he got to his feet.

She stared at him. "Why does that surprise you?"

"You seem to have difficulty counting, *ma-*

dame. You have only been back in this country for a month!''

''Yes, and I'm eight weeks pregnant,'' she said, waiting impatiently.

His eyes glittered. He looked as if he might explode. ''If you were eight weeks pregnant, the child would have to be mine. And it cannot be! It is impossible! You are lying!''

''Lying!'' She got up, too, her fists clenched at her side. ''You think I got pregnant here? And just how could *that* have happened?''

He looked uncomfortable. ''You had said that you had a feeling for your foreman,'' he said harshly.

''Yes, and in case you didn't notice, Katie's fifty-five—her husband, Connor, is fifty-seven! I had a crush on him when I was six years old!''

He was looking more murderous by the second. He was losing ground. ''So? You have had a male visitor, have you not, a friend of your brother...''

''Damn you!'' she bit off, clenching her small fists even harder. She wondered what the Secret Service would do if she laid his head open with a chair.

He sighed furiously. His mind was whirling. The doctors, the specialists, had said it would be impossible. She knew that. What nerve, to accuse him of fathering her child! "I cannot produce a child!" he repeated.

"And you can't have sex, either," she said with cold sarcasm, "let's not forget that!"

He let loose a barrage of Arabic curses that would have done his father proud. "Just because they were wrong once is no reason to suppose that the prognoses of three international specialists are riddled with error!" he said in English.

She was very nearly reduced to tears, but he wasn't going to make her cry. "Believe what the hell you like, Philippe!" she choked.

"I won't believe a damned fairy tale!" he retorted.

That did it. She threw even worse curses in Arabic back at him, but more enthusiastically. Then, when she ran out of words, she reached out to the reading table beside the bookcase, picked up the heaviest book in the small stack she found there, and threw it at him with all her might. It hit him with a satisfying thud, leaving him stunned.

"What the hell are you doing?" he exploded.

"Showing you my book collection!" she returned furiously. "Did it hurt? Why don't you call the Secret Service to rush in and protect you?!"

She threw another book, harder, and he ducked that one. But the third one was the heaviest in the lot, and it caught him neatly in the shoulder. She was reaching for a fourth when he went toward her and caught her arms, wrestling them behind her.

She struggled furiously and kicked him. He groaned and lifted that leg, and while he was vulnerable, she kicked him in the other one. This time he yelled. Seconds later, the door burst open and two Secret Service agents with pistols drawn and two bodyguards with automatic weapons stood framed for action in the doorway.

"Get out!" Gretchen and Philippe both yelled in chorus.

The men withdrew immediately and shut the door behind them.

Philippe looked down at the little blond fury in his grasp and suddenly burst out laughing. "No wonder the servants have gone around like attendants at a funeral for weeks," he murmured with a sigh, wrapping her up tight when she tried to kick him again. "All right, I withdraw all my filthy accusations," he said softly. "I must confess, I could not really picture you with another man the way you were with me. But I missed you and I was violently jealous when Hassan told me about your visitor."

"You didn't contact me..." she accused angrily.

His lean hands slid along her back, holding her firmly. "I was ashamed," he confessed quietly, grimacing. "I had behaved very badly and I have apologized only once in my life, until now." His black eyes sought hers hungrily. "Brianne is my friend, Gretchen. She was never more. She never could be."

She was weakening. She didn't want to. But it had been a very long time since he'd held her, and she'd been lonely and a little frightened of her condition. She studied his silk tie. "Judd is Marc's friend. He and I grew up together. He's like my brother."

"I apologize wholeheartedly for my base suspicions," he said softly. His fingers lightly brushed over her mouth. "I want to make amends."

She was still bristling, and glowered at him. "Do you? Hand me another book," she murmured. "I'll show you how!"

He laughed again, and bent quickly, finding her mouth with his. She resisted, but only for a few seconds. Her body, starved of kisses and caresses, flowed into his like a wilting flower welcoming a spring rain. She moaned, tugging her hands from his grasp so that she could loop them around his neck and lift herself even closer. He kissed her back with raw passion, immediately aroused. He gasped against her mouth and his strong arms held a faint tremor. She moaned and he eased her back urgently against the desk, groaning as he levered her down fiercely on its hard surface while she moved eagerly under his hips.

"This is insane," he choked, but even as he said it, his mouth was on hers again and he was reaching for fastenings, so excited by her after the long weeks of abstinence that he could barely get his fingers to work the hooks and buttons.

When she realized his intent, she pulled her lips from his. "Philippe, no! Darling, we...can't...!" she gasped, but he already had. The weight of his body pressed hers into the laminated wood of the six-foot desk and his powerful body was already invading hers even as she protested. She looked up, shocked speechless, into his glittering eyes as he moved urgently on her, shuddering with the force of his desire.

He pinned her hips with a lean hand as his mouth ground into hers. "Don't cry out," he managed jerkily.

"I wouldn't dare," she whispered, biting her lip to keep from moaning as he increased the pressure and the rhythm and she felt the familiar, delicious spiral of ecstasy beginning.

"Gretchen. My darling!" His body rippled with the fierce movement of his hips and he caught her mouth with his as a harsh groan broke from his throat. The heat and potency of him brought her to a shocking onrush of fulfillment in scant seconds.

She felt his body tense as her eyes opened and looked straight into his as he stiffened and convulsed. It was the most intimate thing she'd ever imagined. The starkness of it increased the pleasure until she sobbed helplessly, certain that she was going to die.

Her eyes closed and her nails dug into his hips as they pressed together in one last fierce spasm of ecstasy. Long seconds later, she felt his beloved weight in her arms as he collapsed.

She sighed shakily, aware that her straight skirt was up around her waist and her briefs somewhere on the floor. He was barely covered from the waist up. He lifted his head and looked into her eyes and cocked an eyebrow.

She blushed to her toes.

"See what you get when you throw books at me?" he asked lazily as he tried to get his breath.

She touched his hard mouth with her fingertips. "I'll have to buy a few more books to take home with us."

His eyes softened. "And I thought I might have to tie you up and put you in a sack to get you to come back."

She looked down the length of their bodies, still joined. "Oh, no," she replied, lifting her eyes back to his. "I love you."

He caught his breath audibly and his body became violently capable. He bit off a harsh word as she lifted sinuously against him.

"Yes, you like that, don't you?" she whispered, and did it again. "Here, darling, hold me...like this...!"

It was too soon, too soon, too soon. He felt the explosions like fireworks all over him, under him, around him. He thought that he could not survive the depth of the pleasure she gave him. But all too quickly, his body spent itself, and she laughed, the little blond witch. He bit her shoulder in fierce delight, and she wrapped her long legs around him and laughed secretively in his ear while he convulsed.

"You witch!" he groaned when he could get his breath.

"If I keep you happy, you won't let me leave you again," she said on a contented sigh, stretching under him. "Darling, I love you, but I'm very uncomfortable."

He moved slowly away from her and stilled deliberately, grinning at her faint shock when he drew back.

"So much for all that bravado," he accused gently and kissed her before he got back to his feet and rearranged his disheveled clothing.

She laughed softly as she did the same, her eyes wicked when they met his.

"I will never again look at desks in the same way as before," he mentioned. His dark eyes twinkled playfully "And I shall have some very interesting anecdotes for our children when they are old enough to understand them!"

"Our children." Her face softened as she moved close to him and met his eyes. "You didn't believe this was your child, when you came here," she accused gently.

His lean hands caught her shoulders and he actually winced. "I was afraid to believe it. But after that," he added mischievously, glancing at the desk, "it becomes impossible to believe you have let any other man touch you. You were starved."

"So were you," she retorted.

"Of course. I have not touched a woman since you left me."

She stared at him. "But, Brianne Hutton...?"

He drew her into his arms and held her gently. "She could not arouse me. Not that she knew I was even thinking of such a thing," he confessed. "For a day, two days, perhaps I tried to go back into a past when we were both single, a past when I was not under the spell of a woman who aroused me past bearing and weakened me so badly that I ached for her day and night," he added with a meaningful look that made Gretchen smile with triumph. "But my body was dead when Brianne was near me. Of course, it did not help that she missed her husband and spoke of him relentlessly the whole time," he chuckled. "Or that I could think of nothing but you, and my unspeakably terrible treatment of you, especially after you left me."

"She didn't arouse you?" she asked, aghast. "But you loved her!"

"Did I?" He brought her hand to his lips and searched her eyes. "She was kind to me, at a time when I desperately needed kindness. But you build fires in me. I am alive with you, as I never was before, even when I was whole. You are part of the fabric of my life. I must have you, or I can never be truly happy."

Her eyes lit up. "You're sure?"

His hand reached down and touched her belly tenderly. "I'm sure." He smiled wickedly. "One of the specialists who told me I was sterile practices in Paris. We must invite him to the christening."

"An engraved invitation," she agreed wholeheartedly, grinning.

His eyes adored her and he sighed. "And I thought I would go through life alone and incomplete. Those miracles we spoke of—I think I believe in them now."

"I always did," she said simply, and she reached up to kiss him.

* * *

They walked out into the living room together, disheveled, and several heads turned enquiringly.

"Are you ready to leave, sir?" Russell, the Georgia member of the Secret Service asked politely.

Philippe shook his head. "Not until tomorrow. I'm sure that my wife has loose ends to tie up before we leave the country again." He pursed his lips and smiled amusedly at the uncomfortable-looking men in suits. "Surely a night on a real Texas ranch will not trouble you?"

"I'm from the Bronx," one of the suited men said miserably. "I hate cattle."

"And I'm from Los Angeles," another one added. "Horses scare me to death."

"Sissies," the Georgia agent scoffed.

"Oh, yeah?" the Bronx agent retorted. "Well, I didn't notice you rushing out to stop that Bahama bull that damned near trampled the Soviet premier at the president's summer home near Fort Worth, Russell!"

The Georgia man roared. "Brahma, you idiot, not Bahama!"

"If that Texas Ranger hadn't rushed in, we'd have had World War III for sure!"

"It wasn't a bull, either, it was a milk cow," the taller agent scoffed. "It was just playing with him!"

"Took ten stitches and the president had to buy him a new pair of trousers," the third agent remarked. "And we heard the next day, they sent you to the Okefenokee Swamp to guard the vice president when he was on holiday."

The Georgia agent glared at him. "I asked for that assignment! I like swamps!"

The Bronx agent chuckled. "Sure you did."

"You can all sleep in the bunkhouse," Gretchen said, interrupting them.

"No, we can't, ma'am," the Bronx agent debated. "We have to be where His Highness is."

"In the bedroom?" she exclaimed, horrified.

"Ma'am!" he exclaimed, and blushed. "It's not that kind of agency!"

Philippe laughed heartily. "He means that they have to be within shouting distance," he said. "We can have cots delivered for the living room, surely."

"Of course," she said, placated.

"My bodyguards will sleep in front of the door, with Hassan," Philippe continued, watching her blush. He chuckled. "We should be quite safe."

"Speak for yourself," she murmured, watching the other men. "They've all got guns."

Russell, the Georgia agent grinned. "It's okay, ma'am, they only let us have one bullet apiece, and we have to keep it separate from our guns."

The Bronx agent hit him. "They'd never be stupid enough to give *you* a bullet. Let's go out and scout the perimeter."

"Suits me."

They left, and Philippe motioned his own bodyguard to follow. That left "Elvis," who grinned from ear to ear at Gretchen.

"You never said a word about being able to speak English," she muttered at him.

"You never asked," he drawled smugly and, bowing politely, stalked out behind the others.

Philippe drew Gretchen into his arms and held her close. "Alone at last," he murmured.

He was kissing her enthusiastically when the sound of a car arriving was followed by a loud commotion outside.

"Who the hell do you think you are?" came a furious, and very familiar, voice from the front yard.

There was a commotion. Gretchen rushed out on the porch just in time to see the Secret Service trying to wrestle her big, angry brother to the ground. He was giving them hell on the half-shell, holding his own against all of them in a free-for-all punctuated by grunts and cries of pain and thuds.

"Marc!" she exclaimed.

He lifted his head, diverted just long enough for

the Secret Service to get his hands behind him and handcuff him. He started cursing and one of the men backed up.

Gretchen ran ahead of Philippe down the steps and right up to the Secret Service agent from Georgia. "You can't do that!" she exclaimed. "He's my brother! He lives here!"

"We just did it," the Bronx agent said coldly, mopping a cut on his cheek with his handkerchief. "And he's going up before a judge for assault on a federal agent!"

"You'll be sitting right beside me, you son of a bitch!" Marc told the man. "I'm FBI!"

"No," the Georgia guy drawled slowly as he began to connect the name and the state. "Oh, no. No, you couldn't be *that* Brannon!"

Marc's gray eyes narrowed in his lean, tanned face, and his wavy blond-streaked brown hair seemed to stand on end as he glared at the other man. "The hell I couldn't be. I am! And you're really going to get it this time, Russell." He held up his big fists and shook the handcuffs binding them together. "Get these damned things off me!"

Russell swallowed. "You'd better do it," he told the Bronx man. "He's related to the state attorney general, two United States senators, and the vice president."

The other man grimaced as he dug for the handcuff key. "Well, how was I to know? He didn't even introduce himself properly!"

"Introduce myself, the devil!" Marc exploded as he jerked off the unlocked handcuffs and threw them at the Secret Service agent. "You tackled me the minute I got out of my damned car!"

"He was a Texas Ranger for ten years," Russell said uncomfortably. "And the last agent who handcuffed him was transferred to the Okefenokee Swamp to guard the vice president on a camping trip."

"How *was* the camping trip, Russell?" Marc asked with flashing silvery eyes and a mocking smile.

"I had a wonderful time, sir," Russell said with a grimace. "I never knew snake roasted over a campfire could taste so good. If you see the vice president, you might tell him that," he added hopefully.

Gretchen laughed with pure glee and ran to hug her brother. He swung her up in his hard arms and kissed her soundly, his expression changing to one of affectionate delight as he put her back down.

"How are you?" he asked softly. "And why aren't you in Qawi doing your job?" he added with a frown, glancing at the tall, obviously foreign man standing close to her.

"She's pregnant," Philippe said with twinkling eyes.

Marc scowled. "Pregnant?" His expression softened even more as he looked down at his sister. "I'm going to be an uncle?"

"Very definitely," she said dreamily. "He's a miracle baby."

"Excuse me?"

Philippe's long arms drew her back against his chest and he smiled at Marc over the top of her blond head. "I was told that I couldn't produce children, among other things," he said easily. "Gretchen has changed my life. I adore her."

"Who are you?" Marc asked. "Her boss?"

"Her husband," Philippe corrected.

"His Highness is the ruling Sheikh of Qawi," the Georgia agent, Russell, said.

Marc's eyebrows arched. He glanced at Gretchen. "You're married?"

She glared at him. "Of course I'm married!" she said indignantly. "Why else would I be pregnant?"

His expression was enigmatic as he studied the other man curiously. "Weren't you on the evening news a couple of years ago? Your country was invaded, I believe."

Philippe nodded. "Invaded and captured, in fact. Some influential friends helped me drive out the mercenaries. But their leader is out of prison and causing trouble.''

"Brauer," Marc said unexpectedly. He glared at the Secret Service. "Now I understand all the security around here. Surely he wouldn't try anything on American soil?''

"We can't guarantee that," the Bronx agent said. "That's why we're here.''

Marc lifted his chin. "Haven't you caught him?''

"He's over the border from my country, in Salid," Philippe said. "We have an elite military force trying to contain him even now." His black eyes narrowed. "There must be a state wedding," he added. "Gretchen carries the heir to my throne. A simple service such as we had several weeks ago is insufficient for stability in the region. We must fly back tomorrow. It would be good if you came with us," he added surprisingly.

"I'll request a leave of absence," Marc said at once, to Gretchen's delight.

"I'll request it for you," Philippe replied. "Considering the extent of our newfound oil reserves, and our favored nation status with your government, I expect I have more political pull than even you do at the moment," he added with a grin. The grin faded. "I also want to invite some old friends along who have experience of dealing with international terrorists.''

Marc raised an eyebrow. "Micah Steele?"

"No. I understand that he's in the middle of something. I was thinking of one from Montana, and a couple more," he agreed.

Russell scowled. "Look here, Your Highness, you can't start exporting mercs to foreign countries!"

"Private citizens," Philippe assured them, drawing Gretchen closer. "Wedding guests," he added with a smile.

Marc looked at the Secret Service. "I could call the vice president if you have a problem with that."

"I don't have a problem in the world," Russell said immediately. "How about you guys?"

"Not us," they chorused.

Marc moved toward the porch. "In that case, we might get Katie to fix some lunch. I'm starved!"

They sat around talking until late. The next morning, the cowboys were gathered at the corral to look over a new stallion Marc had bought while he was in Austin at Texas Ranger headquarters, reapplying for his old job.

"Nice, isn't he?" he asked Gretchen and Philippe, both wearing denims and cotton shirts—

Philippe was of a size comparable to Marc and had borrowed some leisure wear.

"Very nice," Philippe mused.

"Purty, ain't he?" one of the cowboys drawled with a speaking glance at Philippe, who looked elegant even in denim. "Don't suppose Miss Gretchen's husband would like to ride him?"

Russell stepped forward. "Now, listen here," he began.

"Yes, I would enjoy that," Philippe said with a wicked grin, and climbed nimbly over the corral fence.

"Your Highness!" the Bronx agent exclaimed in protest.

"It's all right," Gretchen told him, and Marc, who was looking worried. "Trust me."

"He may buck a bit, mister, and you might get mussed up," the cowboy said with a vicious little grin. "Think you can stay on him, or do you even want to try?"

"I will…try," Philippe said with a returned smile.

He took the reins, stroked the horse gently and spoke into its ear, feeling its fear, its faint tremor. He turned the horse's face into the morning sun and suddenly vaulted onto his back and held on. The stallion bucked like a mad thing, but Philippe looked as if he'd been glued right into the saddle.

He laughed with obvious enjoyment as the horse leaped and bucked around the wide corral several times before his soft voice and slow stroking gentled it. He smoothed its mane and whispered in its ear, and then rode it elegantly around the ring several times before he dismounted gracefully and gave the reins to the shocked cowboy who'd challenged him to ride it.

"I breed thoroughbred Arabians," Philippe told him. "I break them myself. This is a good horse, but he lacks stamina. If you intend breeding him, that should be taken into account."

He climbed out of the corral and dropped to his feet in the dirt. Marc chuckled.

"I should have known better. But you did look a little like a city wimp yesterday," he murmured dryly.

Philippe grinned back. "So your sister thought, at first, until she saw me ride." He held out an arm and Gretchen went eagerly to his side. "One day I must tell you the story of how she came riding to save me with a single action Colt .45 in her hands."

"It wouldn't surprise me," Marc admitted. "She's quite a girl."

"Yes." He kissed her forehead warmly. "I am a fortunate man."

* * *

They flew to Qawi later that day, put on the plane by the Secret Service and cocooned by Philippe's bodyguard in the private jet, along with Bojo, whom Gretchen remembered from Tangier, and three older men that she'd never seen before. Marc was apparently on friendly terms with the mercs, and they spoke quietly during the flight, careful to keep their conversation confidential. Gretchen did learn that Cord Romero had not regained his sight, and that her friend Maggie was still with him, trying to help him pick up the pieces of his life. But more than that, no one said. There was a lot of talk about Kurt Brauer, however.

Gretchen was nervous of the state wedding Philippe had said must take place. But he calmed her fears and promised that things would go very smoothly. She must leave the worrying to him and his bodyguards. All would be well, and Brauer would be dealt with.

She knew that she was as safe as possible, but she worried about Philippe. Brauer was half crazy with thoughts of revenge. The wedding would be televised. It would be the perfect opportunity for a terrorist attack.

Chapter Sixteen

Gretchen thought she'd never seen so many camera crews, satellite trucks, and newspeople in one place in her life. Although she knew the wedding was to be televised, she'd never envisioned anything approximating this scale.

Philippe's unbridled joy in her pregnancy had communicated itself to everyone in the palace, especially to his father, who filled Gretchen's rooms with orchids as a coming-home present. The servants did everything possible to enhance her comfort, and every night she slept in her husband's arms.

The only dark cloud was that Kurt Brauer had become an irritating intrusion on their happiness, and Gretchen hated the very mention of his name.

Philippe's uncle, who'd been helping Brauer spy on him, was conspicuous by his absence. He had gone, along with the former chief of security, to seek asylum in a neighboring country. The man's other allies had gone into hiding, although Philippe was taking no chances. Bojo was noticeable in the palace, along with the mercenaries who arrived on the plane with them from Texas.

The oldest was a sitting judge in Chicago named J.D. Brettman. He was accompanied by a handsome blond rancher from Montana whom the others called "Dutch." The third member of their group was very Latin, with a mustache and a charming manner. He was called Laremos, and he and his family lived near Cancún, in Mexico. Gretchen learned from her husband that the three had literally come out of retirement to oversee security for the wedding—as a favor to Philippe. They also knew some younger members of a group from Jacobsville, Texas, who were involved in fighting a powerful drug lord with his own Mexican cartel. It was a little surprising to be told that reclusive rancher Eb Scott was a member of that ex-mercenary bunch, along with Cy Parks and Micah Steele.

Meanwhile, security at the *Palais Tatluk* was formidable. Hassan went literally everywhere with Gretchen, and Leila was never out of her sight except during the night. The old sheikh, Philippe's father, had the same sort of protection. The mercenaries seemed to be having the time of their lives. For men in their forties, Gretchen thought, they were uncannily fit and expert in their security arrangements. She'd never seen such a conglomeration of electronic gadgets in her life.

She remarked on one, a device that could pick up the sound of an ant walking outside on the concrete beside the fountains and videotape its every move. Even Marc didn't have anything quite so sophisticated.

"Oh, we're thorough," the blond man, "Dutch," told her with a grin. "That's how we've lived so long.'

"You all have families, don't you?" she asked him.

He nodded. "My wife and I have two sons and a daughter. Laremos and his wife have a son and daughter, and Brettman and Gaby have a daughter. Our former boss, Apollo, and his wife Joyce are expecting their second child this coming spring." He chuckled. "None of us ever expected to marry at all.''

"Neither did I, really," she mused, her eyes going to her tall husband who was speaking with his press secretary and two members of the media.

"I suppose you know that your husband has

been the subject of some interesting gossip over the years," he murmured dryly.

She grinned. "He'll be the subject of a lot more when I start wearing my maternity clothes," she told him.

He pursed his lips. "Well!"

She laid a protective hand over her still-flat belly, and smiled.

He finished a connection and glanced toward Philippe. "I thought Laremos was lying when he said your husband could back down terrorists. Amazing, how cosmopolitan he looks until you see him over the barrel of a gun."

She eyed him curiously. "How do you know how he looks over the barrel of a gun?"

"Didn't anyone mention that we were part of the team that came in to liberate Qawi from Brauer in the first place?" he asked. "We were in the first assault, right alongside Philippe and his personal guard." He whistled. "He walked right into the damned bullets," he said, shaking his head. "I've never seen anything like it. He went for the commander of the group, the one he later said had killed his house servant Miriam on the government's island of Jameel. I won't tell you what happened, but even some of the career soldiers backed away from him afterward. He's a man you don't want to ever see in a temper."

Gretchen pursed her lips and flushed. "Well, I have seen him in a temper," she remarked, and wasn't quite brazen enough to add that her husband had ravished her twice, ripping her clothes off in the best tradition of bodice-ripping heroes from the silent films. Of course, temper notwithstanding, he'd been tender and exquisitely loving with her.

Dutch was reading between the lines. He chuckled. "No wonder he takes strips off guards who look lax around you. One of them, I understand, is on extended sick leave. It seems he was injured..."

"Oh, my gosh!" she groaned, hiding her face in her hands. "I didn't think I kicked him that hard!"

"It wasn't exactly a kick that injured him, I hear," he murmured dryly while he fiddled with minute adjustments on his equipment. "It was a very hard fist in his jaw. Several teeth were loosened and he was reduced in rank and reassigned to guard the single elderly camel your husband keeps in his stables. It belonged to his father and was used in the coup that drove out the Europeans and put the Tatluk family back in power in Qawi."

"Philippe hit him?"

"Several times, I believe," he chuckled. "That's one soldier who will *never* question your married status again, much less be insolent to you."

"The things we learn about people we think we know," she murmured absently, and grinned.

He glanced at her amusedly. "Yes, we've learned a few things about you, too. Especially about you riding to the rescue with your trusty Colt .45," he said. "I wish you could meet my wife. Dani helped me foil an air-jacking some years back. And J.D.'s wife, Gabby, actually shot a man who was trying to kill him in a Guatemalan jungle."

She was impressed. "They aren't from Texas, those women?" she teased.

He smiled and she moved on, feeling safe and protected.

The prewedding traditions were fascinating to Gretchen, who threw herself into them with pure delight. Leila and the other women in the palace helped henna her hands and feet and conduct her to the endless parties and conversational feasts that were a prelude to the elegant, ancient ceremony that would see her traditionally married to her handsome husband.

The guest list, like the preparations, was formidable. Gretchen almost shuddered when she read some of the names on it. She wasn't too happy to discover Brianne and Pierce Hutton at the top of it, but she was learning that Philippe really did love her. When he spoke of Brianne now, it was respectfully, but not with any lingering desire.

Along with the Huttons, Tate Winthrop and his wife Cecily had been invited, and his parents, Matt and Leta Holden. Matt was a senator from South Dakota and Leta was his wife. There was quite a story there, which Philippe had told her at length and with some amusement. It seemed that the new Mrs. Tate Winthrop had actually baptized her then-guardian Tate with a tureen of crab bisque at a widely televised live fund-raiser. Gretchen couldn't wait to meet her.

As the wedding day dawned, preparations for security became tighter and more efficient. Metal detectors were set up unobtrusively. Listening devices and cameras were put in place. Philippe's bodyguard was abundantly in evidence, along with quite a number of American men in suits—among them, Russell.

Gretchen, in her wedding finery, caught a glimpse of him darting around a corner to avoid an encounter with her handsome brother. She tried not to grin at the consternation on the agent's face. Her brother had a reputation, much-deserved, for making life difficult for people he didn't like.

The morning seemed to crawl by as limousines ferried guests from the airport. Then, suddenly, cameras were set up and rolling. The ceremonial band was playing. Dignitaries were gathered in the grand cathedral that had been built by the Spaniards four centuries ago. A robed pontiff waited at the altar as Marc escorted elegant Gretchen down the red-carpeted aisle to the altar where Philippe, in his ceremonial robes of office, waited for her.

Incredibly, Gretchen had forgotten all about the threat of Kurt Brauer. The security was so tight that a fly couldn't have managed to get through it. She was certain that everything would go perfectly. She stood by Philippe and spoke her vows in a strong, clear voice and smiled dreamily as he repeated his own with equal fervor. It was much like the ceremony in the desert, because he took his scimitar once more and cut a small loaf of bread in half and handed part to Gretchen. They were pronounced man and wife, but he didn't kiss her at the altar. He smiled at her and turned her to the audience to be presented as his queen.

The sound of the bomb exploding behind them was like something out of time and place. Gretchen heard it and didn't even realize what it was until Philippe pushed her to the floor and spread his powerful body over her.

She felt the carpet rough under her cheek and she coughed as tiny particles of debris crept over the church like a gray cloud. There was gunfire and the sound of hysteria. People ran, being pushed and shoved out of the building as Philippe's personal bodyguard, armed to the teeth and bristling with protective instincts, swarmed around him and Gretchen.

Philippe cursed roundly as he helped Gretchen to her feet and turned to see about the priest, who was just managing to sit up.

Gretchen moved forward to help him. "Oh, dear, are you all right, Father?" she asked, concerned.

"Yes, my child. And are you?" he asked at once.

"I'm fine." She looked at her husband, recognizing the cold fury in him that sent chills down her spine as he tossed orders to his personal bodyguard.

Dutch van Meer vaulted over a wrecked pew and halted beside them, a small automatic weapon in one hand. He looked nothing like the kind, friendly man she'd come to know. He looked as dangerous as her husband, and eyes like cold steel met her husband's.

"Brauer sent one of his spies in with a C-4 charge," Dutch told Philippe, grim-faced. "He concealed it in the baptismal font, of all places, and it was the one thing we didn't check. I'm sorry. I must be getting older than I realized."

"None of my bodyguards thought of it, either, including Bojo," Philippe told him.

"We caught the man who planted the charge and interrogated him," Dutch continued. "He says that Brauer and about thirty men are on their way here in two high-tech military helicopters. They're going to sneak in under radar and land on the helipad, with the intention of kidnapping you in front of the international press."

"A bold plan," Philippe said coldly. "And I need no magic ball to know where he got the funds. My uncle will wish he had never heard of Qawi! As will Brauer, when I finish with him." He shot an order at Hassan, who was always nearby, and went to see about his father, who was waving his hands and shouting.

"Watch yourself," Dutch told her before Philippe and his father joined them. "You can't underestimate this man Brauer. I think you're in more danger than Philippe is."

"Why?" she asked, shocked.

"Because Philippe would do anything to save you, and Brauer knows it. The wedding is proof of his intentions, and his preference for you over Mrs. Hutton."

Gretchen bit down on a curse. "I'll be careful."

Marc came up beside them with a gun in his

hand and fury in his eyes. "You okay?" he asked his baby sister with sharp concern.

"I'm fine. Are you?"

He nodded. He hugged her quickly, while Dutch excused himself and went to speak to Philippe. Marc reached into a holster under the leg of his slacks and pulled out a snub-nosed .38 Smith & Wesson handgun. He slipped it to Gretchen.

"You know how to use that," he said.

She nodded grimly. "If he gets into the palace, he'll be sorry. How dare he mess up my wedding!"

Marc smiled gently. "Don't get yourself shot."

"The same goes for you," she instructed. She studied his drawn face and reached up to smooth his cheek gently. "My poor brother," she said tenderly. "I'm so sorry about the way things worked out for you."

The strain was showing on his face. He averted his eyes. "Life is hard."

"*She* didn't blame you," his sister said.

He glanced toward Philippe. "I blame myself. And now this isn't doing a lot for my self-esteem. I should have checked the baptismal font."

"I'm sure every other federal agent in the place is thinking the same thing. You'll notice that the chief of Philippe's personal guard is trying to look invisible. It won't help."

"Your new husband is a character," he told her with a smile. "I like him."

"You like him because Russell's afraid of him," she accused.

He chuckled and hugged her again. "Here comes the media wading back into the rubble," he said, glancing over his shoulder. "Hide that pistol and get out of here. You don't need to be in the spotlight right now."

"Neither do you."

"Stay close to the bodyguards anyway."

She nodded and made her way through the broken masonry and shattered wood, still shaky from the explosion and the aftermath of relief at finding herself alive.

Philippe came back to her. He checked her carefully for damage before he sighed and kissed her forehead tenderly. "Hassan will stay with you, as will Leila. I must go."

"Go where?" she asked, horrified.

"To catch Brauer before he can swoop down on the palace," he said, motioning to his men, including the three mercenaries, Bojo, and Marc.

"I want to go with you!" she exclaimed.

He took her firmly by the shoulders. "You carry our child," he said gently. "This risk you must not take, for his sake. You understand?"

She touched his mouth with her fingertips, worried and unable to hide it. "I can't live without you!" she said huskily

The very simplicity of the statement made it profound. He ground his teeth together as he brought her palm to his mouth and kissed it hungrily. Life became precious. Terribly precious. He looked at her with fear and torment. He didn't want to leave her, but there was more risk in staying here and waiting for Brauer and his lunatics to attack. "Take care of her, if you value your own life!" he called to Hassan, and whirled on his heel.

"He'll be all right," Dutch assured her grimly just before he followed Philippe. "A man who could unite ten of the most warring Bedouin tribes in all of the Middle East is more than capable of dealing with a terrorist."

She looked up at him miserably. "Oh, I hope so!"

He chuckled. "You really should read a history of this country, Mrs. Sabon," he mused. "I think you don't quite know your husband yet."

"I only want time to get to know him," she said, and meant it.

The palace was like an asylum for the next hour. News media were everywhere, talking to anyone who seemed to understand English or any one of twelve other foreign languages. Gretchen escaped with Leila to the women's quarters, with Hassan close behind, his hand on the automatic weapon he always carried as he looked cautiously from one side of the corridor to the other, pausing to check closed doors.

"He is worried," Leila said quietly. "So am I. This man Brauer is like a cobra, quiet and shrewd. The man who told them about his approach is not trustworthy. I have known him to do many wicked things for money, and I was told that they didn't have to do much to make him talk. They were much too upset and angry to think rationally about what he said."

"You think he gave them false information?" she asked Leila, worriedly.

Leila nodded. "I think it is possible. And while a whole force of men might not be able to invade the palace, one or two men with bribed guards could accomplish much."

Gretchen felt the cold metal of the pistol against her thigh where she concealed it under her wedding robes and narrowed her eyes as she considered what to do.

"We should lock ourselves in your rooms, Lady," Leila said firmly. "There, at least, you will be safe."

Gretchen turned toward her, still frowning. "No. That's the last place we'll be safe," she murmured.

"If I were Brauer, it's where I'd be right now. It's the last place anybody would search for him." She turned to Hassan. "I want you to go and bring that guard I kicked from the stables where the camel is kept."

Hassan's eyes widened. "I beg your pardon, ma'am?" he drawled.

"The rest of the sha-KOOSH are with my husband," she reminded him. "He is the only man of the bodyguard left here. And bring Philippe's father with you when you return. His safety is no less important than mine."

Hassan, to his credit, didn't ask questions. He did immediately as he was told.

"You and I are going to bait a trap," she told Leila. "I want you to go to the laundry and bring back men's clothing for you and me. But I want women's clothing in a size to fit Hassan and that tall guard who was looking after the camel."

Leila's eyes lit up with mischief. "You are bad!"

Gretchen grinned. "I am a Texan," she said glumly. "And even international terrorists should know better than to mess with us!"

The punished guard was uneasy around Gretchen at first and full of apologies. She held up a hand.

"I never meant for my husband to knock your

teeth out, just the same," she said firmly. "But I'm giving you a chance to save all of us, and I promise you, my husband will be very pleased if we can pull this off. I think Brauer is in my suite. Leila and I are going to dress as men and patrol outside my rooms. You and Hassan are going to walk into the room unexpectedly and let yourselves be found by Brauer. The surprise is going to be his, because Leila and I are your backup. And we're going to both be armed." She showed her pistol and pulled one from the guard's belt to hand to Leila. "Can you shoot it?" she asked the other woman.

"But of course," Leila told her. "My own husband belongs to the *sidi's* sha-KOOSH." She grinned.

"Okay, then, we are going to walk in there and give Kurt Brauer the unpleasant surprise of his life. Then we're going to give the international media outside the palace a *much* bigger story than my wedding! Now let's change into our disguises and get moving!"

A few miles away, a furious Philippe was sitting beside Dutch and Bojo in a small helicopter talking to his other military vehicles.

"Brauer's helicopters are nowhere in sight, if they even exist," Philippe said angrily. "But one of the border patrols found evidence of recent movement, and a satellite picked up two Jeeps moving toward the palace. We have been out-flanked. I knew I should never have trusted that informant!"

"We live and learn," Dutch said quietly. "I'm sorry. None of us are exactly standing out as defenders of the innocent right now."

"Gretchen," Philippe groaned. "She and my father were left behind for their own protection. Even now, they may be dead! Turn around," Philippe told the pilot harshly. "Go back to the palace, as fast as you can!"

"Yes, *sidi*," came the respectful reply, and seconds later, the helicopter was on its way back.

The men had changed, in another room of course, into their wispy *gellabias* with the *hijabs* pulled carefully over their faces. The old sheikh, fuming at being left out of the action, was coaxed into remaining in one of the empty rooms for the time being.

The young guard gave Gretchen, in her flowing robes and *igal*, an accusing look.

"If anyone says a word, I'll swear that I ordered you to dress like that, I promise," she told him. "Think of the mission, not the means."

"You sound like my army sergeant," Hassan drawled. He looked very large, for a "woman."

"If you say I look like him, I'll have you guarding sand dunes for the next five years," Gretchen told him.

"I never said a word, ma'am, honest!"

She grinned at Leila, who looked as out of place as she felt. She hid the pistol in the flowing robes and indicated that Leila should do the same. She signaled to the men, who began to walk deliberately toward Gretchen's quarters and slowly entered the room.

From the corridor, Gretchen and Leila moved close enough to peer inside. Sure enough, Kurt Brauer, as she'd guessed, was waiting behind the curtains with two armed men. They came forward. Brauer was wild-eyed and angry, and he looked momentarily perplexed.

"Where is Lady Sabon?" he demanded in English. Arabic, obviously, wasn't one of his languages.

"The Lady? She is being taken to the hospital," the cross-dressed guard said. "She was badly injured, in an explosion in the cathedral! We have come for her gowns."

Brauer seemed to relax. "And her husband?" he persisted.

"With her. Who are you? What do you want in my lady's chambers?" the guard persisted.

Brauer moved restlessly. "Never mind. Where is this hospital?"

The guard told him.

Brauer was frowning at the "women." "You look very odd, for a woman," Brauer said. "Get outside and watch the corridor!" he told the two men with him.

They came barreling through the door and right into the leveled pistols of Gretchen and Leila.

"Say one word, and I'll be looking down the corridor through you!" Gretchen said in a hushed whisper, forcing her captive out of sight of the door.

Leila repeated the command in sharp Arabic, her own pistol in her camouflaged prey's stomach. She added an order for them to drop their weapons.

"What was that noise?" Brauer demanded. "You men...!"

There was a scuffle, quickly over, and Brauer came flying out into the corridor, headfirst. He hit the floor and before he could roll over, the guard who'd insulted Gretchen was all over him. She had to admire that technique. He might have a bad attitude, but he left nothing to be desired as a bodyguard. In no time, Kurt was vanquished, bruised, and neatly tied up with a piece of the "women's" robes.

"Very nice, young man!" Gretchen told the

guard, her green eyes twinkling. "I'm proud of you!"

He actually grinned at her. He and Hassan threw off the robes they were wearing over their own clothing and left them on the floor while they marched the three captives down the hall. Gretchen and Leila took only a few seconds to discard their own disguises and follow along.

The old sheikh peered out the door of the room he was occupying, saw the captives, grinned from ear to ear and joined his daughter-in-law and her servant with such pride that Gretchen had to smother a grin.

"Here," she said, handing him her pistol and urging him forward without actually touching him. Touching him would have broken a local taboo, which she knew. "You get right up there with Hassan and that other guy. It will do wonders for you with the international press!"

He stopped, looking perplexed. "You would do this, for me? After all the insulting things I have said to you about American women and outsiders?"

She shrugged. "You're going to be the baby's grandfather," she reminded him.

"So I am." He smiled with real affection and handed her back the pistol. He wrapped both his big hands around hers. "And you will be his

mother. This story will be told around tribal campfires for the foreseeable future. It will do your child
no little service to have it known that his mother
has the heart of a falcon. Go.'' He urged her up
into the group that was coming to meet the tied,
dejected prisoners.

"Kurt Brauer," Brianne's husband Pierce said
with a cold smile. He motioned to the international
press to join them. "You people from the American press may remember this scalawag. He invaded Qawi two years ago, slaughtered women and
children with his hired mercenaries, and got a short
Russian prison sentence. He'll be tried in Qawi this
time. And I promise you, he won't get out anytime
soon."

"About that, you are precisely correct!" came
a furious voice from behind Pierce Hutton.

Philippe came into view, still wearing his ceremonial robes, with the mercenaries and his personal guard flanking him. He stopped short at the
sight of Kurt and his comrades in bondage. Then
his eyes went to Hassan, the disgraced guard, and
Gretchen with her brother's pistol and Leila with
a borrowed one standing behind them.

He grinned outrageously. "As you can see," he
raised his voice, "in Qawi, even the women are
dangerous!"

Brauer and his two friends were moved aside so

that the press could photograph Gretchen and Leila with their pistols in hand. It was a media event. Philippe folded his arms and smiled with enormous pride as his bride was photographed, interviewed, praised and admired by half the world—including the foreign dignitaries. The U.S. vice president kissed her, and the Russian and Israeli delegates shook her hand warmly. Others surged forward to add their own praise. Gretchen thought she could never withstand such happiness. Sadly, with her condition and all the excitement, it was too much for her. She fainted.

Philippe was at her side instantly, patting her hands, smoothing her hair under the concealing headdress. "Gretchen. Darling! Are you all right?" he asked.

He sounded actually frantic. Gretchen's eyes opened. She was numb and cold and she felt nausea in her throat. She looked up at her husband and smiled gently. "I don't think capturing invaders is good for pregnant women."

He chuckled, relieved. "Perhaps not, but at least you picked the best time to pass out, my own." He bent and lifted her into his arms, brushing his lips tenderly across her eyes as she clung to him.

"Did you say that you were pregnant, Mrs. Sabon? I mean, Lady Sabon?" one of the journalists asked, aghast.

"Very pregnant, indeed," she assured them. "You can all come to the christening. But right now, all I want is my bed and some dill pickles with strawberry sauce."

She grinned at them as they got the joke and started to laugh. Behind them, Kurt Brauer was cursing himself, and his friends. They were taken quickly away to jail. Gretchen was just glad that it was finally over. She reached up and kissed her husband's lean cheek before she slid her lips against his throat and tightened her arms.

"Did I do good?"

"You did good." He kissed her softly. "How did you manage it?"

She hesitated. It was good to have things to hold over men. You never knew when a nice threat would get you something you needed badly. She pursed her lips. "Do you know, I don't remember a lot of it. But Hassan and your disgraced guard saved the day. They surprised Brauer in my rooms and Leila and I pointed our guns at his henchmen. That was all it took."

"Dutch and the others cornered the rest of his men outside. Two were wounded, but the rest are all right. And fortunately for us, nobody was seriously hurt in the bombing. I'm sure Brauer meant it to kill us. It didn't succeed, so he had to do his own dirty work."

"He's not very good at it," she murmured. "Maybe he can learn a useful trade while he's in prison."

"Our prisons have no such facilities," he said without thinking.

She looked up at him with a wicked little smile. "Now, speaking of prison reform..."

His groan could be heard by Leila and his father, who were watching the byplay with broad smiles. But they didn't say a thing.

Chapter Seventeen

It seemed like forever until Philippe came back to their suite. She'd long since removed her beautiful wedding robes and replaced them with the caftan she liked to wear in her suite.

Philippe smiled as he closed the door and opened his arms. She ran into them, holding on as if she was afraid someone might try to tear him away from her.

"Everything's all right," he said softly, hugging her close. "Brauer and most of his men are in custody and they will be tried. It's all over."

She held on tighter. "We can't ever let him get out!"

He kissed her forehead. "Come. I want you to meet some people."

"Wait," she said, and found her *aba*. She drew it over her before she joined him, grinning at his faint surprise.

He caught her by the arm and tugged her along with him to the door. When he opened it, she recognized Brianne Hutton at once, but the big dark man beside her was unfamiliar, like the young blond and the very dark gentleman beside her.

"You've met Brianne," Philippe said, with his arm tight around her waist. "This is her husband, Pierce, and this is Cecily and Tate Winthrop."

"I'm very glad to meet you," Gretchen said in her soft drawl and smiled.

"Well," Pierce Hutton mused. "There is a resemblance."

"Yes, there is a slight one," Philippe said with an indulgent smile at his wife.

"Slight, indeed," Pierce continued, holding Brianne close at his side. "You look well, despite all the excitement this morning," he told Gretchen. "You're none the worse for wear, I hope?"

She leaned close against Philippe's chest and smiled sleepily. "No. I'm just tired, but that's natural."

"Very natural, for a mother-to-be," Philippe said with breathless tenderness.

Brianne's gasp was full of shocked delight. Her

green eyes shimmered with glee. "Oh, my, my, my!"

Philippe chuckled and a ruddy color came along his high cheekbones. "As you once said, miracles still happen in the world. Gretchen has made me believe in them again."

"Obviously," Pierce Hutton said with a low whistle. He gave his wife a curious look and she made a face at him. It was as if she were daring him to have any more suspicions about her friend Philippe Sabon. And it was equally clear that he didn't.

"I believe in miracles myself," Cecily Winthrop said softly, and with a smile at her handsome husband. "Tate and I are expecting our second child. Our firstborn is with his grandparents at the hotel. Thank God we didn't bring him or Brianne's little boy along for the ceremony!"

"The Holdens, Matt and Leta, stayed at the hotel to baby-sit for us," Pierce offered with a smile.

"It was scary," Gretchen admitted, looking up at Philippe with a grin. "But nothing we couldn't handle!"

The guests stayed for a late supper before they went back to their hotel. They were going to fly out the next morning. Marc wished his sister happiness, took back his pistol with a wry grin, and shook hands with his new brother-in-law heartily. Gretchen and Philippe went back to their own suite soon afterward, both tired and ready for bed.

But on the way, they encountered Philippe's father, who was looking darkly concerned and broody.

"What's wrong?" Philippe asked him.

He shrugged. "It is nothing. Well," he amended with a glance toward them, "it is nothing much."

"Father," Philippe prodded.

The old man shifted and shrugged. "Father Felipe has just given me the most intimidating lecture of my life."

"For what?" Philippe asked.

"You knew that your wife insulted your bodyguard. He is the youngest son of the leader of one of the Beduoin tribes, who is very pleased that you have reinstated him and at a higher rank," he said slowly.

"Yes, he was instrumental in saving Gretchen's life," he agreed. "It was the least I could do."

"Well, she said a great many things to him that your other guard overheard and repeated gleefully. Since her American heritage is well-known, along with her newness to Arabic speech, the source of her language was traced to me." He cleared his throat, avoiding the howling amusement in Gretchen's and Philippe's faces. "I have been given penance for the next two weeks and advised to take more care in my choice of suitable epithets.'' He cleared his throat again. ''But besides that, I have recently been listening to my daughter-in-law in an attempt to learn some curses which are more acceptable.'' He grinned suddenly and let loose a barrage of Spanish ranch slang that had Gretchen gasping for breath.

''If you say that in front of Father Felipe, he'll wash your mouth out with lye soap!'' she exclaimed, red-faced.

''I did!'' he groaned. ''That is why Father Felipe has given me two weeks' penance!''

She burst out laughing. Her father-in-law's eyes bulged and he glowered at her. ''You said this language was American slang!'' he accused.

''It is,'' she confessed in a squeaky tone, ''but I learned it from my brother. And there is nobody in south Texas who can hold a candle to him when he loses his temper!''

''There is no cause for concern,'' Philippe said, holding up a hand. ''As a matter of fact, I have been studying old American movies for inspiration in this respect, and I have a curse which will even be appropriate to teach my heir when he is able to speak.''

''Have you now?'' Gretchen asked, still catching her breath. ''Okay. What is it?''

Philippe grinned from ear to ear. "Horsefeathers."

She and his father exchanged a long stare and
suddenly burst out laughing.

Later, as she lay in her husband's strong arms,
Gretchen thought over the past few months and felt
a warm glow under her heart as she savored the
delight of her new life.

"We have so much," she murmured sleepily.
"I never dreamed of being this happy."

His arms contracted. "Nor I. You have made
miracles all around me."

"We made them together." She pulled one of
his hands to her belly and held it there tenderly.
"I hope we can have a palace full of children, but
even one is more than I ever dared wish for."

"And I." He sighed as his lips found hers in
the darkness. "I must remember to teach you some
very intimate French, when I have the time."

She grinned. "I'm sorry I got your father in
trouble. I didn't mean to."

"Yes, you did," he accused softly.

"Well, he did get me in a lot of trouble first
with those Arabic curses."

"And you did know that Father Felipe spoke
Spanish fluently."

"I only taught him just a few little bitty words,"

she defended herself. "It did help clean up his language."

"And yours," he added mockingly.

"I'm reformed."

"Ha!"

She curled her legs into his. "Really. I'm turning over a new leaf."

His own leg curled lazily against hers. He was no longer self-conscious with her, or inhibited about lying with her in the light. She'd made him realize that his scars were far worse in his own mind than in reality. She'd made him realize a lot of things.

He smoothed her cheek against his hair-roughened chest with a sigh. "My pearl of great price," he whispered.

"Hmm?"

He smiled. "Do you remember the story of the poor man who found a pearl of great price and sold everything he had to buy it? I would give my kingdom for you."

"Would you, really?"

"Everything I own."

She'd thought he was teasing. But that didn't sound like teasing. Her hand stilled against his chest. "I love you," she said softly.

His lips brushed against her eyelids, closing them. "I loved you the first time I saw you, standing so worriedly in front of the concierge and trying to look confident. It was like looking into my own soul. I could never have given you up, even then. How odd that it took so long for me to realize it."

She could barely get her breath. "You never said that you loved me."

He chuckled softly and held her closer. "And of course it never occurred to you that I, a man whose body was his worst nightmare, would willingly take off my clothes in front of a woman out of anger?"

Her whole body stilled. That had never even dawned on her. She caught her breath audibly.

"I knew," he said huskily, "I *knew* that you would never ridicule it or berate me when you saw the scars. I trusted you enough to share my disfigurement with you. It was an act of love, even if I didn't quite realize it at the time."

"Neither did I." She felt tears slipping down her cheek, onto his chest.

"Why are you crying?"

"Because I love you more than my life," she whispered.

"I love you more than mine!" he replied at once, with gruff fervor. "More than anything in the world!" He rolled over and his mouth found hers, cherished it, traced it in a silence warm with tenderness. "I will love you until I die. Forever. Forever, my darling!" he groaned against her lips.

She held him close. "You mustn't ever leave me," she managed in a choked voice.

"As if I could!" He wrapped her up tight and kissed her hungrily.

She kissed him back. When the fierce ardor eased a little, she curled closer, feeling loved and cherished and happier than she ever dreamed of being. "Philippe?" she murmured.

"Hmm?" he asked, his lips teasing just at her collarbone.

"That had better not be a line you hand out to all the women in your life," she teased, punching him in the ribs.

He laughed deeply as he caught her hand. "Woman, you insult me!" he said in mock horror.

"Horsefeathers!"

He chuckled as he moved slowly over her welcoming body. "Now, now," he murmured as his mouth settled against hers. "You'll get in trouble if you don't watch your language. I'll tell Father Felipe."

"Is this the sort of trouble I'll get in?" she asked against his hungry mouth.

"Mmm-hmm," he murmured, smiling.

"In that case," she whispered, "I'll see if I can't learn a whole lot of new words!"

It was the last thing she said for a very long time.

Seven months later, Ahmed Rashid Philippe Mustafa was born to the reigning sheikh of Qawi and his wife the Lady Gretchen. Two prominent medical specialists were overheard at the christening discussing an upcoming joint paper about anomalies of fertilization and misdiagnosis of sexual function based on long-standing injury.

The baby's parents had no comment.

* * * * *

Watch for Marc Brannon's story in

THE TEXAS RANGER,

by Diana Palmer.

This tale of romance and adventure will be coming your way in Summer/Fall, 2001— only from MIRA Books!

New York Times Bestselling Author

DEBBIE MACOMBER

Return To Promise

The town of Promise, Texas, is a good place
to raise a family and spend the rest of your days with
the person you love.

Cal Patterson and his wife, Jane, certainly thought so.
But after months of emotional upheaval brought on
by doubts about their marriage, the two separate,
and Jane takes their children to California.

Cal is now forced to confront what he really wants
in his life, what he *needs*. Jane is confronting the same
questions.... How seriously does Cal take his marriage
vows? And how important is Promise to Jane? Is there
hope for a reconciliation—in time for Christmas?

"Popular romance writer Macomber has a gift for
evoking the emotions that are at the heart of
the genre's popularity."
—*Publishers Weekly*

*On sale October 2000
wherever hardcovers are sold!*

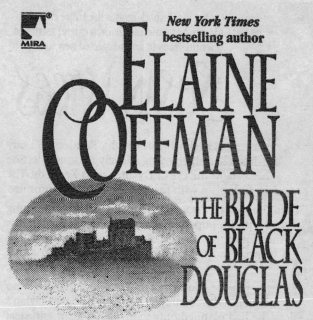

New York Times
bestselling author

ELAINE COFFMAN

THE BRIDE OF BLACK DOUGLAS

Lady Meleri Weatherby is desperate to escape marriage to
her cruel fiancé, and Robert Douglas must find a wife or
risk losing his ancestral home and noble name.

Set against the dramatic backdrop of 1785 Scotland, this
is an unforgettable romance about a marriage that starts
off to defy fate and that just might end in love....

"Coffman's writing is deft, capable and evocative."
—*Publishers Weekly*

On sale November 2000 wherever paperbacks are sold!

One small spark ignites the entire city of
Chicago, but amid the chaos, a case of mistaken
identity leads to an unexpected new love....

Susan Wiggs

On this historic night, Kathleen O'Leary
finds herself enjoying a lovely masquerade. She
has caught the eye of Dylan Francis Kennedy. The
night feels alive with magic…and ripe with promise.

Then fire sweeps through Chicago, cornering the young
lovers with no hope of rescue. Impulsively, they marry.
Incredibly, they survive. And now Kathleen must tell
Chicago's most eligible bachelor that he has married
a fraud.

But the joke's on her. For this gentleman is no
gentleman. While Kathleen had hoped to win Dylan's
love, he had planned only to break her heart and steal
her fortune. Now the real sparks are about to fly.

THE MISTRESS

"In poetic prose, Wiggs evocatively captures the
Old South and creates an intense, believable
relationship between the lovers."
—*Publishers Weekly* on *The Horsemaster's Daughter*

*On sale October 2000
wherever paperbacks are sold!*

DIANA PALMER

66585	FIT FOR A KING	___ $5.99 U.S.	___ $6.99 CAN.
66539	PAPER ROSE	___ $5.99 U.S.	___ $6.99 CAN.
66470	ONCE IN PARIS	___ $5.99 U.S.	___ $6.99 CAN.
66452	AFTER THE MUSIC	___ $5.50 U.S.	___ $6.50 CAN.
66418	ROOMFUL OF ROSES	___ $5.50 U.S.	___ $6.50 CAN.
66168	PASSION FLOWER	___ $5.50 U.S.	___ $6.50 CAN.
66149	DIAMOND GIRL	___ $5.50 U.S.	___ $6.50 CAN.
66056	CATTLEMAN'S CHOICE	___ $4.99 U.S.	___ $5.50 CAN.
66031	LADY LOVE	___ $4.99 U.S.	___ $5.50 CAN.
66009	THE RAWHIDE MAN	___ $4.99 U.S.	___ $5.50 CAN.

(limited quantities available)

TOTAL AMOUNT	$_____
POSTAGE & HANDLING	$_____
($1.00 for one book; 50¢ for each additional)	
APPLICABLE TAXES*	$_____
TOTAL PAYABLE	$_____
(check or money order—please do not send cash)	

To order, complete this form and send it, along with a check or money order for the total above, payable to MIRA Books®, to: **In the U.S.:** 3010 Walden Avenue, P.O. Box 9077, Buffalo, NY 14269-9077; **In Canada:** P.O. Box 636, Fort Erie, Ontario, L2A 5X3.

Name:_____

Address:_____ City:_____

State/Prov.:_____ Zip/Postal Code:_____

Account Number (if applicable):_____

075 CSAS

*New York residents remit applicable sales taxes.
  Canadian residents remit applicable GST and provincial taxes.

MIRA®

Visit us at www.mirabooks.com   MDP1100BL